Saint John Lennon

It's About Time!

I MAGINE!

Daniel Hartwell

Roseanne Bottone

Dearest Marlene,
Wishing you
happy surprises!

Love!
Rosie

Saint John Lennon

Share the love: visit us at www.SaintJohnLennon.com

Author: Daniel Hartwell
Daniel@SaintJohnLennon.com

Writer: Roseanne Bottone
Roseanne@SaintJohnLennon.com

Book cover photo, derivative art and cover design by Gay Stahr
Gay.Stahr@DocStahr.com

Published by: United We Rock® LLC
ISBN 9781947289321

This is a work of fiction.

Disclaimers: See page 267
Thank you: See page 269
Endnotes: See page 270

Dedicated to my big brothers Doug and Dave. Thank you for playing music by the Beatles and John Lennon every day when I was a child. You taught me about peace and love.

*The future influences the present
just as much as the past*

- Friedrich Nietzsche

PROLOGUE

ZEPHYR

Who has seen the wind?
Neither you nor I,
But when the trees bow down their heads,
The wind is passing by.

- Christina Rossetti

The Christmas sky hangs low and sullen over Liverpool this Monday morning. Shivering uncontrollably at the side door of St. Peter's Church, 10-year-old John Winston Lennon turns up his coat collar against a bone-chilling mist. He shoves his fists into his pockets and, while he waits for the sexton to admit him to the choir's rehearsal room, clutches his overcoat tightly from within.

A flurry of movement erupts behind the boy as parishioners scurry past the cemetery at the side of the church. Heads down as they take refuge inside their place of worship, the church-goers do not notice the tiniest opening piercing the gloomy clouds.

Outside, the air crackles and whooshes as a ray of sunshine blazes forth and lands at John's feet. The aperture dilates as if it were the iris of an eye adjusting to the darkness below. Lifting his gaze, John's face is bathed in a marmalade warmth.

The sky in this magical place is a cerulean blue where a lollipop sun glows all lemon. The mountains are a sweet purple hue;

trees burst with neon limes and ecstatic tangerines; a brook twinkles diamonds; and fields of colossal ruby-red strawberries stretch on forever.

Musical notes rain down, hover around the boy, and assemble to form playful melodies. The boy jumps to snatch the notes and laughs when they burst like soap bubbles. He leaps three feet into the air and remains there, suspended weightless, until he floats back down to earth and his feet settle gently upon the ground.

∞

It doesn't seem odd that the sky opened up for me. I had been expecting something wonderful to happen. My childhood years were blessed with enchanting little moments all along the way. I talked to the trees and whispered to the stars and paid attention to the extraordinary.

When I was five years old, my mother told me that happiness was the key to life. When I went to school they asked me what I wanted to be when I grew up and I wrote down "happy." They told me I didn't understand the assignment. I told them they didn't understand life.

The world is full of surprises. They are diaphanous spirits coursing through space. But unlike comets following a known trajectory, surprises zip and zing until they find an opening to land. Where some of them alight is purposeful. We attract happy surprises with the thoughts we project; they know how to find us. They pick up our signals and head right for us when we make a place for them in our hearts.

Sad surprises descend on us too. Sometimes it's instant karma and sometimes flashes of randomness occur across the universe, and there's no avoiding them.

I was surprised when the music of my life changed suddenly as I lay dying in front of the Dakota apartment building. I rose from my own body and watched the scene below. Musical notes appeared once more, swirling softly out of focus; this time they became my wings.

∞

The creaking of rusty hinges startles the boy out of his reverie. The heavy wooden church door groans as the old sexton pushes it open.

"Did you hear that, sir?" John asks.

"Hear what, lad?"

"The music, sir. It was beautiful. It came from the sky."

"Are you daft, boy? It's freezing out here. The choir master is waiting. Get into your robe now. Off you go!"

"But, sir, there were musical notes all over and I was floating."

"Imagine! You're such a dreamer!" the sexton says. Hurrying John inside, he lugs the door closed without an outward glance. A few lingering notes rise back into the light, carried away by a wind perfumed with frankincense and myrrh.

∞

Life no longer has a clear beginning, middle, or end. It's like watching a movie on a big screen. The plot unfolds in a linear way and then the end credits roll. The story is supposed to make sense. You think it's over, but it's not.

When the theater lights come back on, out we go, tumbling into the street. We feel the emotion of what we've witnessed and now the new things we experience are affected by that. We continue living, but it's a different life than the one we lived before we went in.

My story isn't over; peace and love are eternal. Long ago, a miracle was reserved for me.

THE EGG MAN

Music is the space between the notes.

— Claude Debussy

What goes through the mind of a man who is about to become a murderer? Of course I wonder, of course; yes.

I'm only human. He waited for me outside my apartment building for hours while Yoko and I were at the recording studio. He knew how he wanted it to play out. Did he think of his wife? Did he think of my wife? My children?

When I stepped out of the limo and walked by him, he heard a voice telling him over and over again, "Do it, do it, do it." He believed a demonic power was at work. Yeah, I know he said he had an abusive childhood. Underneath he was suffering. Still, that's no justification for the path he chose as a grown man. Taking my life was not the solution to anything.

I could ask him about this when we meet. We'll see. It doesn't matter, really. What's done cannot be undone. Some questions can't be answered — we just have to accept that.

Wait a sec... let me pour myself more tea. I want to ask you about this photo. Wait, where is it? Here. This one. Paul Goresh took it. Have you seen it? I was autographing a copy of Double Fantasy *for Mark earlier in the afternoon on the day he killed me. I don't remember doing this. Fans asked for my autograph all the time. He was a bit odd, but there was nothing about him that stood out. He looks happy. It was the last photo ever taken of me in my first go 'round. You might know these things. Hey, sorry if you do. Mark*

David Chapman may be infamous, but it seems I'm the only person who knows nothing of my own murder. It's all a revelation to me.

When Mark read one of my interviews – the one in the London Evening Standard *– he said he wanted to scream out loud, "Who does he think he is, saying these things about God and heaven and the Beatles?" He told the police he was pissed off at me for my comment about the Beatles being more popular than Jesus. It was taken out of context anyway.*

He murdered me because he wanted notoriety. He wanted to become somebody. I mean, how sad is that? Be compassionate when you think about all of this, OK? The chap was delusional. Doctors said he was psychotic. A few years before he shot me, he was depressed and tried to commit suicide. People like you and me who get high on life can't understand the depth of such distress.

Mark wrote a letter to his friend that said, "I'm going nuts" and signed it "The Catcher in the Rye." Supposedly he related to the main character in that book – what was his name? Yeah, Holden Caulfield, that's right. Mark was desperate for the kind of human contact that had meaning, and he craved love.

All we need is love, man. The answer is love. The question is irrelevant. It's the only thing that will save us. That's my gospel. If someone thinks that peace and love are just a cliché that must have been left behind in the '60s, that's a problem.

Yes, I do forgive him – as much for me as for him. Forgiveness doesn't require full comprehension. You're reticent. OK, I get it. Beauty and forgiveness take time to blossom. A bud doesn't just burst overnight into a flower.

∞

A sharp, searing "pop" echoes through the Upper West Side of Manhattan. The metronome ticks. Another gunshot... Tick... Another... Tick... Another... Tick... The last... Tick. Five .38-caliber bullets played in staccato. Mortally wounded, the victim stumbles forward and collapses face down. His pierced lungs empty their last breath without an exhale. His life's blood drains from a destroyed artery. John Lennon is dead.

In the presence of light, however, there can be no darkness. The song of his existence hasn't ended; it has merely reached a sacred measure where a full rest requires four beats of silence. The pause between notes is filled with grace and the infinite wisdom of the universe. It's where miracles dwell.

Four decades pass, each an ephemeral memory. Tick. The planet makes 3,650 predictable rotations as it orbits the sun. Tick. Yoko's broken heart beats 420,480,000 times. Tick. Every living creature progresses 5.2 million minutes into the future. Tick. Half a billion souls depart for the heavens; John's is not among them. But for the count of one and two and three and four, time stands still for him.

Forty earthly years later, he opens his eyes.

John's face is pressed to the sidewalk. A small crumpled piece of paper tumbles along the ground in front of him. He sees a man's black shoe. His eyeglasses lay next to him, but he can't move to reach for them. He contemplates his translucent hand, paralyzed and not yet living. A sparkling, iridescent magma fills the space where his bones and muscles should be. The outline of his human body shimmers, illuminating the entranceway to the Dakota.

Sounds of the city begin filtering into his semi-consciousness; honking horns, a snippet of conversation, the thud of a car door slamming, a pulsing siren, a burst of loud music – but he cannot make sense of what is happening.

Is he on the subway, lulled into grogginess by the clickity-clack of the tracks and sway of the car? *Where am I?* he thinks.

He watches his hand as his flesh quickly restores itself to its perfect familiar form. The train explodes out of a dark tunnel into daylight as it climbs the El. His back rises with his first breath of winter air.

∞

John sits up as if he has just awakened from a good night's sleep. He puts on his glasses and surveys the scene around him. Hundreds of people waiting to see Yoko are standing behind police barriers and are transfixed by him. Some kneel and begin to pray. Others cry. A few dance and jump for joy. Several push their way out of the crowd and run away along 72nd Street. Almost everyone has a small device pointed at him.

NYPD Officer Dove extends his hand and helps John to his feet. "I've seen some crazy shit during my years on the force, but what the hell was *that?*"

John asks, "What happened? What's going on?"

"You just appeared out of nowhere – like beam-me-up from the old *Star Trek* movies. I wouldn't have believed it myself if I hadn't been standing right here when it happened. Who are you?"

"I'm John Lennon."

The crowd buzzes. "Did he say 'John Lennon'? Can it be? Imposter. What the fuck? I knew it. Miracle. Trickery. This will go viral. Unbelievable. John Lennon! Give peace a chance. Magic. Let's get out of here. Crazy. Looks just like him. Back from the dead. I saw it with my own eyes. Oh! My God!"

The murmuring begins as a gentle ripple, and then swells as it undulates over thousands of miles of ocean until it crashes to the shore. A human wave surges for a closer look.

"Don't be crazy! John Lennon is dead. You can't go around claiming you're him. Let's get you inside before you're mobbed." Officer Dove gestures to the doorman to unlock the door and ushers John into the reception area.

"What the hell are you talking about, man? Look at me! I'm John, alive and well! Where's Yoko?"

"She's across the street at Strawberry Fields speaking at a peace rally for the 40th anniversary of John's death – ah, supposedly *your* death."

"My death? Forty years? What's today's date?"

"It's December 8th."

"Yeah, right. Me and Yoko just got back from the studio. I was going in to say good night to Sean—"

"Not exactly, mister. It's December 8th… two thousand and twenty."

∞

#JohnLennon is trending. A world-wide celebration to commemorate his death and share his words of love unfolds in all 196 countries. People can no longer bear the sadness of war and terrorism and come together to say "no more" to violence. Throughout a 24-hour period, human peace signs form at 10:50 p.m., the approximate time John was shot. A surge in global consciousness is evident, so powerful is the united human spirit.

Yoko leads a minute of silence in remembrance of her husband when the clouds, like lush velvet curtains in the grandest theater, part to reveal God's resplendent creation; the moon shines to bless the revelers with the bright light of hope. The hair on her arms stands up and her skin tickles with goose bumps. A shiver runs up her spine. A commotion riles the 40,000 New Yorkers in Central Park. Something is blowing up social media.

"Yoko! Yoko! Have you seen the videos?"

The crowd chants, "John's alive! John's alive!" The good news reaches the heavens and the angels who helped orchestrate John's return are pleased with their work.

Yoko's bodyguard thrusts his iPhone at her. "Look! Oh, my God, look! It's on YouTube."

Tens of thousands of smartphone screens glow. Every star in the heavens twinkles with happiness and is reflected in its own mirror on earth. The witnesses' comments are re-tweeted around the globe in record time. Thousands of photos document John's miraculous appearance. Facebook, Instagram, and Snapchat crash.

Sirens blare in the city as one NYPD tactical squad surrounds the Dakota, and another encircles Yoko and her entourage.

"Oh! Yes! Yes! Yes! Yes! Tell me it's true!" Yoko cries.

∞

Yoko rushes into the Dakota to behold John standing before her. She knows his equine nose, small heart-shaped lips, and soulful brown eyes by rote, having created thousands of paintings of her ardently desired reunion with him. Her last memory of him had been indelibly imprinted on her mind. There is no doubt. She takes his face in her hands and says, "I've been waiting for you for a very, very long time. I knew I'd see you again."

John covers her hands with his. He strokes them and notices her wrinkled and thinning skin. Her face, fuller and blessed with the evidence of her 87 years, impresses upon him the enormity of what Officer Dove has been trying to explain to him. Yet here she is, the woman with whom he has his most profound connection − his beloved wife. He says, "I'm so sorry, my love. I didn't even know I was gone."

∞

Me? The second coming of Christ, or something? No way! I'm 159 pounds of ordinary flesh and bone and I don't know what to make of this any better than you do.

Yes, I do believe in God, but not as one thing, not as an old man in the sky. I believe that what people call God is something in all of us. I believe that what Jesus and Mohammed and Buddha and all the rest said was right. It's just that the translations have gone wrong. I'm not any kind of prophet, though. I'm finding my own way for this second go-round. Maybe what I have to say is divinely inspired, I just don't know.

I am thoroughly discombobulated. From my perspective, the entire world, and everyone I knew, fast-forwarded four decades in the blink of an eye. You've all had time to adjust. I asked my son a question and he didn't know the answer, so he said he'd ask Goopplezon. Goopplezon? He had to explain the whole concept of the internet and tell me the story behind Google, Apple, and Amazon and their merger. I'm bloody amazed by what's happened with technology.

The only reason people know this miracle isn't a hoax, though, is because hundreds of witnesses filmed and photographed my return with their mobile phones. Just a second before, my phone was attached to the wall with a cord.

Bloody right I will stay with Yoko! Anybody who claims to have some interest in me has absolutely misunderstood everything I ever said if they can't see why I'm with Yoko. And if they can't see that, they don't see anything. She's beautiful – amazing, really. Have you seen her? There's nothing more important than our relationship, nothing. Without her I'd be on a raft alone lost in the universe. And we dig being together all the time. Both of us could survive apart, but what for? I'm not going to sacrifice love. I've been through it all and nothing works better than to have someone you love, hold you. Yoko said, "Some people are old at 18 and others are young at 90. Time is a concept that humans created." Love is an eternal language.

I always liked a poem by an American poet – can't remember his name right now. Anyway, I never knew it would have such meaning for me. Let me grab my notes and read it to you:

> *Time is*
> *too slow for those who wait*
> *too swift for those who fear*
> *too long for those who grieve*
> *too short for those who rejoice*
> *but for those who love, time is eternity.*

Great lyrics for a song! When I sleep at night I can feel the beating of Yoko's loving heart. As powerful as music, that love reached beyond the heavens to pull me back.

Yes, I am quite disoriented. To say the least. I seek comfort from the familiar. I asked Goopplezon to play a Beatle's song, and the first one I heard was "In my life." I took that as a sign of synchronicity. Yes, I will remember some places forever; some are gone and some, I hope, will still be the same. People I've loved are dead, and, thank god, many are still here. I don't think I could bear this without Yoko and my sons.

I know you have a million questions. Who wouldn't? But, listen. I'll tell you more, later. Right now, I have to get ready for a photo shoot. Annie Leibovitz is coming over to do a session with me and Yoko. It was supposed to have been just for Yoko, but now Annie gets two for one.

ENIGMA

Truth is stranger than fiction,
but it is because fiction is obliged to stick to possibilities.
Truth isn't.

- Mark Twain

On Wednesday morning, televisions up and down the East Coast are tuned in to NBC's *Today Show* expecting to see the predictable two hours of news and talk. Instead, the early winter's day − 40 degrees with light winds and bright sunshine − holds the promise of something big. The banner at the bottom of the screen reads, *Breaking Overnight: Is John Lennon Alive?* The subtitle declares: *Strange appearance in front of the Dakota.*

Live from Studio 1A at New York City's Rockefeller Center, anchor Hoda Kotb begins the broadcast in an uncharacteristically excited state. Looking polished in a cropped black suit jacket, white shift, and a colorful scarf, she appears on the left side of the split screen.

"Welcome Officer Justin Dove," Hoda says. "Thanks for being here."

On the right, the 30-year-old uniformed NYPD officer is at the ready. "Thanks, ma'am. Kind of otherworldly circumstances, right?"

"I'll say. So last night at 10:50 p.m., exactly 40 years to the minute when John Lennon was shot dead outside of the Dakota apartment building, you claim to have observed something virtually unexplainable. Can you tell us what you were doing at the scene?"

"Yes, ma'am. I was on duty working crowd control on the northwest corner of 72nd Street and Central Park West," Officer Dove says. "Yoko Ono was across the street in Central Park at a peace rally in remembrance of John Lennon's death. There were a few hundred people waiting for her to return home so they could get a glimpse of her and maybe an autograph. It was a peaceful group and, at first, not much was going on; a little chatter, some guitar playing and singing, that kinda stuff."

"OK. Let's take a look at some footage of what purportedly happened next," Hoda says. "I say purportedly because, frankly, it's hard for me to wrap my head around this. We obtained this video late last night from a witness. Preliminary scrutiny indicates it's genuine, but we haven't had a chance to finalize authentication." The video lasts about 30 seconds. It shows the miraculous appearance of the outline of John Lennon's body, a close-up of glowing colors, and his flesh filling out to become his living form.

Hoda shakes her head. "I don't know. How can this be real?"

"That's my foot in the picture," Officer Dove offers.

"So, you're asserting you were right there?"

"Yes, I was. I was standing right over him. It was the wackiest thing I've ever seen in my entire life. He stood up, like he had just tripped, and asked what was going on. He was a little out of it. When I asked him his name, he said, 'I'm John Lennon.'"

Off camera, Al Roker, the show's jocular weather man, makes circles with his finger at his temple and mouths, "Cuckoo, cuckoo."

"He was shot before I was born so I only know him from photos," Officer Dove continues. "But I'll tell you, he looked exactly like the guy in all the Beatles pictures I've seen. I don't think he's an imposter."

Hoda, the consummate professional, ignores her co-workers making faces off camera at her side and stays focused. "You're a well-respected and decorated officer. How long have you been on the force?"

"For nine years."

"Don't you think this is beyond far-fetched? Even for New York City?"

The girl-next-door beauty and co-anchor, Savannah Guthrie, playfully mimics "duh" and rolls her eyes.

"Damn right it's far-fetched. Oh, excuse me, ma'am."

"That's all right, officer. I've heard far worse."

"I have no freakin' idea what the hell is going on. The only thing I'm sure about is that it really happened. I watched it with my own eyes. A human being just…I don't know, what's the word? Morphed into existence."

"Do you sincerely believe John Lennon came back from the dead?"

"I'm on desk duty at the precinct. Off the streets 'til the shrinks can make sure I haven't gone zonkers. But, yes. Just don't ask me how."

"Well," Hoda says, "there are hundreds of other witnesses to back you up; you weren't alone. Here are additional corroborating short clips and photos, several of them shot on devices from different angles and from across the street. They've been blowing up the internet all night."

John Lennon comes to life over and over, the tentative evidence transmitted to hundreds of thousands of living rooms at seven the next morning. Hoda muses, "Really. I wonder if this is a brilliant hoax." She continues with her guest, "Tell me how the crowd reacted, Officer Dove."

"It was crazy. Chaos. Some people freaked out and split, and others wanted to touch the guy, like he was the messiah or something. I rushed him inside before he was totally mobbed. My partner came running from around the corner, and we called backup to control the situation outside."

"Were you with – what should we call the guy? John? Were you there when Yoko saw him for the first time?"

"Yes, I was chatting with him, trying to bring him up to speed when she came into the lobby. I swear she recognized him, you could see it on her face. She lit up, if you know what I mean. He was confused when he saw her. They had some private words, and then she and her little entourage whisked him into the elevator and took him upstairs. And that was it."

Hoda addresses her own skepticism with, "You seem like a credible guy; a regular guy."

"The feds were spooked by it too. An FBI S.W.A.T. team swooped in and took over jurisdiction. There was no crime, and no one was hurt, so I don't know what that was going to accomplish."

"Quite a few governmental agencies are already investigating this phenomenon. We'll see what happens and keep everyone apprised. Thanks for joining us."

"My pleasure, Ms. Kotb," Officer Dove says.

During the commercial break, Savannah and Al allow themselves to laugh uncontrollably. Al has tears in his eyes. "Hoda, Hoda, Hoda," he says, shaking his head and stamping a foot. He catches his breath and asks, "You're kidding. An elaborate joke, yes?"

Hoda looks past the makeup artist powdering her forehead. "You never know, Al," she says seriously. "If we'd never expanded our thinking to consider odd possibilities, we'd still think the earth was flat and the center of the universe."

Al takes a handkerchief out of his pocket, dabs his eyes, and blows his nose. "It's so improbable, though."

"Yeah, but improbable is not the same as impossible," Hoda says. She fiddles with her big hoop earring. "Can you imagine if that guy really is John Lennon? I mean, can you imagine?" She hooks the heel of her pink shoe behind a rung.

The stage hand calls, "We're on again in three, two," and holds his finger up to silently signal "one" and rolling.

∞

President Trump tweets:

Donald J. Trump
@realDonaldTrump
John Lennon alive? Another liberal hoax
to deflect from real issues. More FAKE NEWS
from Hoda and NBC. Shameful.
7:14 AM 09 Dec 20

NOW

The World Trade Center is a living symbol of
man's dedication to world peace...
a representation of man's belief in humanity,
his need for individual dignity, his beliefs in the cooperation of men,
and, through cooperation, his ability to find greatness.

- Minoru Yamasaki

A pair of tamed beasts stretch their wings and skim the azure sky. They dip behind clouds of cotton and reappear with their silver scales glinting in the morning sun. Their underbellies, vulnerable and open to the spectators below, belie the beasts' imminent destiny. John watches them soar closer to the great towers; his heart races and his breathing quickens as he anticipates what he already knows.

The devil waves his scepter and the creatures crane their necks to look at John. The faces of the beautiful beasts transform into ugly snarls of sharp teeth and forked tongues. They let forth ferocious growls that shake the land. Now controlled by sinister forces, the beasts turn back to their targets and attack.

The towers scream with shock as if they are living beings when the beasts rip through their skin. Fire sears their innards and spreads like cancer, killing slowly, cell by cell. Billowing smoke signals the kingdom below that the world as they knew it is no longer.

The structures writhe in pain — they twist and groan and shriek with unimaginable anguish; they hold on as long as they can. The weight of their injuries becomes unbearable and, in turn, each collapses into heaps of bleeding rubble. John is coated with the debris raining from above. He is suffocating and thrashes about.

"John! John!" Yoko gently prods her husband. "You're having a nightmare again. Wake up."

When John hears Yoko's voice, he leaves his dream state. "OK." He opens his eyes, gets his bearings, and turns to her. "I'm ready to see ground zero for myself. Let's go."

"Now?" Yoko asks.

"Yes, now," he says. "It's all we have."

∞

John and Yoko get out of bed and bundle up for John's first sojourn outside the confines of their apartment since his return. "Four o'clock in the morning. The FBI, CIA, NSA, Homeland Security, and who knows what other agents are out there to follow you around are going to be thrilled," Yoko says. She pulls a sweater over her head. "You always were a pain in the ass to the man. I bet they never thought you'd literally come back to haunt them."

John makes a boogeyman pose and goes after Yoko. They tumble back down onto the bed laughing.

"Maybe the crowds won't be as bad at this hour," John says. He kisses Yoko and holds her face. "The postman wanted an autograph. The cab driver wanted a picture. The waitress wanted a handshake. Everyone wanted a piece of me. That was before. It's going to be worse now, isn't it?" He doesn't expect an answer. He sits up and puts on his boots.

Yoko speaks into the air and says, "Goopplezon. Connect with Julio. Julio? Sorry to wake you at this hour, we really appreciate you being here for us 'round the clock. Get the car ready, will you? Put the diversion plan into action. We'll be down in ten minutes."

Yoko, John, and four bodyguards slip into the back of the limo. "Where's the driver?" John asks.

"We don't need one, John. Our car drives itself."

"Kuruma, ground zero," Yoko commands the car. "Swing by Rockefeller Center first via Fifth Avenue. Slow down to view the tree. Sightseeing mode, please."

The car repeats her command for verification, "Is this correct, Ms. Yoko?" They turn right off 72nd Street and ease down Central Park West. A light snow falls; enough to reflect the moonlight and muffle the music of the city.

"Kuruma?" John asks.

"'Car' in Japanese. I had to call him something. First thing that came to me when we were programming him."

"What's that?" John nods in the direction of a Starbucks.

"It's a coffee shop, John. Since the 1990s, they've been popping up everywhere–"

"No, I mean that," John interrupts pointing to a pedestrian on the sidewalk. "What the hell is that? Look, there's another one. What is that?"

"Those are cellphones with holograms. When you're talking to someone, you can choose to have their 3-D image hover in front of you. I could have done that when I called Julio on our home system, but I didn't want him to pop up in the middle of our bedroom and freak you out."

"I appreciate that, babe." John laughs. "This is incredible."

Thirty or so objects fly overhead toward them as they approach Columbus Circle. John looks at Yoko and throws his hands up as a questioning gesture.

"Drones," she says. "Amazon – oh, yeah – that was an online store where you can order anything you want to buy on the computer. They are the "zon" in Goopplezon today. Anyway,

Amazon was the first to use them to deliver packages to apartment buildings and special drop boxes – often within an hour. Now a lot of stores use them, and you'll see the overnighters flying off-peak."

"What are those? Rolling coolers?"

"Bots," Yoko answers. "They deliver packages and takeout food. We still live in the city that never sleeps."

John points to two pedestrians standing at the curb. "Why are their cigarettes glowing different colors."

"They're e-cigarettes – electronic," Yoko explains. "Vaping, ah, inhaling flavored vapor with nicotine in it, became all the rage five or six years ago."

"Every time someone walks past a store window, the advertisement changes. Why does that happen?"

"The store reads a chip in your i-Watch or cellphone and knows who you are. The ads change to something you were searching for online or something to complement what you've already purchased. If you recently bought a bathing suit in New York in the winter, the computer program figures out that you're going on vacation and shows you luggage or sunglasses."

"That's a bit intrusive, wouldn't you say?"

"Rockefeller Center, ETA five minutes, Ms. Yoko," Kuruma announces. They sit lost in thought as they drive by the elaborately decorated store windows – each its own commentary on current culture. "If everyone demanded peace instead of another television set then there'd be peace," John says. His growing apprehension is palpable.

"Pull over, please," Yoko tells the car. "Look, John, the tree. There's something to be said for enduring traditions. This hasn't changed."

"If I sit here and look at the angels, and toy soldiers, and the Christmas tree lights, I can pretend that everything is the same," John says, "like we're going to see the Twin Towers instead of the site of a mass grave."

"Don't be afraid, my love. You are strong. Don't rail against the changes around you, embrace them."

"The future came a little sooner than I expected, that's all. But now belongs to us, doesn't it?" John is pensive. "Thank God you're here, Yoko. I don't know what I would have done without you. Everything will be OK in the end. If it's not OK, it's not the end." Caressing Yoko's face he says, "Alright, babe, let's see what's going on in our little town."

With a heavy heart, he hums "I want to hold your hand" and takes his wife's hand in his.

∞

It's been forty years! Forty, for Christ's sake, and I come back to this? Sure, technology has advanced in leaps and bounds, but what good is that? Everyone is still killing each other over religion. Boko Haram, al-Qaeda, ISIS, Hezbollah, Hamas. This is crazy. I've been watching videos, documentaries, the news, and all sorts of stuff to catch up on what I've missed. The world went to hell in a hand basket while I was gone.

Did you know that Boko Haram means "Western education is sin"? They reject the fact that the earth is round because it's an idea propagated by the West. They think they are rebels with a cause for the greater good. How is their insatiable thirst for blood lifting the human condition in any way? What they are capable of doing to fellow human beings is detestable.

I freaked out when I was down at ground zero. Such a travesty. And what did it accomplish? More hatred, that's all.

We've got to take action. This can't continue. Peace is not something you wish for; it's something you make, something you do, something you are, and something you give away.

I'm not claiming divinity. I've never claimed purity of soul. I've never claimed to have the answers to life. I only put out songs and answer questions as honestly as I can, but I still believe in peace, love, and understanding. I will get back to my music, yes. It's how I can inspire people to a higher purpose.

Listen! There are two basic motivating forces: fear and love. When we are afraid, we pull back from life. When we are in love, we open to all that life has to offer with passion, excitement, and acceptance. We need to learn to love ourselves first, in all our glory and our imperfections. If we cannot love ourselves, we cannot be fully open to loving others or to our creative potential. Evolution and all hope for a better world rest in the fearlessness and open-hearted vision of people who embrace life.

We are all one. You are me and I am you. You think my message is naïve? Really? Tell me; how has the alternative been working out so far?

I hope you will join me in the name of peace.

LIKE A GAZILLION SUNS

It is not known precisely where the angels dwell —
whether in the air, the void, or the planets.
It has not been God's pleasure
that we should be informed of their abode.

- Voltaire

John's reflection stares at him from the large oval mirror hanging in his bathroom. He looks directly into the stranger's eyes and asks, "How can I go forward when I don't know which way I'm facing?" He splashes lukewarm water on his face and sighs while contemplating the water dripping off his chin to kerplunk into the sink. He swishes his brush on soap in a shaving mug and applies lather to his cheeks, upper lip, and neck. With a stainless-steel razor, he continues with the ritual of shaving in preparation for venturing out into the world.

"Daddy? Daddy?" John hears the sweet voice of his five-year-old son Sean.

"Look! I drew a picture for you," Sean says. The boy stands on the cold marble floor in his stocking feet, a drawing in his outstretched hand. His socks are pulled over his chubby calves and he wears black boxers and a brown short-sleeved T-shirt. His straight, sandy hair hangs almost to his shoulders. The flow of time is an illusion. The past, present, and future converge.

Startled by the sight of his little boy, John nicks his skin with the razor. A poinsettia red droplet of blood rolls off his face, but gravity has no effect; it hangs suspended in front of him. Like the mitosis of a zygote, the droplet divides in two, then into four, and then into eight, until there are countless droplets in front of him. Together, they form the shape of a small heart, each containing a shimmering point of light. They disperse and drift around the room to surround him and give him a sense of security.

The 5-foot 9-inch tall Sean leans through the bathroom doorway. "Dad? Are you OK? You're staring into space." He's wearing his tweed coat with a scarf around his neck. His tussled, curly black hair and round glasses complete his signature look. He is five years older than his own father.

"Did you hear me?" Sean asks. "I drew this picture for you when I was little; it's of us shaving in this bathroom. Here." He places the yellowed, partially crumpled sheet of paper on the counter in front of his father.

John nods in recognition. "You always said you wanted to be just like me."

"I've kept this for forty years! You remember it, dad?"

"Yes. You drew this yesterday."

"In a way it feels like it was just yesterday for me too," Sean says. "Listen, dad. Your appointment is at 9, but you don't have to do this if you don't want to. We know you are you. That's all that matters."

"I'd usually say 'up the establishment,' son, but I want answers about myself as much as everyone else does. Almost ready."

John looks back into the mirror and watches the lights twinkle bright and disappear one by one. "Thank you," he whispers to his visitors. The last light lingers and fades.

"No problem," Sean replies.

∞

The guards admit John, Yoko, Sean, and their group of bodyguards to the Vim Vitae Medical Imaging Center on Madison Avenue.

As they enter the lobby, facial recognition software scans the visitors' faces. A 3-D hologram of a young male nurse dressed in white scrubs and a lab coat appears in front of them.

"Welcome, Mr. Lennon." The nurse smiles warmly. "We've been expecting you."

John, unsure how to interact with the hologram, hesitates to answer.

"I can see you and hear you," the nurse says. "You can talk to me as if I were standing in front of you."

"Ah, right then. Hello."

"Hello! Please proceed to the elevator with the open door in front of you and take a seat."

John and his group enter the stark white elevator car illuminated by soft, electric blue and emerald green recessed lighting. Built-in seats line its perimeter. There are no buttons. The nurse's voice says, "Floor 40, please." They feel the effects of g-force and arrive at their destination in 20 seconds. The pneumatic doors hiss open and the nurse, in the flesh, greets them as they stand up.

"Mr. Lennon, you'll come with me. The rest of you, please follow our guest attendant to the observation room."

John and the nurse-receptionist holding a Goopplezon-pad walk side by side down a long hallway that makes John think he has been kidnapped by aliens and whisked away from Earth on their spaceship.

The nurse says, "I have a high-level security clearance, so I've been briefed about your circumstances, sir." In a reassuring tone he adds, "I saw the videos too. I believe it's real. I mean, you're real. Well of course you're real, you're right here in front of me. Oh, sorry. I'm a little nervous; I can't believe I'm talking to one of the original Beatles!"

"Are you a fan?" John asks, trying to put the young man at ease.

"My grandparents are. Do you think I could get an autograph for them?"

"Sure. Got a pen?"

"Ah, no sir. If you use this stylus, I'll be able to send it right over to them."

They enter a well-lit room that looks like NASA's mission control center. A glass capsule, large enough for a person to stand in, occupies the middle of the room. "Mr. Lennon, this is Dr. May Belle. She'll take the lead on the examination and explain the procedure."

"Welcome, Mr. Lennon. This whole procedure will take less than 10 minutes and we'll have instantaneous results. Today's advanced technology allows our computers to run parallel algorithms to process data at astonishing speeds."

"I missed the whole computer revolution, doctor," John says.

"No worries. You'll step into the scanning pod. It uses the best elements of technology you may be familiar with: X-ray and computerized axial tomography, magnetic resonating imagery, positron emission tomogra—"

"—Doc! I just want to know if it will hurt."

The doctor laughs and says, "No, not at all. You'll have to remain still and the hair on your body will stand on end. You'll hear a gentle whirring. That's it. We'll generate a complete 3-D picture of all your internal organs. We'll be able to see them as clearly as if we cut you open to take a look.

"We've already acquired a blood sample from police crime scene evidence to develop a comparative DNA model. It was in good enough condition for our purposes. That's the hologram model of John Lennon's DNA across the room."

"Wow! Everything that makes me, me."

"John Lennon is the only human being who has ever lived, lives now, or will live in the future to have this exact DNA sequence. We'll get a swab of cells from your skin and create a new model to compare the two. In a few minutes, we'll know with 100 percent accuracy if it's a match. Our sampling experts are witnessing chain of custody protocol."

"Don't let me down, doc."

∞

"Mr. Lennon. You are indeed who you say you are. There is nothing unusual about your body. We can't explain what happened to bring you back to us, but there is no doubt you are an ordinary 40-year-old man. Just a regular human being."

"I knew that, doc," John says without sarcasm.

"At your request, we've provided all of them with copies of the data to scrutinize." She gestures toward the observation gallery where representatives from several U.S. governmental agencies, the World Health Organization, and the international scientific community observed the proceedings. "The data is impeccable and redundant. Maybe now you'll be able to move forward with the business of living."

"Back to sex, drugs, and rock and roll."

"I counsel my patients to embrace a healthy lifestyle, Mr. Lennon. Exercise and music can help you reach your maximum life expectancy!" Doctor Belle adds, "We've isolated the gene responsible for aging and we are able to accurately predict how long you will live under optimal conditions of self-care. Do you want to know?"

With his quintessential smirk, John replies, "You mean if no one shoots me?"

"Right." Doctor Belle chuckles. "I'm glad your sense of humor is intact. We're talking natural causes. How you nurture your body can either support or undermine nature."

"I think I don't want to know. I'm going to live my life as if I don't have much time. And if I'm still around when I'm an old geezer, I'll consider that a bonus."

"Good luck to you, Mr. Lennon."

"Thanks, but how lucky am I already? Miracles are happening all around me."

∞

Angels in my bathroom. A strange place for them, eh? No, I don't hear voices – it's not like that. They speak to me in a different way. Think of a time you've had an epiphany. The answer just comes to you, right? Out of the blue. Angels are around us, all the time; wherever we are, they are there too. You just have to allow them into your life.

Sometimes they come to us in disguise; a stray animal that finds its way to your front door, a whisper in your dreams, a person you meet on the beach that changes your life, a brilliant idea that pops into your mind from nowhere.

They talk to us in a million ways. Has a book fallen off a shelf in front of you and opened to a page with a meaningful message? Did your phone ever ring right when you were thinking of someone you missed? Happens all the time, right? That's not a coincidence. I bet you've desired something – information, a contact, or even money – and somehow it appeared exactly when you needed it. Angels.

Their message? Hate is not vanquished by hate. Love can be the only everlasting victor. The great English poet Robert Browning said, "Take away love and our earth is a tomb." I mean, this isn't a new idea – we've just lost sight of it. Our world view is all askew.

We think of ourselves as separate from one another, but we're not. You've heard of the butterfly effect? Everything is connected. Goopplezon says, "A minute localized change in a complex system can have large effects elsewhere." What a concept! A gentle flutter of the wing – like a random act of kindness or a promise of healing within your own family – can ripple forth and cause a tsunami of a peace revolution around the world.

I have a sticky note on my bathroom mirror – great invention, by the way – with a quote by Sophocles that guides my continued life's mission: "One word frees us of all the weight and pain of life. That word is love." I look back on everything I've ever believed, and this is who I've always been. Looking back helps me know how to go forward.

Some people will think I'm crazy. Or I'm not who I say I am. There will always be skeptics. I'm not going to change the way I look or the way I feel to conform to anything. I've been a freak all my life and I have to live with that, you know. I'm one of those people. But it's OK.

I feel powerful energy emanating from people all around me. They light up the universe like a gazillion suns. It's the work of peace that's important. I'll channel my angels and live fearlessly.

A FUNDAMENTAL PROBLEM

To imitate the hatred and violence
of tyrants and murderers
is the best way to take their place.

- Pope Francis

John receives the finishing touches on his hair and makeup.
His classic Romanesque nose is powdered, and his hair looks chicly
nonchalant. He and Yoko lounge on the sofa in the green room at
the HBO studios in Rockefeller Center draping themselves over
one another into a tangle of indistinguishable limbs. They laugh at
Real Time host Bill Maher's monologue. John is dressed casually in
jeans, a buttoned-down sweater and his beloved New York T-shirt
made famous by a 1974 photo by Bob Gruen. In a few minutes he
will appear as an unannounced guest on the show.

A backstage techie announces, "Two minutes, Mr. Lennon.
Do you need anything?"

"No. I'm good, love. Thanks."

John unfolds himself from his wife and takes his place
outside the green room door to wait for his cue. He turns back to
Yoko and says, "I miss this. We need to get back to performing
live."

∞

Out front, standing on his mark on stage, Bill Maher says, "Ladies and gentlemen, we've kept the identity of our guest tonight a secret because he is — without a doubt — the most controversial guest I've ever invited to the show; you may have noticed the extra security in the house. He's a talented singer/songwriter, one of the legendary Beatles, and he has recently returned to the world after being dead for 40 years." He pauses to compose himself. "Wow! In all the years I've been doing this show this has to be the weirdest intro to come out of my mouth! So, without further ado, please give a warm welcome to Mr. John Lennon!"

The applause sign lights up but the surprised audience does not react. An audience coordinator waves his arms wildly to encourage them to clap.

John walks down a short hallway leading to the stage and stands behind a partition. He shivers when a tickle rolls up his spine from his buttocks to the base of his neck. His hands tingle as energy pricks his fingertips like a frostbitten hand warming up after an afternoon of making snowballs.

He watches, perplexed, as his body fills with static. He hears Bill calling him, but with his next step he emerges into silence… and is alone. The studio is gone, and darkness engulfs him, save a sliver of light from a nascent moon hanging low in the sky.

Salted ocean air warms John's face. He stands motionless atop a sand dune anchored by clusters of grasses and reeds. Palm trees twist and turn, left and then right, forward and back, as if they dance to music only they can hear. Approaching the water's edge, he watches the waves gently roll to shore. The lapping is hypnotic.

John plops down crossed-legged in the sand, removes his glasses and wipes off condensation with the tail of his shirt. When he brushes his windblown hair out of his face, he is startled by a blinding flash of light on the horizon. An eighth of a beat later he feels the shockwaves of a great explosion rush past him.

A ball of hot gases expands outwardly in all directions, rises up into a funnel and, within 30 seconds, plumes out to form a mushroom cap. The detonation of an atomic bomb suffocates its target with a sickening, thick black smoke. John forgets to breathe as he contemplates what he is witnessing.

Tiny points of twinkling light appear above his head and tumble down around him. He senses they are not threatening. "Who are you?" he asks. "Please, tell me! What are you? Why have you shown me this?" The lights surround him and lift him to his feet.

∞

From far, far away, he hears a woman yell, "We love you, John!"

"John? Where are you? Don't be shy now!" Bill turns from the audience and waits to shake John's hand.

John blinks and once again finds himself behind the partition. His body casts a warm glow as he transitions to the present.

Noticing the unusual light, Bill asks, "What the heck was that? Helloooo?"

John, steeling himself to be fully in the present as is his custom whenever he sets foot on a stage, is unaware of the missing blip in time. He sings "Hello, hello!" in response and steps forward to the house erupting into wild applause.

Most of the audience stands for an ovation; the audience coordinator can't get them to settle down.

"Now, now," Bill says. "Take it easy. We don't have all night."

A few people are overcome with emotion. Others roll their eyes and look annoyed.

John and Bill shake hands, and Bill says, "Good to see you. Thanks for being here."

"That monologue was funny stuff, Bill. Not an easy act to follow."

"Are you kidding? Your appearance will upstage anyone at any time. You've returned from the dead, for goodness sake. And the first thing I really want to know is…did you meet God, John?"

"No, I didn't!"

"See, I knew it," Bill says. He gives his audience an "I-told-you-so" look and they laugh.

"I'm not saying there's no God," John says. "I'm just saying I haven't met him yet."

"So, what were you doing while you were dead for 40 years? And don't tell me you were decomposing, because by the looks of it, you're still pretty fresh."

"Gee, thanks for the compliment, Bill. I'm feeling just fine. I don't know where I was or what was happening. I wish I could remember."

"You didn't visit heaven…or hell?"

"If I ever get to do that, I'll give you a sign," John jokes. "Can you imagine closing your eyes for a second and, before you open them again, forty years goes by. That's what it feels like to me."

"What do you *think* happened?"

"Maybe I was temporarily in another world. I'll tell you something, *this* feels like a different world. Dick Tracy used to talk into his imaginary gadget and we thought that was wild. Now people are talking into their watches for real, and out into the air, and it looks like they're talking to themselves. Everything is different. Well, in a way, *nothing* is really different. I don't know which is scarier."

"Has this experience changed your ideas about death? I mean, do you fear death?" Bill asks.

"No, I'm not afraid. I haven't actually experienced death; we can be aware of the process of dying, but actual death is only experienced by the living."

"True, true," Bill says.

"If you're going to be afraid of something it shouldn't be of death; it should be of not living big," John says. "How many people do you know who don't create anything? *All* their free time is in front of the TV. They spend hours a day commuting over to the office to do a job they hate and work with people they don't like. They're stuck in loveless relationships, and they're too afraid to do anything about it. They don't go to the beach or walk in the park. No music. No art. I even know a guy who has never read one book in his life. That's what we should be fearful of – not living while we're alive!"

"Speaking of creating and music, how do you feel about a Beatles' reunion?"

"I've been writing music. And I'm on my piano as usual. I'd love to sing with Paul again. He's like a brother, I love him. We certainly had our ups and downs and our quarrels. But at the end of the day, when it's all said and done, I'd do anything for him. And I think he'd do anything for me. I'm going to see him and Ringo soon and I can't wait. It's a shame George isn't with us."

"Maybe he'll be back tomorrow!" Bill and the audience laugh.

"Trust me, there's a lot we don't know, Bill!"

"So, now that you're back, you are once again promoting love and peace."

"As far as I know, I never left. I'm just continuing what I've always been into."

Bill says, "When I was a kid I used to watch the David Frost Show. You were one of his guests back in 1969. We've got a clip. Watch this."

John spoke to David Frost and said, "We're trying to sell peace, like a product, you know, and sell it like people sell soap or soft drinks. And it's the only way to get people aware that peace is possible, and it isn't just inevitable to have violence. Not just war — all forms of violence. People just accept it, but we're all responsible for everything that goes on, you know, we're all responsible for Biafra and Hitler and everything.

"So we're just saying, 'sell peace.' Anybody interested in peace, just stick it in the window. It's simple, but it lets somebody else know that you want peace too, because you feel alone if you're the only one thinking, 'Wouldn't it be nice if there was peace and nobody was getting killed?' So advertise yourself that you're for peace if you believe in it."

When the video ends, Bill says, "There's been some crazy shit happening in the world over the past 40 years, John."

"You're telling me! The actor Ronald Reagan became president, and someone tried to assassinate him, too. And the Soviet Union collapsed. And this AIDS virus thing; whoa! There was a famine in Ethiopia. And a poison gas attack in Syria."

"I haven't thought of those things in so long," Bill admits. "You have a lot of catching up to do."

"Some good things too. The Berlin Wall came down. The first woman went into space, Sally—"

"Sally Ride," Bill says.

"But mostly a lot of bad shit is happening. We're going to destroy the world if we don't do something different — I can feel it. It's like I've seen the future somehow. We're on that path. I believe our future is not predestined, though. We can change the outcome. Working for peace, well, some ideas are timeless, don't you think?"

"Speaking of timeless, I saw Yoko in the green room before the show. Wow! She just doesn't age like a normal human being.

How's that going for you? Suddenly you're married to a much older woman!"

John laughs. "It's an adjustment for both of us. She always had a presentiment that we'd be together again. A dream you dream alone is only a dream. A dream you dream together is reality. This is our new reality. We're working it out. We're cool together."

"Thank you so much for being here with us, John. I'm a big fan. This was a thrill for me. Unfortunately, I know you have to go, and that's all the time we have."

As the *Real Time* theme music plays, Bill shakes John's hand, stands and says, "OK. Let's go over to our panel."

∞

Morning light floods John and Yoko's living room at the Dakota. John sits on the sofa and sips tea. "Here you go. Bill's people emailed this for you. I made a copy," Yoko says. She hands him the transcript from the *Real Time* show.

John removes a binder clip and reads the following:

HOST MAHER: All right, let's meet our panel. Here they are. He's an astrophysicist, cosmologist, science communicator, and author. Neil deGrasse Tyson is with us tonight. (*Applause*)

The always controversial and outspoken conservative social and political commentator, my friend and nemesis, Ann Coulter. Hey, Ann, how 'ya doin? (*Applause and boos*)

He's the incomparable Emmy Award-winning actor and liberal activist, Mr. Martin Sheen, is right over here. (*Applause*)

HOST MAHER: Well folks, unless you've been living under a rock, or maybe you've been dead temporarily yourself (*laughter*), you know that John Lennon has returned and is encouraging the citizens of the world to embrace love as the answer to our problems. So let me ask my panel what they think of this very controversial event.

COULTER: Bill! This is ridiculous! It's completely implausible that John Lennon has returned. That guy is an incredible look-alike, and he's asking us to suspend belief in everything we know about life and death.

SHEEN: What do we really know about life and death? I'm willing to at least consider the possibility there's more to the universe than I can comprehend. And then there's the DNA evidence, and all the videos and photos.

COULTER: As if! You think all that can't be faked? That's supposed to convince me? It's just not possible that someone can come back from the dead. Come on! Give me a break.

SHEEN: Gee, there are only more than 2 *billion* Christians in the world who already believe that's possible.

COULTER: What are you suggesting? A second coming?

DEGRASSE TYSON: Hold on, hold on. This doesn't even have to have religious implications. Maybe there are powers at work that can, at least partially, be explained by science.

HOST MAHER: Thank God. You know what I think about religion. Oh, wait, who am I thanking?

SHEEN: Oh, Bill. What are we going to do with you?

DEGRASSE TYSON: The answer may lie with the concept of time. Einstein said the distinction between past, present, and future is only a stubbornly persistent illusion. He posited that they all exist concurrently – at the same moment.

SHEEN: So, maybe John Lennon wasn't "resurrected" but somehow time stood still for him?

DEGRASSE TYSON: Exactly, Martin! Perhaps the rest of us experienced a different reality – or rather, sense of time – simultaneously.

SHEEN: Like he just continued living his life from one second to the next, and the event that killed him was only something *we* experienced?

DEGRASSE TYSON: Einstein proved that time is not absolute; it's relative. You've heard the example about sending someone into space in a super-fast spaceship and comparing his experience to someone waiting for him back on Earth? While the space traveler experiences a few minutes or hours, the earth dweller would simultaneously live through much more time – it could be days or years. The faster the person in the spaceship travels, the slower his time will pass relative to someone on Earth. If the space traveler could reach the speed of light, time would cease for him and he would be in a state of timelessness.

SHEEN: Wow weeee! That Einstein guy was smart! (*Laughter*)

COULTER: I'm sorry! I just can't wrap my head around someone coming back to life for *any* reason.

HOST MAHER: Call me crazy – it wouldn't be the first time – I believe he *is* John Lennon. That's always going to be debatable, though; I can't imagine the world coming to a consensus. Let's move on then and discuss his message. My guest – whoever you think he is – is spreading the word that love is the answer to the challenges we're facing around the world. What do you think of that?

COULTER: Well, I'm playing the role of Debbie Downer today, aren't I? Do you think that's what terrorists are looking for? Some kumbaya, feel-good psychobabble is going to make them say, "Gee, I'm feeling all warm and fuzzy inside. I'm not going to cut the head off my hostage today?" You people need to get real.

DEGRASSE TYSON: There's a difference between feelings of love and actions. Dropping bombs on them is proof we have failed miserably at diplomacy. Communication and negotiations have failed. And our efforts for deterrence have been woefully inadequate.

COULTER: What's the alternative?

DEGRASSE TYSON: Their hatred of Westerners and Christians is based on ignorance and intolerance. Education might be a good place to start.

COULTER: Oh, like star shows and podcasts, Neil?

SHEEN: Have you ever heard of Dr. Benedetta Berti? She's done some fine work in the area of peace building.

COULTER: The only thing that is going to create peace is to annihilate all the terrorists. We have to obliterate Hamas,

Hezbollah, ISIS... While they're walking the face of the Earth, there will be no peace.

HOST MAHER: Can you name one place where U.S. military intervention has been successful at doing that... after all these years? Insanity, Ann, insanity. Doing the same thing over and over and expecting a different outcome.

SHEEN: Dr. Berti says the reason these groups flourish is because they provide public health services – they build hospitals and schools and garbage and sewer systems. They step in to ensure safety and security where governments have fallen short. They've built effective communication systems – radio stations, TV channels, websites, social media channels, and even an English language magazine to recruit for ISIS.

COULTER: Dabiq.

DEGRASSE TYSON: I can understand how those services are enticing to people.

SHEEN: Then they create legitimate and profitable businesses and use them to raise funds, increase their brand awareness and recruiting capabilities.

COULTER: Oh, good God! And we're going to coddle these animals?

HOST MAHER: That's why the Hamas party won the Palestinian elections back in '06. The people weren't voting for terrorism per se, they were voting for the basic necessities of life.

SHEEN: Winston Churchill said something in 1899 that is still relevant today. He said, "Individual Muslims may show splendid qualities, but the influence of the religion paralyzes the social development of those who follow it. No stronger retrograde force exists in the world. Mohammedanism is a militant and proselytizing faith...raising fearless warriors at every step."

COULTER: We agree on something! I think it is naïve not to deal with this threat severely. And by that, I mean with military intervention. There can be no doubt that their violent behavior will not be tolerated.

SHEEN: Listen to what you're saying! Use violence because we won't tolerate violence? How does that make sense? There are millions of peace-loving Muslims. Their religion has been hijacked by a relatively small number of evil-doers. "Hate is not conquered by hate. Hate is conquered by love." Buddha said that.

COULTER: Buddha didn't live in our world! The Islamic terrorists place zero value on life – even their own. They're demanding Christians denounce their beliefs and, when they refuse, murder their children in front of them. Then they behead the parents. They are publicly raping women. They wear bombs and commit suicide, taking out as many innocents as possible. Shopping malls, universities, and random public spaces are under siege. I just don't see how love and compassion could possibly be a solution to such tyranny.

SHEEN: Let's face it, the issues are complex.

HOST MAHER: When John Lennon speaks of love, I don't think he means overlooking horrific acts. What is love? Is it treating people with compassion? Dignity? Respect?

DEGRASSE TYSON: We're on a dangerous, slippery slope to world annihilation, my friends; unless *we're* the ones who work with the goal of improving the quality of life for the less fortunate.

SHEEN: That's always been the motivation for U.S. foreign-aid. Dr. Berti suggests we invest more in non-military tools to fill the gaps of inadequate governments. She says it's the way to encourage a transition from violence to non-violence.

HOST MAHER: So it boils down to problems like poverty, hunger, displacement and homelessness, global warming, and the mistreatment of women?

DEGRASSE TYSON: And religious intolerance. The extremists' violent behavior causes the loudest roar and creates the greatest fear as a result. But the problems you listed, Bill, are the underlying issues, and they are insidious. Collectively, they are debilitating.

SHEEN: Do not be overcome with evil, but overcome evil with good. Romans 12:21.

HOST MAHER: John would be happy to hear that, Martin.

COULTER: Who? That guy you had here?

HOST MAHER: Oh, boy. Let's not circle back on that. Not that I don't love a controversial challenge. (*Laughter*)

DEGRASSE TYSON: You have to give him credit for the work he's doing, Ann. My favorite saying is "Be ashamed to die until you have scored some victory for humanity."

HOST MAHER: And on that note…I'd like to thank my panelists—

DEGRASSE TYSON: —May I leave the group with a final quick thought, Bill? It's something we keep in mind in the scientific world. Thomas Edison said, "When you've exhausted all possibilities, remember this: you haven't."

HOST MAHER: Thanks, Neil. And now it's time for "New Rules."

John tosses the transcript onto the glass coffee table in front of him. He moves to his piano and teases Yoko with a silly ad-lib to the tune of "Watching the wheels."

So many bloody questions, am I lost in delusion?
Well, I can deal with my confusion, there will be a resolution
Well, they wonder 'what the fuck,' has he lost his mind?
I tell them don't worry, now I've got more time

Yoko plants her elbows on the baby grand and rests her chin in her palms. She says, "The world needs your music, John."

THE CROSSING POINT

Good friends are like stars
You don't always see them,
But you know they're always there

- Author unknown

They stare for a long minute and remain motionless across the living room from one another. For any other pair of friends, this might be awkward, but this is no ordinary reunion. John is leaning against his white baby grand piano with a look on his face that Paul will describe later as "a bloody stupid grin."

Paul approaches slowly, fascinated by John's familiar face. He knows it by heart. He grips both of John's shoulders and takes a good look. "I read the news reports and saw the videos and photos. I caught you on *Real Time* and studied the evidence online. I thought, 'A bunch of poppycock, all of it. It has to be.'" He takes a deep breath. "When Yoko called and told me to come by to surprise you, I thought she'd lost her mind. Holy shit! If I hadn't seen you myself, I never, ever would have believed this! It's really you, though, isn't it?"

John nods, and the two old friends embrace.

Choked with emotion, Paul sobs, "Damn it, mate, you went and died on me!" He takes a step back, tears streaming, and demands, "Tell me, please – how did you do this?"

John shrugs and throws up his hands. "The tears are killing me, mate. You look like a bloody old man."

Laughing and sobbing, Paul replies, "For the rest of us, life went on."

"The last time I saw you, we were watching *Saturday Night Live* right here, and we almost got into a cab to go down to the studio. Do you remember that?"

"Do you have any idea of how long ago that was?" Paul hugs John again. "I've missed you, auld fella." His voice cracks with emotion.

Speaking over Paul's shoulder, John says, "From when I died to when I returned, it barely felt like a second to me."

Paul steps back again and holds John's arms. "No shit, man? What was it like? What did you see on the other side?"

"You know what a lemniscate is? The sideways figure eight sign for infinity? I think it's a brilliant symbol. Imagine time moving in every direction at once – with no beginning and no end. And sometimes you cross back over the same point. That's where I am now. I can't spend any of my mental or emotional energy trying to figure it out. I'll leave that to the philosophers and scientists."

"But what did you see?" Paul demands.

"Nothing that I can remember."

"Come on, man. Don't be blaggin' me 'ead! I can handle it."

"Nothing," John insists. "It's like I didn't even have time to open my eyes and look around."

"But you were gone so long."

"Only if you think time moves in one direction. And you think it's the same for all of us."

"Maybe you're just a beat-up, old LP, mate," Paul says.

"What do you mean?"

"There you are, a diamond-tipped needle is moving through your groove, your music is playing all nice-like, when, wham, the needle hits a scratch and jumps back. Or ahead. Or all over, willy-nilly, and you never know where the music will start again."

"Good one, Macca. Some of the music has already played and some is yet to come. But it's all already there."

"I don't know," Paul says skeptically, "I don't really believe in the pre-destiny thing. It takes away the idea of free will. Too depressing a thought. There's gotta be choice. Someone can change the record too."

"Or maybe this: What if we have many lives at one time? Like you're driving on a highway, hop off at an exit and then drive the service road right next to where you were a minute ago? Know what I mean? Cars are still zipping by on the highway, only you're gone, but you can get back on at any time after you have this other adventure. Parallel lives."

"Too much for me, mate. This stuff makes my brain hurt." Paul puts up his hands in resignation. "The only time I think about time is when I notice that it's going faster and faster the older I get."

"I wonder why it feels that way," John says.

"When you're a 2-year-old, a year is half your life. When you get to my age, it's just a drop in the bucket in the big picture. Time probably isn't moving at all—"

John interjects, "That's what Einstein says."

"—but it feels like it's running out. And then you go and show up for a second visit. Damn! How cool is that?"

Paul embraces John, his lifelong friend, his childhood buddy, now half his age. Letting go and relaxing, Paul says, "We can write a song about it." He pinches away persistent tears in the corners of his eyes.

"Yeah, man. That's one of the things I want to talk to you about." Gesturing to his sofa, John invites Paul to sit for a chat. "But first, tell me what's going on with you. How's ya bird, Linda?"

"Oh, boy. This is going to take a while."

"Sozz, Macca I'm catching up as I go along. Fill me in."

John and Paul settle into the comfortable space of old friends picking up where they left off, as if no time had passed at all.

∞

I hadn't seen Paul for four and half years — according to my warped reality. Four and half, forty-four and a half — what's the difference? In my first life, I was busy with a new baby and there wasn't time to hang out. We're all busy, though, right? Still, that's no way to be a friend.

Paul made fun of me smiling at him when we finally got together this time. He told me, "Don't stick your tongue out or you might wet your ears."

I knew you'd ask that! Yes, we did talk about a Beatles reunion. George's son, Dhani, can stand in for his pop if he's available. That would be a fitting tribute. Ringo is going to come by for a visit soon. I talked to him, but he doesn't believe it's me. I hear his son, Zak, is a great drummer. Of course, I'd bring in Sean and Julian. Paul's son James too. And any of the other kids who might want in on the project.

I agree with you; the mysterious coincidence of me being here at this time in history has some sort of meaning. The world is on the precipice of a renaissance of sorts — one that's essential for our ultimate survival. The Beatles and our music can bring a message of peace to encourage a new worldview.

Do you really think you're powerless? A big mistake to think that! Everyone can do something to make a difference! There are countless examples of one person having a huge impact — either directly with their work or by influencing other people to follow in their footsteps.

Ghandi, Martin Luther King, Jr., Mother Teresa, Steve Jobs, Jonah Salk, people who volunteer in a community soup kitchen, care for the elderly, shovel snow for a neighbor. The list can go on and on. We have the power to shape the world; how you relate to people in your own sphere can add love to the planet. Can you imagine if everyone reached a little further out of their circle and loved just a little more deeply?

Paul is totally into this. There's going to be some rocking and rolling happening. Our music is going to speak for us.

So, let me ask you this: Do you have the courage and conviction to be a part of this? The planet is in big trouble. I know, I'm stating the obvious. We've got to get everyone to wake up and do something about it, really get in their faces. When you're drowning, you don't say 'I would be incredibly pleased if someone would have the foresight to notice me drowning and come and help me,' you just scream.

I'm screaming! Help me! I know you can!

DEATH TOLL

The stars are scattered all over the sky
like shimmering tears,
there must be great pain in the eye
from which they trickled.

\- Georg Buchner

Stepping outside the Dakota into the balmy winter twilight dressed head to toe in black — a turtleneck sweater, wool pants, a long coat and scarf — John becomes invisible. Compelled to visit his own memorial, he crosses the street from the Dakota and slips into Central Park. He looks down at the circular black, gray, and white tiled mosaic on the western end of the garden's grounds and contemplates the word at its center. "Imagine," he says out loud.

A thud to John's right startles him. He approaches a nondescript heap on the grass and gasps as he realizes he is looking at the dead body of a young man. The deceased is dressed all in white — a tunic and loose pants — his skin the ashen gray pallor of extermination. He appears to be a teenager and perhaps Middle Eastern.

Another thud. John spins around to discover a second corpse dressed the same way, has fallen from the sky behind him; a young Vietnamese man. Next, a little girl falls in front of him; her long blond hair shining in the moonlight. To his left, an old woman, her gnarled hands land at rest over her heart. Three Hispanic men.

A gangly black man. Several Japanese men. One by one they fall, like the first raindrops announcing an impending deluge.

And so, the storm begins. Men of all ages, dead from war. Decapitated. Limbless. Their guts spilled onto the battlefield. Millions and millions of them throughout the ages.

Women. Raped. Crushed. Pierced by bullets. Dead of broken hearts. Schoolchildren blown to bits. Babes in arms, obliterated. All of them robbed of their futures.

Warriors, terrorists, soldiers, victims, innocents – soulless bodies now whole before John, equal in death, lay at his feet.

John runs to flee the horror. He leaps over a body that lands in his path and takes flight. The tails of his long coat flap loudly behind him as he soars. Piles of bodies mounting in the park quickly fill the two-and-a-half-acre, teardrop-shaped Strawberry Fields below him.

John dodges the inundation of death, dipping left, rising right, circling around – a frightened bird whose heart beats furiously. He collides with a falling body that sends him spiraling out of control and he plunges back to earth.

John hits his head. He opens his eyes and realizes he is on the floor next to his bed.

Yoko bursts into the room. "What happened?" She rushes to John's side.

"It was something terrible, my love. Was I dreaming?" John asks as he sits up rubbing his head. "Or did I leave again?"

"I don't know," she says. "I was in the kitchen."

UNITED WE ROCK®

So many of our dreams at first seem impossible,
then they seem improbable, and then,
when we summon the will, they soon become inevitable.

\- Christopher Reeve

♪

The world's three most influential corporations merged, when? In
2018, right? That was before I came back. None of them even existed at the
time of my departure. Ha! That cracks me up – the time of my departure. Like
I just got on a bus and went on a trip or something. Yeah, so Sean explained
that Google, Apple, and Amazon came together to form Goopplezon. The
merger was spearheaded by the CEOs of each company, young hipsters, and
forward-thinking "old timers." Yoko and I have a meeting coming up. They
seem very cool. They're committed to bringing music, art, and technology to the
people to foster global peace-building. Right on!

∞

A Goopplezon team member ushers John and Yoko into a
state-of-the-art conference room. "Right this way, Mr. and Mrs.
Lennon. We're all so excited to meet you in person this afternoon."
John had expected a roomful of stuffy, corporate suits. Instead, he
meets a relaxed group, dressed casually, conversing happily.

Calling the meeting to order, a handsome African-American
man with an infectious smile welcomes John and Yoko. "Mr. and
Mrs. Lennon, I am Robert Johnson, a former CEO with Black

Entertainment Television, founder of RLJ Companies, and presently the chief operating officer for the three co-chief executive officers of Goopplezon. Allow me to introduce you to product manager and former CEO of Google, Sundair Pichai; industrial engineer and developer and former CEO of Apple, Tim Cook; and entrepreneur, founder, and former CEO of Amazon, Jeff Bezos." Each gentleman stands and shakes hands with John and Yoko and welcomes them warmly.

The lights dim, and using voice commands and physical gestures, Mr. Johnson fills the room with 3-D images to support his presentation – a visually stunning example of technology coupled with surround-sound background music that is crisper than anything John has ever heard. "I think it will become evident shortly why we've invited you to this meeting," Mr. Johnson says.

Tim Cook takes the helm. "Although Goopplezon follows a traditional profit-making business model, we invest heavily in social programs consistent with our corporate philosophy, 'Peace is a basic human right.' While these initiatives are typically expense items that detract from a company's bottom line, we have found the resultant good will has had the opposite effect on Goopplezon's revenue. Socially conscious investors can't get enough of Goopplezon stock, and consumers want to spend their money on quality products made and supplied by a company whose culture is in line with their own ethical inclinations."

A pause sign lights up over the door, the 3-D images disappear, and the lights come up. "Ah, yes," Mr. Johnson says. "Tea service has arrived, and we'd like to introduce you to a few of our Peace University students – we've been supporting and mentoring them."

"Tea! Is right, mate! Appreciate the kindness," John says.

After some pleasant chatter and feasting on an artfully presented selection of sandwiches, cakes, and scones, the group returns to the topic at hand.

Jeff Bezos continues the meeting. "In addition to our traditional business units, Goopplezon plans to fully support its own, newly forming Peace Department. Many of our most progressive employees hold degrees in peace and conflict resolution from prestigious U.S. universities or are graduates of the United Nations-mandated University for Peace in Costa Rica."

Mr. Johnson says, "Goopplezon employees demonstrate a concern for the future of our planet. The company roster includes former Peace Corps volunteers, environmentalists, social workers, directors of non-profits, artists, student activists, and other visionaries of all ages and races, and without regard to gender. Our student interns Alyssa, Lexi, Gigi, and Anthony will continue."

The youngest members of the Goopplezon team beam with confidence and take turns speaking.

Alyssa begins. "Goopplezon's peace-building and conflict resolution mission has three key elements. One: To develop and manufacture the tools necessary for the free flow of information and remote access to education. Two: To help build efficient delivery mechanisms for supplying basic needs, including health care and clean water. And three: To support political candidates, policies, projects, and lobbying for laws and regulations to protect the environment and prevent violence."

Lexi elaborates. "About 90 percent of the world's 7.7 billion inhabitants have access to some sort of portable communication device: old-fashioned cellphones, ear bud phones, wrist watches, clothing chips, hologram transponders, pocket computers, obsolete Google glasses, and now the 3-D Goopplezon Lenses. We can use all this technology for educational purposes."

"Progress, civil liberties, a functioning government, and effective political participation require an educated populace," Alyssa adds.

John leans over to Yoko and whispers, "Google glasses?"

Yoko whispers back, "I'll explain later." Because of circumstances like this, the public nicknames Yoko "The Interpreter."

Gigi sees John has a question and volunteers to help. "Google glasses? Just a second, I'll show you." She pulls information up on the screen, and an assistant brings a pair into the room for him to examine.

John shakes his head in amazement. "And these are obsolete now?"

Tim Cook responds. "Yes, they've been replaced with the 3-D Goopplezon Lenses. We're perfecting a miniaturized version too – sort of a contact lens operated by sequence blinking. We have an extensive technology museum collection on premises. It would be my great pleasure to give you a guided tour." He clears his throat. "You left us in 1980. Good way to put it, right? Anyway, our first clunky Mac computer wasn't even rolled out until 1984. This must be overwhelming for you."

"Sean told me he had one of those. My friend Steve Jobs gave it to him as a gift."

"My predecessor at Apple," Tim says. "I'm sorry you weren't able to see your friend again. He certainly would have been thrilled to see you. He believed everything is possible."

"I'm living proof of that," John agrees. "Some things haven't changed at all and others, like all this technology, just blows me mind."

Anthony stands up and gestures. Photos of global devastation scroll around the room. He says, "Of the 77 million deaths worldwide within the past year, approximately 40 percent are attributed to environmental factors, such as water and air pollution and exposure to toxic chemicals. Here at Goopplezon we strive to provide practical solutions for tackling cleanup, restoration and the prevention of pollution. We are hoping that Sean and Ms. Yoko will collaborate with us as we tackle the issue of fracking, and we're already working with Julian's *White Feather Foundation* on an ocean cleanup project in the Pacific."

Sundair Pichai interjects, "We have instituted a systemic, eco-friendly approach to manufacturing and distribution practices. We aspire to a 'zero-landfill' approach to waste disposal and have implemented extensive waste minimization practices."

"Through advertising and education, we promote an awareness of climate change and the fragility of the planet," Gigi concludes.

Mr. Johnson thanks the students and, as they sit down, he adds sobering information: "During the 20th century, more than 100 million people died in wars and conflict. In the U.S., 8,000 veterans commit suicide each year after they return home from war. Another 300,000 people around the globe are killed every year because of gun violence."

John leans over and whispers to Yoko again. "That dream I had? I see them falling from the sky. You can't imagine how many of them there are!" Yoko squeezes his hand.

Mr. Johnson asks, "Why not use Goopplezon's technology, resources, and ingenuity to promote peace? This brings us to why we've invited you here, Mr. and Mrs. Lennon.

"First, Mr. Lennon, we want you to head up our Peace Department."

Raising his eyebrow, John says. "Thank you, but I don't think I'm much of the corporate type. I prefer to do my own thing."

"Perhaps you'll like our terms," Mr. Johnson counters. "We will fully fund your projects and give you a staff of peace ambassadors to help with coordination. But, you run the show autonomously. We'll back whatever plans you have regarding peace initiatives with our technology, resources, and advertising. You're the boss with final say."

"I'm the boss of me?" John laughs. "That sounds like something I might consider. Can we get back to you on this?"

"Of course. But there's more," Mr. Johnson adds. "We also want to form the Give Peace a Chance Party and back you to run for president of the United States!"

The attendees hoot and holler and burst into applause. They chant, "United we rock! United we rock! United we rock!"

John and Yoko look at each other with amusement.

Finally, John speaks, "Misters Johnson, Pichai, Cook, and Bezos, I'm flattered. Really flattered. I don't know what to say. I'm just a regular bloke. I make music, ya know."

"With the work you've done in the past and your earnest dedication to peace – coupled with your notoriety – you are the perfect person to lead our country in a new direction," Mr. Johnson says. "You can be the face of peace representing the U.S. to the world. Please think about it."

"I have a question," Yoko says. "Don't you have to be a natural-born citizen of the United States to be president?"

Mr. Johnson gives her a conspiratorial look and says, "We thought of that. Yes, you do. But the John Lennon born in Liverpool died in 1980. You, however—" He looks directly at John and pauses for dramatic effect. "—were re-born in New York City on December 8, 2020. Our lawyers are prepared to argue the case."

ZUG ZUG

A man who becomes conscious of the responsibility
he bears toward a human being who affectionately waits for him,
or to an unfinished work, will never be able to throw away his life.
He knows the 'why' for his existence,
and will be able to bear almost any 'how.'

- Viktor E. Frankl

Holding up two fingers to make a peace sign as he saunters into the Dakota living room, John says, "Peace and love!" and opens his arms to embrace another of his beloved brothers.

Ringo staggers back three steps — as if a mere few feet could shield him from the most shocking thing he's ever seen — and trips over Yoko and falls. Looking up from the floor, he screeches, "Good God! Hooooooooly shit!"

"This isn't like you, Ringo. You're usually much mellower," John says as a matter of fact. As John approaches, Ringo tries to scoot away. "Come now. It's OK," John cajoles. "It's just me; your old mate, John. There's nothing to be afraid of."

John offers his hand and waits patiently. Ringo reaches up with trepidation, expecting a monster to rip off his arm. He's been living a clean and sober life for years but fears he is hallucinating.

Ringo moves in slow motion, hindered by the gooey molasses of fear. The four seconds it takes in reality to rise to his feet, stretch to four protracted minutes in his mind's eye. While

Yoko helps steady him and John holds his hand, the sounds of the city subside and Ringo's brain floods with memories. They wash over him like euphoria — or an all-consuming terror.

A mélange of images floats by, snaps into place, fades slowly, and flickers: Ringo is in the "acoustik" booth at the Kirchenalle Recording Studio in Hamburg again, where in 1960, he sat in with John, Paul, and George for the first time as background musicians for another recording artist; John wears a silken lime-green top coat adorned in elaborate red trim and matching pants for Sgt. Pepper's Lonely Hearts Club band, while Ringo stands next to him, regal in fuchsia; a bitter wind blows as it did in 1969. John is in front of Ringo's drum set wearing Yoko's fur coat and working his rhythm guitar in "Don't Let Me Down" during their rooftop concert at the Apple Building in London; Ringo and John sit next to one another on a golden velvet sofa in Ringo's suite at the Plaza Hotel, carrying on and having a fantastic time three weeks before John is murdered.

Ringo stands up. Yoko steps away and John lets go of his hand. Ringo faints and is back on the floor.

∞

It's funny now, but it wasn't at the time. When we revived him, he was worse than Yoko, my sons, and Paul all rolled into one; he balled like a baby and was inconsolable for quite some time. He was always the sensitive one. It broke my heart to see him like that. He kept hugging me and saying over and over, "I love you, man. I love you."

Me, Yoko, and Julio piled into Kuruma and took Ringo back to the Plaza. He was dazed. We gave him tea and scones and put him to bed. We rang up Barbara; she's his wife, you know.

Barbara flew from across the pond to New York straight away. Ringo didn't trust himself. He wanted her to tell him I was real. Don't misunderstand;

he knew it was me all right. He told me later he could tell by my nose and ears. My nose, OK. But my ears? Ha!

We had to spend weeks with him — chatting, eating, walking, playing music — before he finally came 'round. When Yoko and Paul had insisted my return was the real deal before Ringo saw me in person, he thought it was an elaborate ruse by Paul. For the past forty years, they've been going at it. They're quite the pair of jokesters.

Ringo said to me, "I always thought you had a nice place up in heaven and were just fine. I knew you were waiting for me, and I expected some day to play the kit in a big band in the sky with you."

Bullocks, heaven can wait! We can't leave the planet yet with things being such a mess. I told Ringo, "Let's do it on earth, you big cry-baby!"

As serious as could be, he said, "Sorry, I'm retired," and stood there all self-controlled.

Me? I said, "What the f—," and he started laughing. It was worth the wait.

YOU SAID GOODBYE, I SAY HELLO AGAIN

We are eternal beings,
Endings are not in our destiny.

\- Dieter F. Uchtdorf

Much remains the same since the last time John had stepped into the lush, velvety-red lobby of Radio City Music Hall. The smooth lines of geometric art deco motifs create a sense of timelessness, and in a world that had evolved at hyper-speed without him, this classic ambiance is comforting. High-gloss blond wood, framed in black-lacquered trim, form the sweeping staircases. John admires the architectural aesthetics of the room and comments to Yoko, "Maybe this is where we should have the Beatles' reunion."

"Oh, my dearest, if you think the Beatles were big when you were alive, you can't imagine what it's going to be like now that you've returned from the dead." She caresses his arm lovingly and adds, "You're going to have to think bigger. Much, much bigger."

Luxurious chandeliers hang from ceilings gilded with gold. Their light shines on pillars featuring photos of the Rockettes. "I love New York," John says.

"You know the media is going to ask about a reunion," Yoko says.

"Right, then! I'll give them the scoop! Don't know where or when just yet, but it's going to happen. Paul and Ringo want to do it."

A Radio City skeleton crew is at the ready to help John with his first press conference since his return. There is always a lively debate about how to refer to his "return." Was it a resurrection? A reincarnation? A publicity stunt? Something else?

A privately contracted security team deals with an overflow situation, screening attendees who are now seated inside and excitedly awaiting John's appearance. In addition to representatives of U.S. news and entertainment TV stations, internet outlets, magazines, newspapers, a contingent of foreign media have flown in. Only the pope has ever garnered such interest by the media and adoring public.

Several ambassador Rockettes escort John and his intimate entourage into the "powder room." They sit in a well-lit, circular, fully mirrored room drinking tea and submit to primping by a hair and makeup artist. In just a few minutes, Ioni, John's newly hired press secretary, will be the moderator stepping onto the legendary stage to reintroduce John to the world.

∞

The house is abuzz with anticipation. Ioni takes her place center stage and the loud hubbub of animated conversation settles into an electrifying murmur, and then, save a cough or a shuffle, a respectful quiet.

"Ladies and gentlemen, thank you for joining us today for this historic meeting," Ioni says. "John Lennon is here to share some information with you, and then we'll open it up for questions. Photos are unnecessary. We'll provide a link to a recording of this meeting and full surroundings. You'll have the rights to video and stills. The room is fully wired for on-demand sound for our Q&A session.

"Also, we have a random numbers generator corresponding to your seats, so we'll take your questions that way to keep this organized and fair. If you're selected, please step out into the aisle and stand in Mr. Lennon's hologram field so that your image will be picked up around the room too.

"OK, without further ado… I present a founding Beatle, singer/songwriter, progressive thinker, and self-described peacenik, Mr. John Lennon!"

Entering from the wings, John and Yoko walk hand in hand to take their bar stool seats behind a clear, Plexiglas podium. The applause, shouting, and whistling rise to deafening levels. Waving a heartfelt hello, John has a flashback to the Beatlemania he experienced when he, Ringo, Paul, and George landed at JFK Airport for the first time in 1964.

A smattering of the media remains seated, in an unequivocal demonstration of skepticism. Later, crime scene investigators will find a note a reporter has scrawled that reads, "Why are so many of these morons falling for this ploy?"

John gestures to the audience to settle down. His image is projected on large-screen television panels and 3-D holograms around the floor, enthralling the audience.

"Thank you. Thank you very much. Please, be comfortable and relax," John begins. It takes a few minutes for more than 6,000 people to gain their composure.

"I know you are curious about my return," John continues. "I'll do my best to answer your questions. But first, I'd like to make an announcement: I've accepted an offer by Goopplezon to head up their innovative Peace Department. Yoko and I are organizing a worldwide bed-in to promote our platform of 'give peace a chance.' Goopplezon will release information to you later about the date, time, and locations. I can tell you, though, one of those places will be in Central Park here in New York City. All right, then. Let's get to your questions."

Ioni calls out, "First mezzanine, K-314."

BBC reporter Lorraine Mersey jumps up and stands in John's hologram field, startling him when she appears on stage right in front of him. "Mr. Lennon, did you meet God?"

"I have no memory of where I was or what I saw during the past 40 years," he explains. "For me, it was a mere heartbeat. I closed my eyes and opened them again. I'm sorry – for you and for me – that I don't know more."

"Orchestra, ZZ-603," Ioni announces.

A young reporter for a small local newspaper in Normal, Illinois, stands up and adjusts his glasses. "Mr. Lennon, can you explain how you came back from the dead? How does this fit into our commonly accepted religious beliefs and concept of God?"

"I didn't come back from the dead," John says. Whispering from the audience swells. "The John Lennon who died in 1980 is still dead. But I think I am time travelling. The version of me that was living right before I was shot is who you see today. I don't know how or why I jumped over to an alternate time line. I've been consulting with Stephen Hawking's legacy team and other brilliant scientists at MIT, and they are working out some mathematics to explain all this based on Einstein's theory of relativity, string theory, and worm holes in space. Way over my head! They may as well be speaking Greek to me; something about our concept of time being arbitrarily defined in a way we can comprehend, but time actually moves in all directions. So, lad, you're asking me how God influences scientific laws. I can't answer that."

"Third mezzanine, AA-106."

Leif Hart, an internet blogger with millions of followers asks, "Now that you're here again, aren't you changing the future that we were supposed to have?"

John laughs and says, "Ah, lad! Do you see the crazy shit that's happening around the world? The violence is worse than ever. I sure hope I will change the future you were supposed to have! That, indeed, is my life's mission."

"First mezzanine L-214."

A pretty TV personality with "World Entertainment" asks, "Will there be a Beatles' reunion? And if so, what will you do about a stand-in for George?"

John says, "Yes, I've been chatting with Paul and Ringo." Abruptly, he stops talking and feels a bit light-headed. His body flickers with static, humming and crackling – like tuning in to a TV station that has stopped transmitting for the night. The media are aghast – the static isn't just replacing his hologram image, but his human body as well. And then, with a snapping pop, he disappears.

Yoko yells out, "Don't worry. Everything–

∞

John opens his eyes. He's on his back on top of shoes and sneakers, knees bent to his chest with his head wedged against a wall. A few shirts and a jacket are hanging above him, and he realizes he is in a small closet. The closet door is ajar, and he glimpses somebody moving about in front of a bed.

A young man, bending over to stash a gun inside one of his winter boots, asks, "Did you hear that? What was that?"

His companion, a young woman in the bathroom and out of John's field of vision, yells out, "Don't get all paranoid on me!"

He grabs his coat off the bed and says, "OK, let's do this."

"Ready," she says, and they both leave the room.

When John hears the hotel door close behind them, he jumps up, runs to the peephole, and watches the couple as they start down a flight of stairs. He grabs the jacket hanging in the closet and follows them. The sidewalks are slushy with dirty, melting snow and, after tailing the couple for a few blocks, John's feet are sopping wet.

The young man and woman each hang a lanyard holding an ID card around their necks and join the throngs of media congregating in front of the main entrance to Radio City Music Hall. Their phlegmatic demeanor reveals nothing about their intentions as they wait to pass through security.

The young woman is stopped when a security officer finds the knife she has planted in her pocket. She creates a scene that is diversionary – just long enough for her accomplice to slip into the lobby unnoticed.

The marquee above the door says, "Today! John Lennon Meets The Press."

∞

"–will be OK."

A bright point of light radiates like a 4ᵗʰ of July sparkler, and there he is; in the flesh on stage and back in focus. John and Yoko look at one another for a millisecond. As he tackles her and knocks her to the ground, a bullet whizzes by his head and grazes his earlobe.

From underneath John, Yoko asks him, "How did you know?"

"I just had this gut feeling we should duck."

The terrified crowd scrambles for exits, chaos ensuing. As John, Yoko, and Ioni are dragged off stage to safety by security, Ioni asks John, "Where did you get that strange jacket?"

Yoko asks, "And why are your shoes squeaking?"

Saint John Lennon

∞

When the would-be assassins are apprehended by the police, they rant about John's presence on earth being sacrilegious. They fail to see the irony of murder as an appropriate response to their religious complaint.

THE SALVATION OF 81A3860

My heart; a black hole
No escape for beauty or love
Your spirit; unbounded by the speed of light
Enters with forgiveness
And I am redeemed.

- Roseanne Bottone

I was bloody nervous. I mean, no one else has ever come back from the dead — or whatever this is — to have a chat with his murderer. It's not like there's some sort of book written about how to do that. It wasn't a confrontation, no, but it was tense at first. I went in with a desire for reconciliation. That's what I'm all about. I can't preach love and peace for everyone else and not work to have that in my own life; that would make me the world's biggest hypocrite.

Yoko, Sean and Julian gave me suggestions of what to say, but I didn't have anything prepared. I figured, under the circumstances, I'd just have to go with the flow.

This past August, before my return, Mark had another parole hearing — his 11th since he's been eligible. Yoko always weighed in with the board against letting him go free. Yeah, in the beginning, there was some of that; she was angry — she witnessed a horrible, violent crime; it was gruesome. She didn't think he deserved freedom. Part of it, too, was that she thought he could still be a danger to her and my sons. She told me she has softened her position somewhat over the years; Mark has claimed he found Jesus.

You doubt a man can be redeemed? Ah, my friend, human beings have a great capacity to learn and adapt. If that weren't true, what would be the point of living? We're born good but life fucks that up sometimes — people lose their way. It doesn't matter how far astray you've gone. You can always take a left turn or a right turn and get onto another path, or even just double back.

∞

The American flag at the entrance of the Wende Correctional Facility snaps sharply in the winter wind. Glancing up as he walks out the door after his visit with Mark David Chapman, John is struck by the incongruence of this symbol of freedom and justice with the five rows of barbed wire topping the brick wall behind it.

Just a few days ago for John, the prisoner was an awkward 25-year-old in a green overcoat asking for an autograph – a free man with any future he desired in front of him. The young man has transformed instantly into a gaunt, 65-year-old who's lived his entire adult life in protective isolated custody in maximum security prisons.

So many losses, John thinks.

Dressed all in white, John paces while he waits for Mark to be escorted by guards to their meeting room. "*Damn, damn, damn,*" he says under his breath. "*This guy devastated my family. What am I doing?*"

When they finally face one another, neither man knows how to proceed. Mark's body is in a numb dream-like state as if it has been shot up with Novocain; the news about John Lennon's return is incredible. And now his presence is exhilarating.

As an offering of detente, John extends his hand. Mark tentatively walks toward John for a handshake and begins to sob. Becoming emotional as well, John puts his arm around Mark's shoulder.

Noticing the contrast between John's clothing and his own dark prison jumpsuit, Mark asks, "Good and evil?"

68

John smiles and says, "The forces of yin and yang. We are one."

"I can't believe it!" Mark chokes between sobs. "I thought it was a trick. I haven't granted interviews to the media for 28 years, and I thought it was a trick. My God!" Mark drops to his knees and prays. John stands by his side with his hand on Mark's head – a spontaneous gesture of tenderness – and waits patiently.

Rising to his feet, Mark says, "I'm sorry for what I've done. I regret it all. I am peaceful now though; Jesus lives in me. He has forgiven me and loves me. His presence in my life has lifted me up. And now I am doing his work and sharing a message of love with other people who are like I used to be."

They sit next to each other in a couple of rickety beige plastic chairs. John composes himself and asks, "What were you like then?"

"I was a confused, lost soul. I don't know how to explain it; I just needed to feel important in some way. I guess everyone wants that to some extent. But I was profoundly sad, worse than most; I was nobody and nothing. That's why I didn't run away after I shot you. I wanted everyone to know who I was and what I had done. I wanted to be in the limelight."

"Did you have any understanding of what the consequences would be?"

"I was depressed, and I was drinking. That's not an excuse. I'm just trying to explain that I wasn't capable of solving my problems like a healthy person. I was trapped in the abyss of my own mind. I wanted a way out of my doldrums – like shooting up heroin – a total escape from reality. Something to make me feel alive. I wasn't thinking about anyone else, just about me."

"My family, man, I loved them so much. I missed out on 40 years of their lives. My fans missed the music I would have created. And each one of us has unique gifts to offer the world; who knows what good I might have done had I been here? And who knows what good you could have done?"

"I'm sorry for causing such pain," Mark says. "I'm truly sorry. I was weak; the false promise of notoriety seduced me. My self-esteem was non-existent. I thought the bright lights of fame would be the answer – their allure was irresistible." He composes himself and looks directly into John's eyes. "Please, please, forgive me."

"That's why I'm here. I came to tell you that I do forgive you. I don't want to carry bitterness around in my heart. I want you to be free of the past too. It's the only way for us both to heal and move forward with any real possibility of joy."

"Oh, my God," Mark says. His eyes fill with tears again. "Please believe me when I tell you I'm not the same person who shot you. I am a changed man."

"I know."

"How do you know I'm telling the truth? How can you know for sure?" Mark asks.

"I have dreams and visions. I just know."

As John hugs Mark, a dark blur of sadness leaves Mark's body and floats out of the room through a vent in the ceiling. They both feel lighter.

Their conversation lasts 40 minutes. "Maybe it could have been different," John says.

"I could have backed out, but I didn't."

"What if I had talked to you? You seemed so strange and lost. I sensed that, but I didn't reach out."

"You think just talking to me might have altered the course of events?" Mark asks.

"Maybe. Isn't it plausible that words of kindness could influence a person's life?"

Mark closes his eyes as they sit in peace.

Quietly, John asks, "What would you do if you were free?"

Mark opens his eyes. "I am interested in one thing and that's ministering to prisoners. Me and my wife—"

"Your wife? You're still married?" John asks.

"Yes!" Mark says. "We have grown closer to the Lord more now than ever before. He has restored my sanity and protected our marriage as we dealt with unbelievable adversity."

"I know what it's like to have a woman stand by me, through everything. It's empowering."

A buzzer sounds, and the prison guard announces the end of the visiting session. As they say their goodbyes, John asks Mark, "Have you ever heard of a writ of habeas corpus? You can petition for a review of the legality of your imprisonment."

"But, I admit I shot you. Everyone knows that I did it."

"True. But there's no body. You have noticed I'm no longer dead?"

Mark laughs uncomfortably. Then it dawns on him what John is saying. "You? It's you? After all this time, *you* are my salvation?"

∞

"Check out these headlines, Yoko. The media are going crazy." John throws a copy of the *New Age Monitor* onto the coffee table: "'Forgiveness or Folly?'" He tosses the *New York Post* onto the pile: "'Is John Lennon delusional?'" The table groans with the weight of controversy. "This one is disconcerting." Holding up *The Guardian* he reads, "'Lennon loses it.'"

"You're sounding a bit cynical, my love," Yoko says.

"I did the right thing by talking to him and forgiving him. I'm cynical about politics, newspapers, government. But I'm not cynical about life, love, goodness, death."

Yoko sits next to him on the sofa and pats his knee.

"Here's my favorite. It's an op-ed in the *New York Times*."
John shows Yoko a folded over newspaper. "Saint John Lennon,"
he reads.

"You? A Saint? Hardly!"

Making the sign of the cross, John blesses himself, and
brings his hands together for prayer.

"Not buying it," Yoko says.

"I'm not letting it go to my head. I like what the editor had
to say. Let me read part of her piece to you. Ah! Here we go:

> In order to forgive, we are not required to forget
> our personal history. We may remember, but not dwell.
>
> Forgiveness requires accepting the wrongdoing of
> others as human foible and finding the compassion to let
> go. By doing so, we give a most glorious gift to ourselves –
> the release of anger and resentment.
>
> By showing mercy, we take away the power of past
> events to control our emotions and interactions with others
> now. Exoneration does not condone the bad act, but by
> liberating our hearts of sadness, we restore ourselves to
> wholeness.
>
> Forgiveness is a great personal sacrifice; it takes
> meaningful work to wrestle free from a sense of righteous
> indignation and the belief that seething anger is a
> prerogative.
>
> The act of forgiving others is a form of generosity
> – for both the transgressor and the aggrieved. We become
> free to truly embrace life and all its joyful possibilities."

"Beautiful," Yoko says. "Without the capacity to forgive,
the heart cannot truly love."

On the upbeat, they turn to one another and say, "Amen,"
in unison.

LIVE AND LET LIVE

Music is God's gift to man,
the only art of Heaven given to earth,
the only art of earth we take to Heaven.

\- Walter Savage Landor

Cozy in baggy gray sweatpants and a soft white T-shirt under a matching hoody, John paces absentmindedly in his living room. He holds a yellow legal pad in one hand and a freshly sharpened No. 7 lead pencil in the other. Singing out loud, he stops and jots a few words and taps out a rhythm with the eraser against the pad.

Goopplezon pings for an incoming call. "Yes, Julio?" His majordomo's hologram appears, causing John to jump back and fall onto the sofa. "Jesus Christ, man. What if I were sitting here naked scratching me balls?

"Meatballs?" Julio asks.

"Me balls, man. Me balls!"

A conservative and usually unflappable man, Julio stifles a laugh. "Sorry, sir. That makes more sense. The Goopplezon setting in the living room is for instant visuals when you answer calls from preferred contacts. We can reset that if you wish."

"Where are you from, Julio?"

"I was born in Paraguay, sir. I came to the U.S. in '79 when I had thirty years, before you were – ah – killed." The mustachioed

Julio stands tall and slim, his short hair, now salt and pepper, contrasts elegantly with his olive complexion.

"Do your friends and family in South America know of my return?"

"Yes, they do. But a lot of them think it's like the moon landing."

"The moon landing?" John asks.

"Just a big, fake Hollywood production."

"They think the moon landing was fake?"

Julio nods and hesitates to add, "And you too, sir."

"Don't worry about it, man." John refuses to be devoured by his own story. "So, why did you call?"

"Ah, yes. Mr. Paul McCartney has arrived. He's on his way up."

∞

Two notes. That's all it takes to set a heart aflutter. Ask a woman what song was playing when she had her first kiss as a young girl, and she will remember it in the first two notes. When "her" song queues up, it evokes anew the emotions she felt long ago; as if this is the very moment her lover is sliding his arm around her waist and drawing her near.

I'm sure Yoko can tell you what song was playing the first time we made love.

Music punctuates the ordinary days of our lives and frames an entire era in which we live. Did you see me and the lads on the Ed Sullivan Show? *I bet you remember it. It is no wonder every person vehemently insists the music of his upbringing is the best.*

When I write my music, I think of you. There's no real division between the listener and the creator of music. You and I are irreversibly entwined forever.

My lyrics give substance to my new identity. My song is as essential to my life as the air I breathe. The creative process is my refuge – it is the bridge between the man who was exiled from his own life and my new reality; between incredulity and bloody sanity.

∞

Paul saunters into the living room and tosses his scarf and overcoat over the back of a chair.

Still seated on the sofa, John says, "I would have dressed had I known you were coming, mate. But you're up to your old tricks." Sporting a big grin, he crosses his legs and makes a circle with his oversized, white athletic sock.

Paul maneuvers around the coffee table, whacks John's foot, and says, "Shove over, mate. What're you working on?"

"A song for the bed-in. But I'm stuck. Listen." John picks up the guitar and sings, "I'm just a something-or-other coming back from time−" He stops mid-phrase and asks, "What am I, Macca?"

"You're the luckiest son-of-a-bitch walking the face of the earth, is who you are!"

"True," John laughs, "but I need something more succinct. I'm just a hmm, hmm, hmm coming back from time."

"A dead man living?"

"Nah, too macabre."

"Walrus is already taken," Paul says. "I don't know, man. You're just an old hippie."

"Ha!" John plays a few chords and sings, *"I'm just a hippie coming back from time…* Aww, Macca! There you go. Brilliant as usual! Yeah, that works."

I'm just a hippie coming back from time
I stand accused of playing games
with all of your minds
I am a hippie

Saint John Lennon

I came back a man all the same
Yet everything I knew about this world has changed

"Good hook right at the beginning," Paul says. "Oh, man, you know, you just missed George – Martin – he passed in '16."

"I know. 90 years old. He was definitely one sagacious, cool dude. I can't imagine him that old."

Rising from the sofa, Paul says, "Let me tickle the ebony and ivory."

The two friends ease back into a collaboration the universe had programmed into their DNA; a couple of teenagers – the chubby schoolboy and the rakish hoodlum – together again, fulfilling their destiny.

Strumming a few chords, John sings:

I'm just a hippie
Imagine sublime
a world of peace and harmony,
a dream that is mine

Paul picks up the melody on the piano and hums along to follow John.

You want to exalt me
Make me something I'm not
But I am a hippie and a hippie can't be bought
You want my support
in leading many your way
But I'm just a hippie and make nobody pay

"We need a strong backbeat, Macca."

I am a hippie
And I'm doing just fine
Yet there was a time
When just being a hippie was a crime

"Ain't that the truth?" Paul interjects over the top of the baby grand.

I am a hippie
And on love I stand true
I hold onto the hope of
Sweet kisses from you

I'm just a hippie

"Wait, repeat that," Paul says. "Sweet kisses from you. Go back."

"Ya think so?"

"Yeah, go back."

I am a hippie
And on love I stand true
I hold onto the hope of
Sweet kisses from you
Sweet kisses from you

"Good. Keep going," Paul says.

I'm just a hippie
And my dreams are all haunting
I still believe in a better life
For all who are wanting, ya gotta be wanting

"Let's add a bridge here…" Paul sings, "*ya gotta be wanting, ya gotta be wanting…*"

> *I met the Maharishi*
> *In multiple lives*
> *and called him Sexy Sadie*
> *but George said I wasn't right*

"Oh, shit, man." Paul laughs and offers up a little improv. "*What have you done? What have you done?*"

John continues singing.

> *You want to exalt me*
> *make me something I'm not*
> *But I'm just a hippie*
> *and a hippie can't be bought*

Hours pass, and time stands still. The lingering vibrations of the final note glint in the moonlight and are claimed by heaven.

John lays the guitar on his lap. Looking up and smiling at Paul, he says, "Fucking magic."

Paul stands up behind the piano. "Let's make the reunion happen after the bed-in. Life is short, man."

"You're telling me," John says. "I still can't believe the quiet one kicked the bucket. Fucking lung cancer at 58."

"Pity that," Paul says.

"I used to love me French Guitaine ciggy. What a vile addiction. About a year before I was shot, I took a sailboat to Bermuda to make demos for *Double Fantasy*, and while I was in a peaceful state of mind, I quit smoking. Did you know that?" John asks. Without waiting for an answer, he adds, "I wanted to be a good example for me little boy."

"George's boy is a pretty darn good guitarist and songwriter," Paul says.

"Yeah, you told me. Geez, Dhani was two years old the last time I–" John stops abruptly and sighs. "Will I ever get used to this, Macca?"

∞

No other connection rivals the bond between childhood friends. Who else knows me the way Paul knows me? A single path existed for us when we were lads; we had to come together – and it was more than serendipity. Yeah, I think the inevitability of our union was divine will. What chance did we have against kismet? None.

Look at George Washington, John Adams, and Thomas Jefferson. They developed the bloody framework for this nation and changed the world. Those chaps were born at the same time and found one another like ants drawn to a picnic.

Great scientists and philosophers like Socrates, Plato, and Aristotle are another example of superhuman synergy. The Beatles were like that too. OK, don't misquote me here; I'm not saying the Beatles were as powerful an influence as the United States on world events or history's greatest thinkers! But maybe our impact on music was pretty far reaching, wouldn't you say?

I've been accused of being a poseur for my causes. Pisses me off. With the backing of Goopplezon and heading up their Peace Department, meaningful shit is going to happen. There's no way I will be indicted for merely spewing rhetoric.

My style was always anti-something. It feels more beautiful to be for something. I've been doing a lot of re-evaluating since I've returned. In the '70s, I supported radical groups like the Black Panthers, because I thought it necessary to shake up the status quo and wake the sleeping masses. I'm moving toward integrating a sense of grace into my being and music; building and creating are better than tearing down. We can tackle problems from a positive perspective instead. Paul was always the optimistic one. He's a sweet guy. Ha! Don't tell him I said that!

The Sufi poet Hafiz wrote "The place where you are right now, God circled on a map for you." I'm standing in the middle, surrounded by light and hope.

∞

"Goopplezon, turn on *Saturday Night Live,*" John commands into his living room. He pats the sofa next to him and says, "Sit your arse down here, old man. Take a load off, Macca."

"On your bike, mate, with the old man stuff," Paul shoots back playfully.

"My favorite. I can't believe it's still on after all these years – a blast from the past. Sorta makes me feel normal. Except I have no idea about who's who. Who's this singer? This Hailey Knox chick? And Kate Hudson? Some character called the rock? John Boyega?

"Oh, Boyega was in *Star Wars* movies," Paul says. "It's not exactly a doodle to keep up with popular culture even when you're here and alive," Paul jabbed. "The same guy, Lorne Michaels, is still the producer of *Saturday Night.* A few years back Barack Obama gave him the Presidential Medal of Freedom."

"Unusual name. Goopplezon, show me a photo of President—" John looks at Paul.

"Obama," Paul says.

"No shit? A black president?"

"For the first time. Two terms," Paul says.

"Problems with racism are improving here?"

Paul puffs out his cheeks and answers thoughtfully, "Well, the best I can say is, there's hope.

"Hey, you know, it was a big deal that we thought about going down to the SNL studio in '76. They offered us a pittance – a few thousand dollars – for a Beatles' reunion on air."

"Yeah, I remember that," John says. "We thought it would be a great gag if we showed up, but we were too tired."

"They wanted us to sing 'She loves you'–"

"–Yeah, yeah, yeah," John sings. He smirks, and his mischievous nature hijacks his face. "Do you remember the words, Macca?"

"Have you gone barmy? Wait! You're not thinking–? Do you think we should?"

"Why not? Let's do it!" John says. "What do you say, mate? Should we beam our holograms in, or actually go down there? It's only twenty-something blocks from here if we want to show up."

The synchronistic rabble-rousers nod at one another, and stand up from the sofa.

"Let me throw on some decent clothes," John says. "Goopplezon? Connect with Julio."

Julio's hologram appears and John jumps. "Sorry, sir. Yes, sir?" Julio asks.

"Bring Kuruma 'round, will you? Me mate and I are going out."

On cue, "Live from New York, it's Saturday night!" fills the living room as a couple of lads from Liverpool set out to create a little belated rock 'n' roll history.

THE BEST MEDICINE

My mission in life is not merely to survive, but to thrive;
and to do so with some passion,
some compassion, some humor, and some style.

- Maya Angelou

We live in trying times. How obvious; aren't all times trying? Our challenges ebb and flow, like the tide rushing in and out under our feet. Life twists and contorts from bad to worse to better, and back to bad to worse to better again in a different way. If it's not one bloody thing, it's another. And if it isn't that, it's something else. It could be anything, really.

How do we keep from going stark-raving mad? We laugh. At tragedy. At absurdity. At ourselves. I laugh raucously at my own expense. It's the only thing to do.

As newborns, laughter is one of the first instincts we manifest to show pleasure. If we're lucky, it will be one of the last things we experience as we exit the world. For the years that ensue between, and for sure during my bonus years as I like to call this, humor can be the salve that heals the wounded heart and the spice that enhances even the sublime.

∞

Kuruma deposits John and Paul in front of the NBC studios at 30 Rockefeller Plaza. John jumps out first, runs around the back of the car, and offers his hand to his mate. Now in his late 70s, Paul moves a bit slower than the sprightly John. His mental and musical acuity, however, remain as sharp as ever. Julio and the bodyguards follow behind carrying several guitars.

Rumors reach the *Saturday Night Live* cast and studio audience that John Lennon and Paul McCartney are ensconced in the green room and want to make an impromptu appearance on the show. Comments, text messages, and facial expressions are like neurons transmitting information around the studio as if it were a collective brain. The news jumps from one synapse to the next, creating an electrifying sense of anticipation.

The stage clears at the end of a skit, and Lorne Michael's hologram appears. "Ladies and gentlemen," the dapper white-haired producer says, "it's true that Lennon and McCartney may be willing to do a little something here for us tonight." The audience whistles and cheers wildly.

He continues by addressing John and Paul directly as they stand in the wings just off stage. "In my book, the Beatles are the best thing that ever happened to music. It goes even deeper than that – you're not just a musical group; you're a part of us. We grew up with you." He waits a beat for the audience to stop laughing. Those in the know recognize these as his exact words spoken into the camera on April 24, 1976.

"I always believed John would be back," Lorne says. "Just in case this opportunity ever presented itself again, I've saved this." He holds a piece of paper up closer to the camera lens. "The National Broadcasting Company has authorized me to offer you this check to be on our show; a certified check for $3,000. All you have to do is sing three Beatles' songs. 'She Loves You,' yeah, yeah, yeah – that's $1,000 right there."

John and Paul saunter on stage. Shouting, foot stomping, and applause shake the building – an earthquake would be less noticeable. They take modest bows and approach the producer's hologram field. John says, "I know I've been away for a while, but that doesn't mean you can take advantage of me, Mr. Michaels. I'm no dummy."

"Well, whatever can you mean?" Lorne feigns surprise.

"Paul and I were talking. You're going to have to adjust that check for increased cost of living." He turns to Paul and asks, "Isn't that right, mate?"

"Right," Paul says. "Or there'll be none of this." He throws the strap of his guitar over his shoulder, takes out his pick, and twirls it through his fingers for dramatic effect. He strums a few bars of "She Loves You." The audience roars. Before he sings a word, he stops, turns to the audience, and winks.

"Now, now," Lorne coaxes. "I'm sure we can work something out. Maybe we can get you a few hundred more dollars."

John tosses the strap of his guitar over his shoulder. He raises his eyebrows and gestures to the audience as if to ask them, "What should I do?" He strums and sings a little ditty from "Yes, I'm your angel," stops, and winks at the audience when he says, "Go ahead, make a wish!"

Turning to Lorne he says, "Paul and I did a few calculations."

"We did," Paul says. "And we figure that $3,000 is equal to about $14,000 in today's dollars."

"Fourteen thousand dollars? I don't know. That's an awful lot of money," Lorne banters.

NBC's phone lines are ringing off the hook. The audience chants, "Do it! Do it! Do it!"

"OK, then," Paul says. "I guess we wasted our time coming down here." Turning toward the audience, he waves goodbye. He grabs John by the shirt and drags him along. John hams it up, waving as he stumbles under Paul's grip.

"OK, OK, OK," Lorne says. "Don't go. Please. I'll arrange to have the check made out for $14,000."

Paul lets go of John and asks him, "Should we take the deal then?"

John elaborately composes himself by adjusting his guitar, smoothing his hair, pushing up his glasses, and sighing. "No bloody way!" he says, shaking his head. "If NBC makes it *one hundred* and fourteen thousand, we'll donate it all to peace initiatives."

"Wait a second," Paul teases. "Do I have to donate my half too?"

Slowly, and in an exaggerated and persuasive tone, John says, "Yes, you do, mate."

Lorne jumps in, "Hold on there, let me make a phone call." He holds his mobile phone to his ear and says, "You've been watching? I see. Too much money? I understand. OK. Got it."

"Do it! Do it! Do it!" the audience insists.

Lorne turns his attention back to John and Paul and says, "Sorry, gentleman." He busts a grin from New York to L.A. and says, "Just kidding. It's a go, boys!"

∞

Why shouldn't I have a playful nature when I'm on TV or at any other time? With the state of world affairs I came back to, we may very well be facing impending doom. But I believe in honoring the beauty of life. Let's have some fun while we tackle the serious problems, eh?

A sense of humor is my consolation for bearing witness to the unbearable.

THE PERSONAL AND THE POLITICAL

Throughout history, it has been the inaction of those who could have acted;
the indifference of those who should have known better;
the silence of the voice of justice when it mattered most;
that has made it possible for evil to triumph.

- Haile Selassie

Blue and green lights guide the path of American Airlines flight 236 as it accelerates down the runway of New York's JFK International Airport. Excited, like a little boy strapped into a roller coaster as it ratchets up its rails to the promise of the first peak, John watches a flawless takeoff through the window. He remembers a classic *Twilight Zone* TV episode and assigns himself "wing-watch" to make sure no monsters dismantle the wing. His eldest son, 58-year old Julian, sits next to him on the aisle in the first-class cabin; an accomplished photographer, Julian snaps photographs of his father to commemorate their epic trip and catches John's smile of self-amusement.

The dark sky welcomes them as they climb to 35,000 feet; the plane breaks through the clouds and enters the space between heaven and earth. After a flurry of requests for autographs by the crew and fellow passengers dies down, the two settle comfortably into the plush pod seats, fully equipped with the latest entertainment technology, for their overnight flight to Rome.

Fiddling with the pod controls and menu, John asks his son, "Oh, man, how do you choose what to watch or listen to when there are so many options? What the heck are Lollapalooza, Locobazooka and Bonnaroo?"

Julian answers with patience. "They are festivals, pop. They feature all kinds of music; alternative rock, heavy metal, punk, hip-hop, and EDM. Big events."

"EDM?" John asks.

"Electronic Dance Music. All the rage for a while. DJs pumping out very loud music. Sometimes with accompanying drummers. Wild lights, crowds dancing, that sort of thing."

"You know, Jules, a lot of people thought Jim Morrison was a fool for saying what he said about the future of music. He envisioned one person with a lot of machines, tapes, and electronics set up, singing or speaking."

"Yeah, the DJs are considered musicians now," Julian says.

The pair examine the in-flight magazines and safety cards. They rip open the plastic covers to remove their blankets and pillows, and fidget in their seats trying to figure out what to talk about with each other for the next eight hours.

"And every summer, there's a big, big, big Beatles festival in Liverpool," Julian says to break the silence. "Aunt Julia is always there."

"We should go. I'm looking forward to seeing my sister."

Julian says, "Hey, there was even a second and third Woodstock."

"Thank God all the hippies haven't died yet."

"Oh no! There are plenty of them left. Some of them, like Mick Jagger and Keith Richards, are never going to die. Have you seen them? Jagger even has little kids." Father and son laugh easily. "And even if a hippie dies," Julian chides, "he may not stay away."

John sings under his breath, "The pope smokes dope..." and the two of them progress to laughing hysterically. "...God gave him the grass. The pope smokes dope; he likes to smoke in mass. The pope smokes dope, he's a groovy head. The pope smokes dope, the pope smokes dope. Yeah, yeah, yeah!"

Julian has tears in his eyes from laughing so hard. He composes himself enough to say, "This pope must be high on something if he wants to meet with *you*!"

A pretty flight attendant takes their meal order and returns later with steaming, hot towels. Father and son both put them over their faces. John peeks out at the same time Julian does, and they laugh again.

"Son, I'm glad you're on this trip with me." John clears his throat. "I've been doing research about what's happened since I left. I've read so many things about *me*. It's very, very weird; like being present to witness your own eulogy. I know everything everybody ever thought of me and my work." He ventures, "You've had some harsh things to say."

Julian carefully considers his response to the man who is both father and stranger – a man who had abandoned him, but when handed a second chance, is reaching out to reconnect. "I have to say that, from my point of view, I felt you were a hypocrite. You could talk about peace and love out loud to the world, but you could never show it to the people who supposedly meant the most to you: your wife and son. How can you talk about peace and love and have a family in bits and pieces – no communication, adultery, divorce? You can't do it, not if you're being true and honest with yourself."

"I've had to process all this at warp speed, Jules. I haven't had the benefit of living through the progression of a normal life – you know, where you learn things by trial and error, grow and mature, and redefine your principles as you become wiser. I know it was hard on you."

"Yes, it was. It affected my whole life. I remember how you were with me. You were critical. I never felt like I was good enough to be your son. Even when you were right next to me, you weren't really there. I can still feel the rejection, although, when I was little, I didn't understand what I was feeling. And then you left me."

"I wasn't ready to marry your mom. I was young and immature and, selfishly, it wasn't what I wanted. And you represented the reason why I was living a life I wouldn't have chosen for myself at the time.

"That wasn't fair to you, or Cynthia. She was a good woman, and now in periods of self-reflection, I must admit I was a cad. You're right. I was preaching one thing but not living my own life in a loving way. I'm sorry for hurting you, Jules. Truly. There must have been another way, a better way, to handle it all. If I could go back and do it all over again, I would live authentically, so I wouldn't poison my own heart with resentment and burden you with such sadness. I'd be kinder and more affectionate."

A lump forms in John's throat. He barely whispers, "I hope you can forgive me; I hope I can forgive myself." Holding back tears, he says, "I'll be right back, son," and rises from his seat.

Passing behind the flight attendant stacking soda cans onto the beverage cart in the galley, John pushes open the lavatory door adjacent to the cockpit. He reacts in horror to find the tiny room engulfed in flames. The intense heat assails him and, just as he jumps back, the plane hits turbulence. Losing his balance, he knocks over the coffee pot − and disappears in a snap of crackling static.

Hearing the ruckus behind her, the flight attendant turns around to see spilled coffee splattered on the counter and pooling on the floor. She does a quick check of the vacant lavatory and sees all is in order, closes the door, and sets about cleaning up the mess.

∞

John lands face down in the dirt. As he gets up on his knees, his sleeve is singed by a marauder running by dragging a lit torch. John stands up and dusts himself off. The humid air around him glows peachy in the sinister moonlight. Behind him, a young hooligan dressed in filthy, tattered clothing says, "Ye mak a better door than a windae."

John turns, looks down at the boy, and asks, "What? What are you saying?"

"Outta me way, sir." The boy gestures to the front of the rowdy gathering. John turns around again to see a tall, thick wooden stake that has been erected for an execution. Layered straw and wood is piled six feet high all around its base. A narrow, clear path at the front serves as a passage for the victim to reach her place of death.

"Oh, my God," John says. "What the f–"

"Indeed! The witch known as Janet Horne is condemned to be burned at the stake for sorcery."

The old woman is stripped, and her naked body tarred and feathered. She was paraded through town on her way to the execution. Confused by dementia, she smiles as her captors chain and tie her tightly to the stake.

The executioner declares, "Witch, you have been found guilty of turning your daughter into a pony as evidenced by the deformities of her hands and feet; and for riding her through the countryside to do the devil's work. The penalty for consorting with Satan is death by fire. Repent, woman! Ask God for forgiveness so that your soul may rest in peace."

The crowd jeers at the witch and hurls insults.

"No, no, no!" John cries.

"Are you mad, man?" Grabbing John's arm, the hooligan gestures to him to hush. "Keep the heid, or they will come for you next."

"Where are we?" Noticing the odd manner of dress, John demands of the boy, "Tell me! What year is this?"

"We are in Scotland, sir. The year is 1727." The young hooligan promises John, "It's gaein be awright ance the pain has gane awa."

The execution committee lights six torches and fan out around the base of the stake. At the command of the sheriff, they light the pyre from all sides at once.

"Don't watch," the hooligan advises. "It will haunt your dreams."

The flames lick the witch's feet with avarice. Writhing in pain, she cries out for mercy. John becomes light-headed as she is slowly devoured by the very evil she is accused of practicing. He covers his face with his hands and turns away.

"It's a lang road that's no goat a turnin. Soon this practice will be no more. But the world will see new atrocities."

"How do you know this, lad?" John asks.

"I know this because man refuses to learn." A glint of eternal knowledge sparkles in the hooligan's eyes. "He refuses to see how over and over he commits the same sin in a different form. If a man truly is empathetic to another's suffering, he will be moved to be the change."

"Who *are* you?"

With an impish smile, the hooligan answers, "You will not remember even if I tell you, sir. In times to come, a great philosopher will advise, 'Whoever fights monsters should see to it that in the process he does not become a monster.' You must keep this in your heart and teachings always." He hands John a book.

"But—" As he speaks his last word to the hooligan, John's body shimmers a soft transparent blue, and he fades into time.

"Lang may yer lum reek!" The boy says. "May you live long and prosper, John."

∞

John returns to his seat on the airplane next to his son. He puts his hand on Julian's arm and says, "From this day forward, it will be different. I'm here for you now. I can learn from my mistakes. We all can. History does not have to be our destiny."

Julian places his hand protectively over his father's. "What's that, pop?" he asks pointing to a book John holds in his left hand.

"I– I don't know." They examine the cover and read the title, *The Witches' Hammer*. "I must have picked this up in the lavatory without realizing it," John says. He turns the book over and they read the jacket:

Written by the Catholic Church to educate the world of the dangers of free-thinking women, this guide instructed the clergy how to identify them and destroy them. Witches included female scholars, mystics, nature lovers, growers and gatherers of herbs, and midwives who used medical practices to ease the pain of birth.

"Look at this blurb," John says. He reads out loud, "By some estimates, the Catholic Church may have killed five million women during its reign of witch hunts."

"Whoa, what is this?" Julian asks. "The Catholic Church's dirty little secret? Thank God this kind of persecution isn't going on now."

"But it is," John says, "this time, by the Islamic extremists. It's like the witch hunts and the inquisitions all over again. The Catholic Church condemned and tortured Jews, Protestants, and Hindus for heresy. Now the Muslim radicals are doing the same thing to Christians and calling them infidels. History is repeating itself with new players, and the lessons of the past have been forgotten.

"More death and destruction has taken place in the name of religion in the history of mankind than for any other reason. Zealots have once again hijacked a religion to impose their own sense of morality on the masses."

"Mankind is repeating the tragedies of the past," Julian says.

"Keep the faith, son." John points to his temple. "We have imaginations. It starts with the personal. One-to-one. Me and you. We can create whatever future we set our minds to."

Julian grabs John's burned sleeve and twists it around to show him. "Hey, what happened to your shirt, pop?"

"I swear," John says as he looks at his burned sleeve. "Sometimes it feels like I'm living two lives, and I don't know what the other me is up to!"

SHAKE THE WORLD

Do more than belong: participate. Do more than care: help.
Do more than believe: practice. Do more than be fair: be kind.
Do more than forgive: forget.
Do more than dream: work.

- William Arthur Ward

You're throwing some tough questions at me; the primary reason for violence around the world? Let me think. Hmmm. The problem is so complex. I'd say it's because we have forgotten that we're all one sharing a single planet. Oh? That sounds new-agey to you? You asked me for my opinion and now you're making fun of me?

Listen. A few days ago, I snuck into the subway incognito — all bundled up so no one would know me, just to have a good look around. The 21st century has heralded an entire generation of fellow travelers who never meet. Lonely people. Disconnected people. That's it in a nutshell; we're disconnected. They're standing right next to each other — right on the other side of the chasm. The subway is jammed with commuters pressed shoulder to shoulder who are tuned into their electronic devices and not even sensing the human beings at their sides touching them. They're gazing into space through their lenses, watching videos and listening to music — mostly to tune out. They're oblivious to the real world around them.

When will they make eye contact? Smile at a stranger? Notice that the love of their life is walking toward them? Who even hears a simple "good evening"? No one looks up.

More than 10 million crimes are committed in the United States every year. I am not suggesting technology is the culprit. I'm just saying that the way technology is used is symptomatic of how people are progressively withdrawing from one another.

Neighbors don't know each other anymore and don't look out for each other. We don't have a sense of belonging to a community. We're devolving into a compassionless lot. If you're unaware, uninvolved, distanced from family and friends, and feeling like you're walking the earth independently, how can you recognize that every other human being is part of you?

It's worse on a global level. Add to the mix cultural and religious diversity and it's like we view others as interplanetary aliens; they may as well be crazed, bug-eyed, green men trying to take over the planet. So we respond with bombs and assassinations.

What's going on around the world is transmitted into our living rooms every day. We believe, because we're informed, we're connected. The problem is we see what's happening, but we don't feel it because it's out there, somewhere. It's that absence of feeling that's most lethal.

If you kill a man from a distance — with long-range missiles and planes dropping bombs — you will be unaware that you are ripping out your very own heart and soul piece by piece.

But suppose the violence is happening around you, and you are its direct victim. Is it not natural that what you feel is hatred toward the perpetrators?

We are all part of a living, breathing organism. When one organ is injured, the whole being suffers. If you know there is suffering, and you turn a blind eye to it, you are dying your own slow death.

The Syrian refugee tragedy is a blight on humanity. My God, millions of them have been wandering for years only to be turned away by barbed-wire fences and a "not in my backyard" mentality. Have you seen the footage of destruction? Where is the feeling of sadness and outrage for the suffering of these people?

If we're going to have this conversation, you have to be honest with me. To what do you attribute the rise in depression, stress, alienation, violence, and suicide? What do you think people are reacting to? Our bodies are telling us we've become unplugged from our life-sustaining source — one another.

When I sat with Pope Francis, the Dalai Lama was part of our meeting. He's in his 80s — the ageless reincarnation of Buddha. He's still traveling the world teaching his Buddhist beliefs of love, peace, and tolerance; they're universal necessities for the survival of the human race. I'll tell you what the Dalai Lama was like: joyful. He kicked off his sandals, sat on a big sofa with his feet tucked under him with his robes draping over him, and just emanated tranquility — and sunshine. It was contagious. He made us all smile.

The spiritual guru, Sri Sri Ravi Shankar was with us too. I like his title; "ambassador of peace." I'd like to be called that. Oh, stop it! It's not an ego thing. It's rather noble, don't you think? And it is my life's mission. Sri Sri has been asking people to pledge an act of non-violence through social media sites — Facebook, Instagram, and that bird tweet. He has helped mobilize millions of people around the world to launch service projects and take courses on how to create a stress-free and violence-free society. Brilliant.

That's what it takes; each person being aware and doing a small part. Did you know that after 9/11, the Maasai tribe from Kenya wanted to provide support to the United States? They offered 14 of their most important and valuable cattle. I get choked up just thinking about that. The sincerity. The innocence.

The pope is a star! I can see why he was named Time *magazine's person of the year back in '13. What a personality. I greeted him by saying, "Your Holiness, I am John Lennon, and this is my son Julian." He put his hands on both my shoulders, squeezed my arms, patted me on the head, turned to Julian, and said, "Yes, your father is real! Rock on!" He made us laugh a lot. Julian and I felt like we were in the presence of royalty, or saints, or something, and we wondered how we wound up in such company. I don't pretend to be of their stature, but they made us feel welcomed and relaxed.*

Oh, let's see. We started out talking about reincarnation, the second coming, and time travel. We all agreed that I'm still in the same body, I'm no messiah, and so time travel it must be. They were unfazed by this possibility.

The pope said, "Every life, no matter its mysteries, is a blessing." He spoke English a bit slowly, but fairly well. He quoted his favorite author, Dostoevsky: "To love someone means to see him as God intended him."

He believes God intends for me to make music and spread the word of peace. He said, "It's our moral obligation to share our unique gifts with the world, John, and I have plans for you.""

Pope Francis wants in on the bed-in!

BED-IN

*No one is born hating another person
because of the color of his skin,
or his background, or his religion.
People must learn to hate, and if they can learn to hate,
they can be taught to love...*

- Nelson Mandela

"Anderson Cooper coming to you live from New York City's Central Park on this beautiful summer solstice evening." Standing in Strawberry Fields with the John Lennon memorial mosaic below his slippered feet, Anderson speaks into the miniature CNN microphone clipped to his collar. "I'm in my pajamas tonight to celebrate the kick-off of the Lennon-Goopplezon bed-in for peace."

The gentle evening breeze ripples Anderson's light blue nightshirt and pajama pants adorned with fluffy sheep jumping over the moon and blows his snow-white hair out of place.

"Your sheep are adorable, Anderson," Christiane Amanpour says from the studio.

Anderson spins around 360 degrees to show off his sleepwear. "I'm a real fashion maven, don't you think?"

"This is a historic, unprecedented event, Anderson."

"That's right, Christiane. At 8 p.m., the opening ceremony to promote world peace will be led by John Lennon. He will introduce Malala Yousafzai, who will offer a secular invocation. One minute of silence will follow."

"Ah, yes. She's a resilient young woman, an advocate for children's and women's rights in Pakistan. As a teenager, she miraculously survived being shot in the head by the Taliban."

"And when she was 17 years old, she became the youngest recipient of the Nobel Peace Prize," Anderson says.

"A big turnout?"

"Yes, Christiane, about two million people are camped out to spend this cool Sunday night here. Only a quarter of this turnout was expected, but the Goopplezon Peace Department responded quickly; it's so well organized. Plenty of porta-potties, fruit and veggie stands, sandwich stations, juice bars, garbage and recycling bins, first-aid tents – I've never seen an event so well executed."

"What's the mood in the park?" Christiane asks.

"It's peaceful but exciting. Right now, DJ Major Lazer has everyone on their feet dancing.

"We've got every kind of attendee and quite a pageant of sleepwear! Whole families are here with little ones, teenagers, the homeless, college kids, and lots of celebrities. Just before we went on air, I said hello to the former president and first lady, Barack and Michele Obama, who are in matching 'United We Rock' nightshirts. I saw Meryl Streep, Emma Watson, Zac Efron, Jennifer Lawrence, and Josh Hutcherson too. It's a veritable parade of quite a happening crowd. All in PJs.

"I got a kick out of Gal Gadot. She's hanging out in 'Wonder Woman' pajamas and taking selfies with a lot of little girls who had the same idea. We've got veterans from every war; old folks; baby boomers. I'm telling you, Christiane, it's enough to really give you hope to see such a diverse group come together like this."

"Can you give us a little tour, Anderson?"

"Sure. Follow me." Anderson dons his 3-D Goopplezon Lenses, walks a short distance, and scans the scene to share it with

TV viewers. "Oh, look! There's Liam Hemsworth. He's talking to Chris Pine. Ha! They're both wearing Sponge Bob Square Pants pajamas.

"A melting pot of humanity is spread out on blankets, tarps, and mattresses. Goopplezon distributed tens of thousands of air mattresses to pregnant women, the elderly, the infirm and disabled. I didn't see a single person – not one – ask for a mattress that didn't fit into one of those categories. A simple thing like that. Real cooperation.

"They gave out Julian Lennon's children's book too – a well-loved favorite – to the little ones."

"I have the book here in the studio." Christiane holds up a copy of *Touch the Earth*. "It's one of a trilogy he and his co-writer Bart Davis began a few years ago. This one is about loving the earth. It's beautifully illustrated by Smiljana Coh. If we can raise a generation of kids that think like this, imagine what the world could be."

"John is going to sing 'Imagine' first. A lot of people don't know that in 2017 Yoko was recognized as a co-writer of this song. I have goose bumps thinking about the performance," Anderson says. "Both his sons and Yoko are going to sing with him tonight."

"How are people reacting to John's return? That's how we're referring to it, right?" Christiane asks. "His return?"

"Well, yes. If you met him in person, you'd have no doubt at all. I'm sure it's him." Anderson is overcome by emotion.

"Doesn't it make you believe that maybe anything can happen?" Christiane asks.

"Oh, yes, even finding our way to peace. Let's remember what this is all about."

"I see a lot of guitars in your field of vision, Anderson."

"Music is everywhere. We expect two posthumous tribute hologram performances tonight. Michael Jackson will perform 'Black or White' accompanied by live action dancers, and Prince will join Dhani Harrison, Steve Winwood, Jeff Lynne, and Slash from Guns & Roses to honor Tom Petty, for a reprise of their Rock 'n' Roll Hall of Fame rendition of 'While My Guitar Gently Weeps.'

"Jackson and Prince were just budding stars in their early 20s when John died, but evidently he's become a big fan of both since he's been back," Anderson says. "And Tom Petty passed in '17."

Christiane says, "Interestingly, Michael Jackson owned the Beatles' catalog. Some of it has reverted back to McCartney, but the lawyers are still trying to sort out the legalities of the rest since Michael's passing in 2009."

"Oh my, that's a long time for legal wrangling." Anderson says, "I can't wait to see those performances. They're going to be rebroadcast at bed-ins around the world at 8 p.m. in each time zone heading west."

"Right now, we've got cities up and down the east coast prepping. Adele, Justin Bieber, and Meghan Trainor will be wowing the crowds in Boston," Christiane says.

"Chicago, Dallas and Houston in the central time zone will follow an hour later. A giant jamboree that's part of this movement will take place at the AT&T stadium, home to the Dallas Cowboys. John told me he is thrilled by today's hot rockin' country music. Carrie Underwood will be hosting Brad Paisley, Jason Aldean, Sam Hunt, Maren Morris, Florida Georgia Line, Kenny Chesney, and the Zac Brown Band. She'll be in princess pajamas."

Christiane laughs and says, "There's going to be a lot of singing about lost dogs, broken-down pickup trucks and lying, cheatin' scoundrels."

"Indeed," Anderson says. "We'll work our way west through major cities clear across the country to Seattle, Portland, San Francisco, Los Angeles, and San Diego. You'll never guess who's performing in Juneau, Alaska, Christiane."

"Do tell!"

"Jewel, of course. She grew up in Alaska. She'll share the stage with Pitt Bull and Jennifer Lopez, the Weeknd and Lana Delray. They volunteered. I was wondering how they'd have a bed-in up there. Evidently, they're setting up in schools, fire stations, and the Treadwell Ice Arena. Sans ice, I'd imagine."

"That's wild. They're real troopers for the cause. Is it true John Lennon hand-picked all the performers?" Christiane asks.

"That's right. He's fascinated by hip hop, too," Anderson says. "Both Drake and Kendrick Lamar will perform in Los Angeles. Selena Gomez is on the roster with them.

"He loves Shakira's quirky voice and the way she moves. She'll be in Miami with Bruno Mars, Alicia Keys, Gwen Stefani, and the inimitable Ariana Grande. Man, oh, man, oh, man. Wish I could be in two places at one time.

"I spoke to John briefly off camera a little earlier," Anderson continues. "He's captivated by Beyoncé – MGM Las Vegas for her. John thinks she's a goddess." He laughs good-naturedly. "Well yeah. He's the last one to know I guess."

"John must be like a kid in a candy store discovering all this musical talent that wasn't around when he was," Christiane says. "I understand they've set up quite a system of screens, hologram stations, and sound systems. Everyone should be able to see and hear."

"Yeah, it's just great," Anderson says. "An acoustical lineup is in the works for after midnight in New York City to encourage sleep. Celine Dion, Paul Simon, and Billy Joel will sing ballads, lullabies, and classics. John invited younger musicians to be here too. We can look forward to mellow stuff by Ed Sheeran, Justin Timberlake, Imagine Dragons, Miley Cyrus, and Katy Perry. Oh, and I can't forget Sia! And Eminem is going to do his version of "Working Class Hero."

We're supposed to be relaxed and introspective about the state of the world, but I bet no one sleeps a wink."

"McCartney organized the bed-in in Liverpool. He's still astonishing. I hear he and John are practically inseparable; Making up for lost time, no doubt.

"Anderson? Eighteen hours from now, it will be 8 p.m. tomorrow night in Rome. Pope Francis himself will be the keynote speaker for the bed-in and offer a blessing. It's being held in… are you ready for this? Wait for it, Anderson! St. Peter's Square. A sleep-over in St. Peter's Square. With the pope!"

"That must have taken some herculean coordination by Goopplezon," Anderson says. "They've promised to match dollar for dollar the money raised from the entrance fees. Even though that's just $1 per person, world-wide they're expecting a quarter billion dollars' take!" Anderson whistles in disbelief.

"Lennon has pledged the money for outreach programs to help children," Christiane says.

∞

He could be anyone's son, anyone's brother, any teenage girl's doe-eyed boyfriend. The clean-shaven, olive-skinned young man wearing blue jeans and a graphic T-shirt emblazoned with "I love New York" is striking in classical male beauty. His tall, slim muscular build and curly jet-black shock of hair turn heads and inspire envy.

The crowd, spread out around him on blankets, beach chairs, and mattresses, is startled out of its reverie when he jumps to his feet. "Alkuffar min algharb yjb 'an yamut," the young man yells out in Arabic in no particular direction.

He assumes the attack position, feet spread wide, ready to spray a round of ammunition from the Russian AK-9 assault rifle he grips tightly. Poised to begin his long-planned murderous spree, he continues yelling, "Yjb 'an tadfae l bik—"

Bewildered by the lack of reaction, he halts his tirade.

Instead of the screaming and panicked exodus he expects, a swift wave of sleepiness washes over the crowd. They are busy eating cheese and crackers, pouring iced tea, tossing Frisbees, and playing guitars, but − from one instant to the next − two million people begin yawning and stretching, oblivious to the imminent danger around them. Like Dorothy as she frolicked in the Wicked Witch of the West's enchanted poppy field with the Tin Man, Cowardly Lion, and Scarecrow, they slump over and fall into an instantaneous deep sleep.

Two million people, except two.

∞

Hundreds of thousands of the bed-in revelers have an out-of-body experience. Their spirits become untethered from their physical bodies, and their consciousness exists free of constraints. Many of them report hovering over John Lennon and the young man while the pair conversed and are able to repeat the conversation verbatim.

Others rise up, lighter than light, lighter than all that exists, and float away. As they depart from earth, they first see their own slumbering bodies and then a wide, endless sea of humanity − colorful and peaceful − lost in its dreams. Their ascension affords them a view of verdant treetops, the very tips of skyscraper spires, entire continents, and vast water bodies. Upward through the striated layers of cottony cloud puffs, escaping the pull of gravity, they continue on past the waxing moon shining bright with optimism.

Greetings of "hello" in every language rush by: marhabaan, kon'nichiwa, bonjour, hola, zdravstvuyte, olá, and hallå. They hear the sounds of life: a baby crying, laughter, a sneeze, a sob, a crackling fire, the cheering of a crowd, and the sizzle of a steak. Snippets of Beethoven's and Mozart's symphonies swirl among the living spirits. Guitars, flutes, violins, and trumpets. A lion roars, dogs bark, kittens mew, and horses neigh. They smell baking bread, cinnamon buns, campfire smoke, and musky perfume. They taste wine, their favorite meal, and juicy peaches.

From deep into space they look back and see the Earth hanging in nothingness; smaller than a speck of dust floating through a ray of sunshine in an abandoned old house – perceptible only by memory. On this object approaching absolute zero in the great cosmos of all that is flows every river of blood in the history of man.

They feel the pain of knowing earth's inhabitants have suffered millennia of death, destruction, torture, and loss to own a piece of this mote and master the thinking of others.

Possession and control are but an illusion. Love is the only reality.

∞

The gunman stood not more than 20 meters below the stage and stared at me with a fuck-me-sideways look on his face. Bloody hell if I knew what was going on; the peacefully sleeping stretched as far as I could see. We were the only two awake. Crickets chirped, and birds sang. He stood frozen in place gripping his weapon in one hand, while the other swatted at a firefly tickling his ear.

I wanted to reach out and touch him. I didn't believe he had a pulse; how could he be a living, breathing human being and plan to do such a thing? Good God! Surely his heart was made of stone.

I had been sitting on the edge of the bed next to Yoko when she and everyone else fell into a deep sleep. Alert and at the ready – like a warrior – he turned and pointed his rifle at me as I stood up and walked down the stairs. When I approached him, he said, "I am Omar Abadi, supporter of the Islamic State and follower of the great Abu Bakr al-Baghdadi." Pointing the barrel of his rifle directly at my heart, he declared, "You and these filthy infidels must die."

No, I wasn't afraid. I suppose that's what happens when you've already faced death. It's just getting out of one car and into another. The cameramen and news crews slept on the ground, draped over their equipment. The jumbo screens had ceased transmitting. I was the only one who could bear witness to his act and, as long as I listened, I was safe.

He wasn't afraid of death either; he told me over and over that a great eternal reward awaited him for his martyrdom. I wasn't sure if he was trying to convince me or himself.

You use that word psychopath loosely. Only a true psychopath is born without a conscience; children come into this world without the poison of hatred coursing through their veins. Something had diverted his heart to a path of evil. I asked him, "Before you kill me, help me understand?" An abyss of hostility filled the space between our bodies, but he was willing to talk — compelled, really.

A child living in Syria is not afforded any sanctity. Omar's parents voluntarily handed him over to ISIS when he was 6 years old — I assume to raise him as the next generation of jihadists. I'm gutted over this! Bloody gutted! The child was sacrificed by the very people who were supposed to protect and nurture him. Instead, they gave him away to face a certain, gruesome death. Like any little tyke, he was probably happy to go along with the program and please his mum and pop.

I tried to persuade Omar to abandon his mission, but it became clear his ability to reason had been excised from him. It was as if he were deaf. He couldn't hear me at all. He yelled at me in Arabic. He paced like a condemned man. Seething with a festering anger, he began poking at a family sleeping at his feet with the butt of his rifle. The evening was cool, but he was sweating like a pig. And he seemed to be attracting more fireflies.

I thought he might start shooting randomly, so I picked up someone's guitar and started to play. You're looking at me like I'm crazy. Well maybe I am, but not last night. Music was my only weapon of counter-terrorism — I needed some magic.

Sure. I remember. I sang "Aisumasen, I'm sorry." In a way, it was an apology. What are you getting all huffy about? I was sorry for him. Aren't you? Humanity failed an innocent child.

All I could see was a lad whose life was lost the second his little hand let go of his pop's. First he was betrayed, then brainwashed. He was unaware that he, and others like him, had been brainwashed. Any hope of free will had been stolen from him. It would never again be possible for him to participate in shaping his own destiny. The operative leaders taught the children not to question or doubt – the very definition of faith distorted for evil purposes.

ISIS leaders used the strongest desire of the human spirit as a form of manipulation – the desire to belong and have purpose. They used this as a Trojan horse to steal Omar's soul. They snuck right in with a surprise attack against the helpless lad. What's that, you say? The cubs of the caliphate? There's even a name for these children? You've heard of this, then?

Omar told me most of the kids die detonating suicide and vehicle bombs or as foot soldiers. "Praise Allah," he said. He and a few others were spared this fate because ISIS operatives had other plans for them. He immigrated to the U.S. when he was 12 years old as part of a Syrian refugee group. He was here legally and bided his time. Barely 17 years old now, he was a Manchurian candidate for the 21st *century.*

As I sang to Omar, his breathing began to slow, his shoulders relaxed. He stopped his ranting, as if he'd expended his allotment of anger and there was none in reserve. The music I was playing enchanted him. He wanted to resist, but it had a mystical power over him that even I couldn't explain. He lowered his rifle – slowly at first – and then it became too heavy a burden to bear, so he put it down. Just like that.

The fireflies came – four, five, and six at a time. He swatted at them but always missed, because they weren't fireflies at all! I finally recognized them for what they were; I had seen them before in my own bathroom. Yes! Angels! They circled in a swarm around Omar so that they became blurred lines of light engulfing him fully.

He glowed a deep orange like a child's crayon sun. He glowed the yellow of cheery joy and the blue of the tranquil sea. He glowed the passionate purple of laughter and the transforming red of love. The rainbow light lifted him from his feet as if offering him up to God, and then the angels placed him gently, sleeping, onto his blanket. The rifle was gone.

I climbed back up on stage to my bed and whispered to Yoko, "My sweet, my sweet, come back to me." I kissed her, and she woke up — as did everyone else in the park. Yoko and I once again appeared on the jumbo screens, and our holograms were projected around the park.

"Sleeping beauty," I whispered to my groggy Yoko, "I'm sorry, my love. I'm sorry for the lost children. I'm sorry for the sadness in the world." She kissed me, and the crowd went wild. It's known as the 'fairy tale smooch' seen around the world.

When Omar woke up, he looked up at me and our eyes met. I imagined the faintest hint of recognition; or perhaps not. Our connection was interrupted when 50 Broadway singers marched up the stairs to take the stage with me. We sang "What the World Needs Now Is Love," *a song they recorded in the wake of the 2016 massacre in Orlando. Omar sang along. The inexorable rhythm of life continued.*

Are you mocking me? I swear the story of Omar is true. What about the same out-of-body experiences reported by thousands and thousands of people? Mass hysteria? Yoko had this experience too. She described it to me, and I believe her.

Can't you believe something special is happening? And how do you explain the missing four minutes? Nothing recorded or transmitted for four minutes from Central Park.

How do I explain it? Angels again. That's how. Oh, you're such a bloody skeptic. Yes, they do exist. I have no doubt. Time stood still while they averted disaster. Angels swooped in to heal a wound so deep they were summoned by it from another realm.

BORN AGAIN

Humor is perhaps a sense of intellectual perspective:
an awareness that some things are really important, others not;
and that the two kinds are most oddly jumbled in everyday affairs.

- Christopher Morley

"Welcome, welcome, welcome! I'm John Oliver." Debonair in a slim gray suit, lavender shirt, and geeky black-rimmed eyeglasses, comedian Oliver stands before a live studio audience to film HBO's comedy show *Last Week Tonight*. A realistic-looking, panoramic photo of an amalgam of city skylines and fictitious structures under a lush darkened blue sky covers the wall behind him. "Thank you for joining us today. Let's get to a little news straight away," he adds in his charming British accent.

"John Lennon is back in the spotlight." A current photo of the timeless legend flashing the familiar '60s, two-fingered 'V' peace sign pops up in a monitor to the right of Oliver's head. "He came back from the dead," Oliver says as a photo of a zombie pushing up through the mound of a grave flashes behind him "and, may I ask, just how bizarre is *that?*

"No less bizarre, he's now seeking natural-born U.S. citizenship so he can run for president of the United States. It wouldn't be the first time a dead man was running for the highest position in the land."

Laughter swells as clips of 2016 presidential candidates flash on screen: Dr. Ben Carson laconically answering a Republican debate question; Jeb Bush standing idle, hands in his pockets, with his characteristic somnambulistic demeanor, while Donald Trump makes fun of him.

"Even Lennon, after being dead for *40 years,*" Oliver says with a rakish smile, "has more spunk than those two combined!

"The media have lambasted Lennon for claiming he was re-born in front of the Dakota." A montage of video taken by witnesses at the event plays on screen. "C'mon folks! This is *easily* explained." A farcical scene aboard *Star Trek's USS Enterprise* follows.

"Chekov, set the coordinates for earth," Captain Kirk says addressing his navigator. He turns to his helmsman and adds, "Warp 6 cruising speed, Mr. Sulu. Bring us around."

"Ah, there she is: Earth. What a beauty." The planet hangs resplendent outside the *USS Enterprise's* bridge window.

Lieutenant Uhura interrupts, "Captain? We're still receiving distress signals. Earth is in trouble."

"Bones," Captain Kirk addresses his chief medical officer, "Is our ambassador ready to go?"

"Yes, Captain. He's been in deep sleep for 40 years, but he's good as new."

"This is not logical, Captain." Spock speaks in his typically stoic manner. "Of all candidates, we're sending a musician to save the world? A hippie who smokes marijuana for breakfast?"

"For breakfast, Spock? Surely you exaggerate."

"I do not know how to exaggerate, sir. It is not the Vulcan way."

"Never mind, Spock. I've made up my mind."

The pneumatic bridge doors hiss open; John Lennon enters and adjusts his glasses to look around. Several Star Fleet officers walk John over to the transporter where he steps up and takes his place on the pod.

John makes the peace sign and says, "All you need is love."

Spock says, "Highly improbable."

"Beam him down, Scotty," Captain Kirk orders.

John Oliver throws up his hands and asks "Well why not that as a form of birth? Billions of believers think it's plausible that God created Eve out of Adam's rib. Is that any more far-fetched?" A still picture of a naked Neanderthal man wearing only a fig leaf comes up on screen. The man holds a bone adorned with black yarn for hair, with a face and breasts drawn on with magic marker.

"The little boobies there make that so realistic," Oliver says.

"OK, so let's suppose you think the rib thing is a myth and a person can't materialize from space. When it comes to humans living today, we have among us children who began as fertilized eggs in test tubes and were gestated as fetuses in growing pods to viability. If we no longer need a woman's uterus to give birth, maybe what we need is a new definition of birth. This is a big – fucking – deal!

"So, of course we're leaving this extremely important question up to the courts. What could go wrong there?"

A *New York Times* headline reading, "Jurors dismissed for playing Sudoku during embezzlement trial," pops up on the monitor.

"So, they were a little bored. Who could blame them?" Oliver quips.

A *Washington Post* headline scrolls across the screen with a photo of a women being led away in handcuffs: "Mistrial declared in murder trial."

"A juror was charged with having an affair with the defendant during the trial. What is it about women that they're always attracted to the bad boys? She voted for acquittal. Lucky for him he was good in bed. Feisty little vixen, that one. I'd like her on my jury if I ever get in trouble. But I digress."

News footage shows police officers corralling an entire jury into a paddy wagon.

"A full-out, drunken brawl erupted during their sequestered deliberations. Evidently, they entertained themselves with a competitive game of beer pong.

"This will surely inspire confidence in the courts:" A *New York Post* headline declares: "Ouija board verdict tossed." Oliver composes himself. "Hey! Maybe that would work for Lennon? A little consultation with his fellow dead?

"Surely these things were aberrations in our well-functioning justice system." Oliver winks. "John has opted for a bench trial for his petition for citizenship rather than take a chance with an unpredictable jury. So, while he is inside the courthouse at this very moment to receive a ruling, we went out into the street to see who might have been in his jury pool."

A 3-D hologram of a reporter randomly interviewing passersby on the sidewalk outside the CBS Broadcast Center on West 57th Street transmits into the studio.

"Excuse me, young lady. Would you consider voting for John Lennon for president of the United States?" the reporter asks.

A teen steps into his transmission field and appears to the studio audience. "Oh, I can't vote. I'm not 21 yet."

"But you only have to be 18 to vote."

She giggles, "Really?"

Oliver smacks himself in the forehead.

The reporter calls out, "Sir, sir? Can you come over here and answer a quick question?" A sharply appointed, 30-something, metrosexual steps into the field. "If John Lennon is granted citizenship based on being re-born in New York City and he runs for president, would you vote for him?"

"Absolutely! I'm impressed by the meaningful work he's doing with the Goopplezon Peace Department. Maybe he can actually convince people to find non-violent solutions to the world's problems."

Oliver smooths his rebellious purple tie and says, "Well, a man dressed like that can only be sensible."

Approaching a chicly attired, middle-aged woman, the reporter asks, "Ma'am? Would you vote for John Lennon for president?"

"Are you on drugs?" She adjusts her Tiffany-blue shopping bag and continues on her way.

"That might not be a bad idea," Oliver says. "I can imagine President Lennon providing every adult citizen with a dime bag of weed, a Fender acoustic guitar, and a copy of the Dalai Lama's book, *The Art of Happiness*." The audience hoots. "Life in the USA would be a lot mellower."

A montage of comments by pedestrians punctuates Oliver's segment. "Rock on." "You believe that hocus-pocus scam?" "Oh, my God, he's gotta be a fake." "I don't vote." "Who?" "The world would be a better place." "Isn't he one of the Beatles? Are they still around?" "I heard he disappears now and then."

Oliver walks over to sit behind his large desk perched on a platform on stage. "What would be so bad about a disappearing president? Isn't that an American tradition?" he asks.

"In '79, President Carter disappeared at Camp David. Ten days later, he delivered his famous malaise speech declaring that America's problems stemmed from its obsession with consumerism.

"And what about JFK? When he indulged in his little trysts with Marilyn Monroe, didn't he have to,"– and here he makes air quotes – "disappear? At least for two minutes?

"And Bill Clinton? Bill, Bill, Bill! Whenever a certain young intern was in the Oval Office, he would disappear too."

The audience howls as Oliver slides off his chair and slowly disappears under the desk. He knocks his glasses askew and hams up an expression of rapture.

I AM I

Today you are you!
That is truer than true!
There is no one alive who is you-er than you!

- Dr. Seuss

John's bodyguards do their best to accompany him whenever he leaves the Dakota. Adept at putting together disguises – a woman's blond wig, mustaches and bushy eyebrows, dark sunglasses, odd clothing, fat padding – John sometimes manages to slip by them. He amuses himself with the game and teases, "No one controls me. I'm uncontrollable. The only one who controls me is me. And that's just barely possible."

The guards soon discover that John forgets to change out of his favorite red Spring Court sneakers, so they look at people's feet as they step off the elevator into the vestibule. It's all they can do not to laugh when they catch him in one of his get-ups. Pretending not to recognize him, they follow at a discreet distance.

Nine million people occupying 305 square miles of space makes New York City the most densely populated city in the U.S., but John appreciates anonymity even as he moves about on the street. If someone approaches wearing 3-D Goopplezon Lenses and the purple face-recognition light is flashing, he'll look away as they pass in order to preserve his solitude. If he's daydreaming and misses the aversion and a fan recognizes him, he pleasantly complies with an autograph. Selfies with his fans featuring his disguises go viral within minutes, and John has to call Kuruma to come by for a quick pick-up. One on one, New Yorkers are cool. It's the crowds that scare him.

A low-level courthouse clerk, desperate to make a little extra cash, tips off the media about the date of John's scheduled appearance to hear the verdict for his citizenship petition. Thousands of people gather in front of the courthouse, blocking John and Yoko from exiting their car.

The NYPD assembles its crowd-control tactical team, putting up cement barriers, roping off a walkway, and forming a shoulder-to-shoulder human shield.

John grabs Yoko's hand and says, "OK, baby, let's go." Kuruma's door opens and they rush out, running by the screaming throngs. Hands reach through the wall of police officers. A few girls faint but do not fall to the ground as they are propped up by the surge of bodies. The noise is painfully deafening; John and Yoko let go of one another and plug their ears with their fingers.

Safely inside the courthouse doors, John and Yoko lean against the wall to catch their breath. "That's what we hated about touring: the bloody screaming. We couldn't hear ourselves on stage."

"What?" Yoko asks.

"The bloody screaming—" He stops short when he notices her trying to stifle a smile.

∞

John, Yoko, and their Goopplezon lawyers sit chatting quietly at a large oak conference table at the front of the courtroom. John says, "I hope this turns out better than the last time I tried to become a U.S. citizen."

"What a nightmare," Yoko says. "We were traumatized by Tricky Dick and J. Edgar. Remember, darling?"

"Like it was—"

"Yesterday," Yoko finishes John's sentence. "I know, I know."

"Now that marijuana is legal here, they won't want to kick me out for my past evil pot-smoking ways."

Judge Soenso acts as sole fact-finder and ruler of law and procedures in the case of John Winston Ono Lennon vs. the United States of America. As he prepares himself in his chambers, the retirement-aged baby boomer with thinning hair, a slight paunch, and a bum knee remembers vividly where he was at 8 p.m. on February 9, 1964: He sat between his parents on a lumpy sofa in their suburban Long Island den. His older brother and sister were sprawled on the floor in front of them with a big bowl of popcorn. Dad had adjusted the rabbit-eared antennae on top of their black-and-white Zenith TV as part of the family's Sunday night ritual.

The Soensos tuned in to *The Ed Sullivan Show*, along with 73 million other Americans, to see and hear the mop-topped Fab Four dressed in black Edwardian suits perform their first set of "All My Loving," "Till There Was You," and "She Loves You."

"All rise!" the bailiff pronounces. The Lennon contingent stands in compliance.

As Judge Soenso, dressed in a traditional black robe, enters the courtroom, he gestures for everyone to be seated. "Mr. Lennon, I'll never forget the first time I heard, 'Ladies and gentlemen… the Beatles.' I was just a little boy. I was mesmerized by your performance. All year long I begged my parents to let me grow my hair long. I begged them to buy me a guitar too.

"They never relented on doing away with the buzz cut, but in December they gave me a guitar as a gift for my 8th birthday. It was just a plastic piece of crappola, but I was thrilled. I never put it down. The British invasion was changing the course of musical history, and I wanted to be part of it. It is thoroughly exciting for me to adjudicate a motion by you. I've been a lifelong fan."

"Thank you, your honor," John says.

"That being said, I am sworn to uphold the laws of this great nation, and I have addressed this responsibility without bias and with the utmost respect for reaching a fair and just verdict. A great philosopher once said, 'Sometimes the questions are complicated, and the answers are simple.'"

"I love Dr. Seuss!" John says.

"Yes, indeed. I know that about you!"

John takes Yoko's hand in his. She whispers in his ear, "Can you imagine me in the White House? I am first lady, first lady, I am." They both stifle a laugh.

While Mr. and Mrs. Lennon recover from their private joke, Judge Soenso says, "This is going down in my book as the strangest case of my career. Let's get to it, shall we? I've reached a decision."

"All rise," the bailiff calls.

Everyone in the courtroom stands at rapt attention as Judge Soenso rules. "The first issue before the court is to decide whether or not you actually died, Mr. Lennon. If you have lived since you were born, we can all agree that − despite your youthful appearance − your birth took place in Liverpool, England, on October 9, 1940, to Julia and Alfred Lennon. Neither of your parents were U.S. citizens, therefore, you do not meet the requirement to be a natural-born citizen of the United States, and you are not eligible to run for president of the United States.

"There is, however, overwhelming evidence that you died on December 8, 1980. I have in front of me a certified copy of the death certificate for one John Winston Ono Lennon. We have the time of death declared by Dr. Stephan Lynn in Roosevelt Hospital as 11:15 p.m. The cause of death was multiple gunshot wounds of the left shoulder and chest; left lung and left subclavian artery;

external and internal hemorrhage. And shock. It was ruled a homicide."

Yoko, agitated, squeezes John's hand, her usual composure shaken by the memory.

The judge clears his throat and continues, "In addition, there were numerous doctors and nurses who witnessed the end of your life who were previously deposed for these proceedings. I found their testimonies to be credible. We also have verification that you were—" He hesitates, shakes his head, and takes a deep breath before continuing. "That you were cremated at the Ferncliff Cemetery in Hartsdale, New York, on December 10, 1980."

Shuddering, Yoko concentrates on keeping the tears welling in her eyes from spilling over. She fears if she cries she will never stop; if one tear should escape, the torrent will drown them all. Their corpses will float away in a river of sorrow.

Tipping down his reading glasses to the edge of his nose and peering over them, the judge says, "I must say, Mr. Lennon, considering your ordeal, you're looking remarkably well in my courtroom today."

The laughter restores a sense of levity to the room. Yoko catches an errant tear shaken free before it escapes with her sad memories and the promise of disaster.

"Look what you've done, your honor. My wife is laughing and crying at the same time. What's a man to do about that?" John asks.

"Ah, Mr. Lennon, now that's a question I could never answer! This was much easier."

Yoko dabs at her eyes with a tissue, and John pulls her close. "I'm here, my love," he whispers.

With your indulgence, Mrs. Lennon," Judge Soenso continues, "based on a preponderance of evidence, it stands with this court that John Winston Ono Lennon is deceased."

The judge looks at John and shrugs. "What a quandary! You're presenting yourself to this court as the same John Winston Ono Lennon, and clearly you're not dead now."

"No sir!" John says. "I'm feeling super-fantastic! I can't explain it either, your honor. I'm just happy to be here. Every day is getting better and better."

"OK, then. The next question to resolve is: Are you really the same John Lennon? The FBI, CIA, and World Health Organization stand behind the sampling, testing, and results garnered by Vim Vitae Medical Imaging Center that compared your DNA to that of the deceased John Lennon.

"We were able to track down a fan that had purchased a bloody shirt – a shirt your doorman had worn the night you were shot that was stained with your blood – and we used that as an alternate source of base comparison DNA for further verification."

"Someone bought a bloody shirt?" John asks.

"Oh, yes. Anything at all associated with you has always been coveted. Anyway, we used several other independent labs for quality control – and I thank you for indulging the court by providing the blood and tissue samples we requested. It was necessary so people wouldn't think this was some big, deceptive conspiracy–"

John interrupts and says, "I know a thing or two about conspiracies, your honor. No problem."

"I'm sure you do, Mr. Lennon. I'm sure you do. Based on this extensive corroborating evidence and additional videos, facial and iris recognition software, photos, and testimony by the eyewitnesses present at your return in front of the Dakota, it is the ruling of this court that you are John Lennon, one and the same."

John turns to Yoko and teases, "See, my love! It's really me!"

"I would know your kiss anywhere," Yoko whispers as she slips her arm around John's waist.

"By virtue of this fact, I declare that you were born in New York City on December 8, 2020. And guess what! You and I share a birthday! Same day, different year."

"So that means I'm a U.S. citizen?" John asks Judge Soenso.

"Automatically!"

As John hugs Yoko, he says, "I'm going to play my buddy Alice Cooper's song 'Elected' during the campaign." John improvises, "You and me, my darling Yoko. We're gonna get elected, baby!"

"Not so fast, Mr. Lennon," the judge interjects. "Since you were born just last year, you haven't yet reached your first birthday."

Unable to resist, the judge tips down his reading glasses to the edge of his nose and raises his eyebrows. "I dare say, Mr. Lennon, considering your tender young age, you're looking very mature for an infant. You have to be at least 35 years old to be president. You'll have to wait until 2055 to be eligible."

"Bullocks!" John says under his breath.

"I'm sorry. It would have been a rousing campaign. Definitely rivaling the controversies of the Trump-Clinton election back in 2016. You missed that lunacy. Look it up. Unfortunately, you can't have it both ways. Either you're 80-something and not a natural-born citizen of the U.S., or you were born in New York and are automatically a citizen but cannot meet the age burden. I've ruled for the latter." He bangs his gavel.

Judge Soenso rises. "Mr. Lennon, would you indulge the court? May I have your autograph?" He holds up his weathered copy of the *Double Fantasy* album cover.

"My pleasure." John approaches the bench, takes the Judge's pen, and, with a flourish writes, *Happy birthday to us. John L—*

John freezes in place. The pen falls out of his hand, hits the judge's desk, and bounces to the floor. He closes his eyes.

"Mr. Lennon? John? Are you all right?" the judge asks.

Yoko rushes up to the bench to stand beside John. His body fills with flickering black and white static and begins to shimmer and fade. With a gentle, crackling buzz, he disappears.

Judge Soenso jumps back and bangs against the wall. "What. The. Fuck?"

Yoko looks up at the judge and says, "Uh-oh."

LOVE AND THE ODDS OF YOU

*For small creatures such as we,
the vastness is bearable only through love.*

- Carl Sagan

You're in a philosophical mood today, I see. What forces, unseen and powerful, are at work to shape our stories? Well, I'd say love is the number one, essential life-sustaining elixir. It is the most influential of all.

In the absence of love, death festers and destroys the spirit in increments. It eats away at self-acceptance, creativity, the soul, and our sense of humanity. Yep, love. The antonym for death. Its nourishment gives us strength — the steel girder supporting the tower. We should fill our lives with all forms of love. It's bloody good stuff.

∞

The synchronization of traffic lights and driverless cars programmed to pull over for emergency vehicles open a clear path on Manhattan's Second Avenue. An ambulance speeds southbound toward the Gramercy Theater, sirens blazing in declaration of doom.

A commotion unfolds at a table to the side of the dance floor. A young man has collapsed and is in respiratory distress. A DJ keeps the music pulsing and most patrons are unaware of the life hanging precariously by a thread just a few feet away.

Someone calls for emergency services. They create a hologram field around the victim lying on the floor for medical technicians to assess him. Since the EMTs can't actually touch him, they ask for assistance and give direction to a Good Samaritan who steps forward to help.

Sean and his friend, bass guitarist and lead singer of *Primus*, sit on a sofa backstage chatting during a break from their performance. Several neat stacks of tables and chairs piled in a corner behind them inexplicably tumble over with a loud clatter, interrupting their conversation. Sean stands up and sees his father entangled in the mess.

"Dad! What happened?" He gives John a hand, getting him up on his feet. "How did you get in here? Why are you here? I thought you wanted to keep a low profile after your court case for citizenship was all over the news this week? Dad? Dad? Are you OK?"

"Ah, yeah, I think so," John says as he gets his bearings.

Sean ushers him over to the sofa. "Dad, this is Les Claypool. Les, my dad, John Lennon." The two men shake hands.

"Jesus Christ, Sean. Jesus fucking Christ! You weren't shitting me. I didn't believe you. Jesus Christ almighty." Les paces, uncertain about what to do with this revelation.

"Yeah, I have that effect on people sometimes!" John teases. "It's cool."

"Let me get you a drink, dad. What'll you have?"

John asks for a Brandy Alexander and razzes his son when he brings back a Smirnoff green apple and cranberry cocktail for himself.

With his drink in hand, John walks to the door and peeks into the dance hall. "Half the people out there look like they're walking zombies."

"They're high on love, no doubt," Les says.

"Love? They're high on love and they look like that?"

"It's the newest boutique drug devastating the city. It's everywhere. And it's more addictive than crack and meth," Les says.

"Crack and meth?"

"I'll tell you about them later," Sean says. "Love is addictive the first time you use it. Euphoria consumes you. It makes you think you love everyone and everything in the world. But you need more and more each time, and it affects your breathing and heart rate."

"Sounds exactly like love," John says.

"The irony is not lost on me. But it's really bad news. Instead of making connections to experience real love, users are going for the substitute and killing themselves. They know how dangerous it is, and they do it anyway."

"That's because people think love is a feeling that can fill a void. It's not a feeling; it's a way of being alive. You have to feed it," John says. "The basic thing nobody asks is why do people take drugs of any sort? Why do we have these accessories to normal living, to live? I mean is there something wrong with society that's making us so pressurized, that we cannot live without guarding ourselves against it?"

"What about you, dad? Your year-and-a-half-long lost weekend?"

"I learned the hard way. I wasn't coping with the hatefulness and criticism me and your mum were dealing with from everyone. Yoko and I thought I needed a diversion. You know she and I split for a while before you were born, and she gave me her blessing to go off and have, ah, a thing, with May Pang," John says. "I was drinking heavily and stoned a lot of the time.

"I wasn't exactly lost, though. I mean, I spent some fun time with Julian. We went to Disney World! And I was pretty productive. I released three albums, and I did some producing for Ringo and Harry Nilsson. I guess I just needed a temporary escape.

"Part of me suspects that I'm a loser, and the other part of me thinks I'm God almighty." John laughs. "I didn't have love for the loser part of me. But I was delusional to think that's how I'd find it. It was like looking at life through a scrim – all I could see was muted outlines. You can't find love in the shadows."

"This drug is poison," Les says. He pushes himself to talk and pretends he's part of a normal conversation.

The music stops mid-beat. A hush settles over the Saturday-night revelers. "What's happening?" Les asks. The three men interrupt their conversation and reach the doorway to the dance hall to see the paramedics stop resuscitation procedures.

A milky apparition swirls up from the warm and lonely body of the young man sprawled on the floor.

"No! No! He can't die," John insists. "He has to live. He has to marry his childhood sweetheart. They have to conceive their only child, Kerri, so she can marry your son, Kibo, Sean. And Kerri and Kibo's child Heiwa must be born to become a great world leader and champion of peace."

Sean and Les exchange looks. "Dad. Are you losing it? Take it easy. How can you possibly know all this? My son? Kibo? Kerri? What are you talking about?"

"I have no bloody idea," John answers truthfully. "Just get out there and make them keep trying until they revive him." He pushes Sean through the door onto the back of the stage. Les runs out after him. John disappears.

∞

The occupants present in the courtroom are fascinated and terrified as John's body re-forms into ordinary flesh and blood before their eyes.

John blinks and notices he has dropped the pen. "Oops," he says, as he bends over to pick it up. He finishes signing Judge Soenso's album cover with a flourish.

"What?" John asks looking around at everyone staring at him.

"You disappeared again, my love," Yoko says.

∞

What are the chances that you are here to participate in this human experience? By age 25, the man who might be your father could potentially meet 200 million women in the world but meets only 10,000 of them.

There's a mere one-in-10 chance any of these women will talk to him. If one does, there is only a one-in-10 chance she will go on a second date with him and a one-in-10 chance from there she will keep dating him. Your eyes are glazing over. Bloody statistics. Hang in there with me.

There is another one-in-10 chance they will have a baby together. Kind of unlikely, wouldn't you say? Are you following me on this?

We also have to consider the probability that the sperm carrying your unique DNA out of billions will meet her egg. By now we're up to a one-in-400 quadrillion chance that you, as you, will exist. I don't know about you, but I can't even write that number.

But we're not done yet, because the same odds had to happen for each set of your grandparents, and each set of their parents. The prerequisite for your existence on earth today includes the miniscule likelihood of a continuous series of events since the dawn of man.

Sean's existence is predicated on the fact that I remembered Yoko didn't like lima beans. Be patient; you'll understand what I mean by that later. The point for now is that we are all extraordinary creations; unique and outrageously improbable.

The odds you are here to read my story are closer to zero than the human mind is capable of comprehending. If love – real love – is the answer, shouldn't we begin by loving ourselves? Shouldn't we honor the unlikely miracle we each represent and keep the chain unbroken?

TABULA RASA

Imagination is more important than knowledge.
For knowledge is limited,
whereas imagination embraces the entire world,
stimulating progress, giving birth to evolution.

- Albert Einstein

John sits in the dark in his den; elbows perched on his sprawling desk, his cheek resting in the palm of his left hand. Behind him, a large painting of a leopard hangs on the mahogany wood wall and a spray of wildflowers in a crystal vase adorn an alcove.

The pen in his right hand awaits its master's command. John twirls it over one finger and under the next, and back again. He switches on an overhead lamp and his drawing book beckons.

John's heart races as the blank page sets her sights on seducing him, like a provocative temptress sitting on a desk with her legs crossed and dangling a shoe, enticing him with a come-hither invitation. The hypnotic din of city traffic, the susurrus of John's own breath moving in and out of his lungs, and the sound of a clock's tick-tock, tick-tock, tick-tock serenade the lovers.

A man never forgets his first love − drawing is John's, before poetry, before philosophy, before music. She is always welcome to visit. From her he learns to express love openly. She teaches him to be free.

John places the tip of the pen on the paper and, without thinking, his hand moves of its own volition. He works quickly, with inspiration from the heavens flowing through him; playful curlicues in the corner, buildings with hearts for windows, crisscrossing lines forming the cables of a bridge and two towers topped by eyes with lashes; creativity uncensored.

In a few strokes, he creates a skinny man with long hair and round glasses. Next to him on the bridge, a similar but shorter and slightly rounder figure. John scribbles a title at the bottom of the page, "Me beautiful boy and me."

Yoko comes up behind John, places her hands on his shoulders, and looks over the top of his head. "Who's that?" she asks pointing to a third figure standing alone further back on the bridge.

"Ha! I don't remember drawing her." He knows she is a "her" by the two little "U's" he drew to form her breasts. He has given the girl a mop of tight curly hair and shaded in her sad face.

"Can you guess?" Yoko asks.

"Well, she must be someone important or she wouldn't be there."

"Who do you think she might be?"

John rolls his desk chair around to face Yoko. "My love," John says quite seriously, "we have to accept that some things just don't have an explanation."

Yoko laughs heartily. "Oh my God, you're telling *me* that?"

John laughs too. "Come here!" He grabs Yoko's belt and pulls her onto his lap. "I have something important to explain to you."

"What's that?"

He whispers into her ear "I love you." John kisses Yoko's neck, he kisses her cheek, he kisses her lips, and the clock stops ticking.

REASON FOR LIVING

The two most important days in your life are
the day you are born and
the day you find out why.

- Mark Twain

Cotton-candy softness surrounds him. Aware of slow, weightless tumbling, John's instinct is to tuck into a fetal position. A veil of soft pinks and powder blues tickles his skin with a barely perceptible touch as he floats through the haze. The second hand on his watch stubbornly refuses to move. He feels no fear — only warmth and a sense of being protected.

Before he arrives, he hears a lullaby far off into the distance. Or is it far off into time? The voice of enchantment sings:

Hey there, it's time for bed, lay down your weary head
Don't worry 'bout a thing, listen to the angels sing
There now, close your eyes and watch the curtain rise
On yet another dream

When the doctor needs a break from her test tubes, microscopes, chemicals, and calculations in the hospital research laboratory, she sings to the newborn babies upstairs in the nursery. They remind her of her reason for living. The nursery, serene and decorated with photographs of grown children who have passed through, serves as a source of inspiration.

John opens his eyes to find himself standing behind her, a slim black woman in a lab coat cradling a newborn swaddled in pink. His presence touches the doctor's heart – she knows it is him before she turns and smiles. "Mr. Lennon?"

"Yes." He looks around at the sleeping babies in their bassinettes. "Where am I?"

"You're in the neonatal unit of the Memorial Sloan-Kettering Cancer Center in New York City," she answers calmly. "I'm so happy to see you again."

"How did I get here?"

"I wish I could tell you. Einstein's theories of the space-time continuum are beyond my level of mathematical expertise."

Not recognizing her he asks, "We've met before?"

"Yes, we have – twice actually." Untroubled by his inexplicable visit, she re-introduces herself as Dr. Jacqueline Love.

John stares intently at her face. He estimates the doctor to be in her mid-50s. He wracks his memory for any lingering tidbit of their previous encounters. Unnerved by her green eyes, the vaguest sense of familiarity teases him like a missing word on the tip of one's tongue. Still, he comes up short.

Dr. Love hands John the baby. "I'm not surprised you're here. This is your great-granddaughter. She was born today."

John's eyes widen as she places the infant in his arms.

"Her name is Heiwa. It means 'peace' in Japanese," Doctor Love says.

A terrible thought occurs to John. He asks, "Does she have cancer?"

"No, no, Mr. Lennon. None of the babies do. They would have had cancer, but today we have the capability of testing and treating them in utero and in growing pods so they are born cancer-free. We deliver them here just so we can observe them for a few days after they're born. Heiwa is healthy."

John cradles the baby in his arms and kisses her forehead.

Dr. Love explains, "You helped us make that a reality. The second time I saw you, back in 2040—"

"What?" John interrupts. "*Back* in 2040? What year is this?"

"We're in October of 2060. You were traveling through time," she says nonchalantly. "Don't be frightened." She places her hand gently on John's shoulder and strokes the baby's head. When Heiwa reacts with a tiny smile, John's shoulders relax.

"Twenty years ago, I had been conducting some protein and DNA experiments for a cancer vaccine and was baffled by my unexpected results. You appeared, just like you did today. Honestly, you scared the hell out of me then. You had a piece of paper in your hand with a formula on it. You didn't know where you got it or how you had traveled to my lab station. You handed it to me, we chatted briefly, and, in the next instant, you turned into static and disappeared. You left behind the answer I needed to solve the puzzle of my research."

"And you say Heiwa is my great-granddaughter. How so?"

"She is your son Sean's granddaughter. The baby's father is his son — your grandson, Kibo."

John tenderly kisses the baby's nose. "What happened the first time we met?"

"Oh, Mr. Lennon, I wish you could remember. You saved me." An energy surge pulses through her body as she hugs John. He and Heiwa begin to fade. Their silhouettes fill instantly with black and white static. They flicker and disappear with a tiny pop.

Dr. Love inhales; she barely has time for a fleeting thought of worry. In the beat of a quarter-note, John and the baby reappear as a kaleidoscope of swirling color until their flesh becomes normal.

John's instinct is to hand the baby to the doctor. Dr. Love turns around to place Heiwa in her bassinette. She removes an arrangement of an olive tree sprig tied with a silk ribbon and adorned with a tiny ceramic dove from on top of the baby's blanket. She places it at Heiwa's head in the bassinette.

Saint John Lennon

Dr. Love sings to John's great granddaughter.

Some dreams are built to last,
Others disappear too fast,
Whatever yours may be,
Like you, they're dear to me

While her back is turned, John disappears again with no time for goodbyes. The doctor's mellifluous voice penetrates his subconscious while he is in a state of nothingness.

JACKIE, DEAR, IT'S A WONDERFUL LIFE

The meaning of life is to find your gift.
The purpose of life is to give it away.

- Pablo Picasso

The beauty of life — and its most loathsome wickedness — is that nothing remains the same. Change is inevitable. Constant and erratic, we pray for its postponement during times of joy and for its speedy arrival to relieve us of pain.

Perspective is life's most sovereign force. It is so powerful that a purposeful crafting of frame of reference is capable of bringing into existence a new reality.

What do I mean? Just think about it. Within every human being is the capacity to change the world with a shift in focus and belief.

∞

Kuruma cruises down Broadway, turns left, and deposits John and Sean onto Chamber Street at City Hall. Father and son tuck their long hair into woven wool hats and put on a couple of Sean's 3-D Goopplezon Lenses. John steps out of Kuruma first and catches his reflection in the side view mirror. "All we need are those fake mustaches and big red, wax lips, and no one will recognize us."

They make their way around the corner to access the pedestrian walkway on the Brooklyn Bridge. Majordomo Julio and the car continue to Brooklyn Heights to pick up a pizza from Grimaldi's before closing time and to wait for John and Sean's arrival on the other side.

"This was a great idea, dad," Sean says. "After spending an entire day in a courthouse, it's good to get out. I've never done this walk. You know, when you live someplace you just take for granted the special thing will always be there."

"Yeah, we do that with people too," John says. "I've been thinking about what I would have missed if I hadn't returned." After some introspection, he adds, "It's you, Sean, and your mother, and your brother, and Paul, and Ringo. It's the people I love. That's what it's all about." He puts his arm around Sean's shoulder and squeezes.

The grand neo-gothic towers of granite are tethered to four massive steel cables rising up to their apices and down again, to support the bridge's span of 5,989 feet. Stepping onto the wooden promenade above the roadway, John says, "I want to know more about you, son. Tell me about your work with Artists Against Fracking. What is that?"

"Ah, lucky you, dad! Here's my little elevator speech: Hydraulic fracturing, or fracking, is a process of drilling down into the earth, and then injecting a mixture of water, sand, and chemicals into the rock at high pressure. It fractures the rock, which allows the release of oil and gas that flows out of the well."

"Well done, my boy! Why are you against it?"

"Because the chemicals injected into the earth are toxic endocrine disruptors and carcinogens. You should hear the terrible stories of the people who live near these sites. Their voices have been marginalized, and the corporate spin is heartbreaking. Methane, which by the way is one of the major contributors to global warming, is leaking from the wells."

"Oh, my God! That is so cool!"

"Cool? What are you talking about?"

"Sorry, son. When I look at you steadily, all this info about you starts scrolling in front of me."

"Ooops! I forgot. Turn off facial recognition," Sean commands. He puts his 3-D Goopplezon Lenses on. "Now you should just see stuff about our surroundings. Check it out."

"Ah, there we go. That's better. So, tell me more about this bloody fracking," John says as he strolls beside his son.

"OK. Well, the process uses millions of gallons of water; some farmers are competing with the energy companies for local supplies."

"Farmers are being cut off from water? How are they supposed to farm without it?"

"Exactly. And get this: Fracking causes thousands of micro-earthquakes when the rock containing oil or gas is fractured apart and when they inject the toxic waste into underground injection wells. Geologists have registered seismic activity. Earthquakes caused by humans. Can you believe that?"

John feels Sean tense up as he speaks. He takes his arm off his son's shoulder and asks, "What about all this wind and solar power alternative energy stuff I've been reading about? After all these years, you'd think we'd be further along with that."

"You know what I don't understand, dad? People make up corporations, right? So why is it that some of them come together and form companies that have heart? Like Goopplezon. They make money for their shareholders, and they incorporate a philanthropic aspect to their operations and a philosophy of environmentally friendly practices. This makes people want to do business with them.

"Then there are other companies, also formed by regular people, who develop a soulless culture devoid of compassion. What happens to them? How do companies take on good and evil lives of their own like that?"

As John thinks about this, he removes his 3-D Goopplezon Lenses and turns around to take in the midnight view of Manhattan the old-fashioned way. To the south, the twinkling lights of downtown Manhattan light up the sky as if they were nearby stars.

The South Street Seaport below teems with tourists and locals celebrating the end of the work week with a beer, comedy show, and stroll on the piers alongside the bobbing sailing ships. The last Staten Island ferry of the night glides past the Statue of Liberty as she holds her torch high.

To the north, the Manhattan Bridge traverses the East River and the Empire State Building is majestic lit in red, white, and blue. John, proud to be a U.S. citizen, has goose bumps run up his spine.

"That's a big question, Sean. I think the answer is the same for a company as it is for an individual; it's a matter of chosen consciousness and a willingness to speak up. Silence is an injustice. I understand the fear behind shaking up the status quo, I really do. So many of my troubles were directly related to me protesting war."

"I know, dad. You were vilified for being against war! Unbelievable."

John puts his Lenses back on and flashes a peace sign. "Seriously, there can be personal repercussions. But that's what it takes; somebody fearlessly, or maybe despite the bloody fear, to stand up and say, 'This isn't right.' If one person does it, then someone else may join in, and someone else. Before you know it, a little snowball picks up speed as it rolls down the mountain, grows into a boulder, and then causes a thunderous avalanche of change."

"Yes. Just one person can be the catalyst."

"You're preaching to the choir, me boy. I'm curious to know, why this, Sean? Why is anti-fracking your cause? Why did you choose this over, say, saving abused animals, or digging wells for people without access to water, or finding missing children, or something like that?"

"In my case I met a beautiful family from Pennsylvania whose home and lives were ruined by fracking, and their plight touched me. But it almost doesn't matter what we do, dad. If everyone just did something, anything, big or small, to contribute, we'd have it all covered."

"Regrettably, I wasn't here to help raise you. I wanted to be here, believe me. And still you grew up to think about the world the way I do. Amazing!"

"It must be in my DNA!" Sean gives his dad a playful, light punch in the arm. "My mother was a positive influence on my philosophy of life too, you know. And the two of you were attracted to each other for a reason."

One of Sean's dreams comes true when John says, "I'm proud of you, son."

"Look!" Sean points to hundreds of padlocks fastened onto a cable. "Love locks. People attach them there and throw away the key to represent eternal love. The city hates this. It damages the bridge and they have to be removed."

John reads the information streaming into his field of vision.

As they approach the locks, a slim, black teenage girl, noticeably underdressed for the unseasonably cold and windy night, clicks a lock closed, kisses a key, and throws it, along with a scraggly bouquet of flowers, over the side of the bridge.

The girl watches her offerings fall 135 feet from the east side of the bridge into the river and wonders what will go through her mind as she plunges to her death. She does a calculation in her head and figures it will take three and a half seconds to impact. When she hits the water, will she live long enough to register how cold it is? She carefully assesses her options and choses the girder she will scale to take her final leap.

Sean stops and points to something on the river.

When John takes his next step, the rest of the world around him and the girl fades away. The stars above, the expanse of the bridge in front of and behind them, the skyscraper lights, building silhouettes, and the boats below disappear into a milky blur around their little bubble of space. The last sounds he hears are of a subway train whooshing by and clicking over the tracks and the din of traffic below them; the toot-toot of a tug boat, a snippet of conversation, and Sean's laughter. Then, silence.

He notices an odd, jagged aura surrounding the girl. It flickers as if a storm's blustering wind were interfering with power lines. Thinking it a malfunction of his 3-D Goopplezon Lenses, he removes them. But even to his naked eyes, her aura persists in its angry indecisiveness.

The girl is more terrorized by the world suddenly fading away and leaving her isolated with a solitary stranger, than the prospect of suicide had elicited in her just a second earlier.

John intuits her initial intention, but her eyes, green and determined, betray an underlying sense of self-preservation.

"What's your name?" John asks calmly.

"Jackie." She grips a cable on the railing behind her. Tears tumble down her ashen face, tracing a path of anguish.

"Why are you so sad?"

"My mother died today. Cancer." She tries unsuccessfully to muffle a sob. "Multiple myeloma. She was in a hospice for the last three months. It's all over."

"I'm sorry. No wonder you're sad."

"I lost my dad six month ago. He was an alcoholic and died of sclerosis of the liver. He loved me though. We were a family. We all loved each other. We had each other, no matter what. Then everything and everybody I cared about, gone. Just like that. Our apartment too. I miss them. I miss our life together."

"Oh, you poor thing. Do you have family?"

"Just an aunt. She took in my little brother, but there is no room for me."

"So where are you staying?"

She thinks, *it doesn't matter if he knows*. "I live in the basement of my high school. I found a secret way in and out. I know the routines of the guards. When my family got evicted, I dragged my old mattress over in the middle of the night, so I have a nice bed. It's hidden. No one knows.

"I use the bathroom to stay clean and wash my clothes." Defiantly Jackie adds, "I have pride, you know." John listens without judgment. "There's a lot of food in the dumpsters out back. Lots of food. It's not too hard to find what I need."

"You sound like a very smart, enterprising girl."

"I am smart. I do my homework in the stairwell at night because they leave those lights on. I get good grades." Jackie stands a little taller.

"If you can do all that under these circumstances, imagine what you are capable of accomplishing. Your parents must have been so proud of you. Don't you want to live to honor them?"

Jackie, conflicted and overwhelmed, says, "It's so hard. I'm lonely. And alone." She hesitates. "But I do wish I could find a cure for cancer."

Her spirit has spoken. It sees a future for her. Seizing on this glimmer of hope, John says, "Then that's exactly what you should do. That can be your gift to the world — how can the rest of us possibly live without it, Jackie? A cure for cancer? So many people I knew aren't here now because of cancer. We need you."

Jackie steps away from the railing.

"How can I help?" John asks.

"I— I don't know right now. I'm not sure."

John takes out a mini pad and pen from his pocket. "Here is my phone number. I want you to call me anytime when you decide what I can do for you. You're not alone."

"John Lennon?" She looks at him closely now and recognizes him. "John Lennon? No joke?"

"No joke!" John pulls his wallet from his back pocket and takes out all the cash he has, $228. "Take this, and promise you'll call if you need me. It's up to you."

"I promise." Jackie places her head on John's chest and closes her eyes as he embraces her.

Angels, omnipresent and tirelessly working their miracles, swoop by to capture her troubles and carry them off. Jackie's whole body tingles as her life-force is energized with a new resolve. Her aura softens and glows steady, blanketing her and John. Hints of jasmine, rose, and lavender perfume the air.

Jackie lets go and opens her eyes. As fast as the speed of light, the world rushes back into focus. John is now standing a few feet away behind Sean, all memory of the tragic and beautiful Jackie evanescing into the universe.

Jackie never calls. She is a fiercely independent spirit, and it is enough for her to know she has a lifeline. She uses the money John gave her toward her college application. Her grades and astounding essay about her life win her a full scholarship, including living expenses, to John Hopkins University's pre-med program.

"Dad? I thought you were right next to me. How long was I talking to myself?" Sean asks.

John contemplates the empty wallet in his hand and slides it into his back pocket. Shrugging he says, "I must have been lost in thought." They continue on, crossing over to the other side. Arm in arm, they step over the words, "Welcome to Brooklyn."

DOUBLE FEATURE

It would be almost unbelievable,
if history did not record the tragic fact
that men have gone to war and cut each other's throats
because they could not agree as to
what was to become of them after their throats were cut.

- Walter Parker Stacy

In an undisclosed desert where the air is dead and oppressive, the video camera is placed on a tripod and set to record. The clear, deep blue of the sky is the only color, a backdrop to the drab landscape bereft of life and compassion.

A group of 20 or so Daesh radicals prepare a large pile of their weapons of death in anticipation of the execution. The stones must be of an appropriate medium size, perhaps the diameter of a peach or plum. If they are too small, they will be ineffective. Too large and they can cause the death of the adulterous woman sooner than desired, without her suffering adequately.

The condemned must live for about an hour to fully experience the deserved humiliation and relentless pelting for her crime. Justice is better served if she screams to fuel the executioners' lust for blood; they are more satisfied if she begs for forgiveness. Even if she does, they will kill her anyway.

They set their shovels aside and survey the pit they've dug; at about 4 feet deep it is the correct depth to bury American Jenny Smith up to her waist.

Jenny's boyfriend, 22-year-old Jack Miller, is led into frame and pushed to his knees facing the hole, 10 feet in front of her — a strategic position from which his captors force him to watch the proceedings before he is slaughtered in the name of Islam. His head is shaved, and he's dressed in an orange jumpsuit with his hands tied tightly behind his back; he is numb with sadness and barely present. Jack has seen the video posted online with a "message to America" featuring the beheading of journalist James Foley. He is certain of his fate.

The same four-person terrorist cell, called "The Beatles" by their former captives because of their British accents, is responsible for kidnapping Jenny and Jack as they stepped out into the sunshine from their hotel lobby in Baghdad. The adventurous couple, naively ignoring the State Department's warning discouraging U.S. citizens from traveling to Iraq, had set off on an around-the-world trip after completing their university studies.

A Jeep approaches. The leader of the cell, Mohamed Emwazi, also known as "Jihadi John," comes into view and directs his comrades who are carrying Jenny to lower her into the pit.

Jenny is wrapped head to toe, with only her face uncovered, in a white shroud that will be soiled with dirt and blood – a canvas for the atrocity about to befall her. Jenny's hands are tied behind her back and the shroud is bound with rope around her ankles, knees, thighs, waist, and midriff.

Her judge, jury, and executioners fill the pit with sand around her, leaving her exposed only from the waist up. Gagged, her wild-eyed terror and tears speak the language of abject despair for her as she and Jack see each other for the first time in three days.

Jihadi John takes his place on camera behind Jack. He expounds Islamic Sharia Law. "These infidel Americans have been charged with and convicted of fornication between unmarried people. They are a disgusting affront to our Muslim way of life and represent one of the many reprehensible things about Americans that we cannot – will not – tolerate. Their punishment must be death."

Jihadi John is dressed in black cargo pants tucked into light tan work boots, a long-sleeved black tunic, and a black mask covering his head except for an opening that reveals the windows to his monstrous soul. He grabs Jack's chin and holds a serrated six-inch steel hunting knife to his throat. "And now, before you die, you will first see what is right and just for a woman who–"

∞

Jared Kushner and members of the National Security Council, including the secretary of state, rush into the situation room with President Trump. The chairwoman of the joint chiefs of staff paces nervously. A video is displayed on the big monitor when the secretary of defense begins the briefing. Addressing the president, he says, "Sorry, sir, this footage just came to our attention less than an hour ago and it's in an old format." They stand around a big conference table, gripping the tops of the high-backed leather chairs.

President Trump watches for a minute and asks, "Isn't that asshole with the British accent that Jihadi John guy Obama killed with a drone strike back in '15?"

"That's right. We did a voice analysis and iris comparison. This video was made at the end of 2014," the secretary of defense says. "Right after these scumbags beheaded journalist Steven Sotloff and aid worker Peter Kassig and two workers from Great Britain, David Haines and Alan Henning."

"So why the big brouhaha now?" the president asks.

"We've verified that these two prisoners are U.S. citizens, Jenny Smith and Jack Miller. They met as students at Cornell University and did the backpacking thing together after graduation. Now they're married and living on Long Island with three kids. We didn't even know they had been taken hostage. They were in and out within a few days."

"In and out? How the hell did they escape *this*?" President Trump asks.

"Our agents just finished interviewing them. The woman – well, she freaked out – and that's putting it mildly. She refused to talk. Her husband Jack corroborated what we see here. Watch sir."

Jihadi John holds Jack's chin, and looking directly at the camera, says, "First, you will see what is right and just for a woman who–" He stops mid-sentence, lets go of Jack, and waves his knife. He yells orders in Arabic at his comrades.

Two men, also in black, push a new prisoner over to him within view of the video camera.

President Trump looks around the room and throws up his hands. "Is that who I think it is?"

"Yes, sir. It's John Lennon," Jared says.

"Are you wasting my time with some sort of joke?" President Trump demands.

"No, sir," the secretary of defense says. "We've had this video authenticated by Quantico and two other labs. It's the real deal."

"What the fuck? He's been dead since 1980. And even if you believe this nonsense that he – what? Reappeared? I thought that just happened," President Trump says.

The secretary of state says, "You better see the rest of this, Mr. President."

∞

Emwazi shouts angrily, "How did you get here?" He holds the point of his knife precariously close to John's eye. "Where did you come from?"

"I can't say," John answers. "I'm a little confused." He is barefoot and wears light blue, draw stringed pants, and a loosely weaved, white cotton tunic adorned with intricate white embroidery at the ends of the sleeves and hem.

"You are a spy!" Emwazi yells.

"No, I'm not. I'm a musician and promoter of peace. I'm John Lennon." Surveying the scene, he asks, "What is going on here? Are you mad, man?"

A flash of recognition crosses Emwazi's face. "This is American trickery. And these adulterous swine do not deserve to live."

Appealing to their British commonality, John says, "Listen, mate. If you want peace, you won't get it with violence."

"The Islamic State cannot have peace until all the world's infidels repent and convert, or die."

"But 'Islam' means 'peace,'" Lennon insists.

In a fit of rage, Jihadi John thrusts his knife at Lennon's heart. Lennon doubles over as the knife penetrates his skin, and his body fades to transparency. His silhouette fills in with pieces of multi-colored kaleidoscope glass that swirl to form changing patterns and reflect the light of the brilliant sun. A breeze carries the glittering pieces away; John dissipates into who knows where.

The jihadists run screaming. They flee over the dune behind Jack. Emwazi drops his knife and runs for his jeep behind Jenny. In the commotion, someone knocks over the video camera; it tumbles, lands close to Jenny, and continues to film.

∞

"Look at those pussies scatter as soon as they get spooked. They're running away like little girls," President Trump says. "They should all blow themselves up."

The security advisor picks up the briefing and says, "The camera caught how Jack and Jenny escaped."

Jack stands up and runs to Jenny. He drops to his knees behind and facing away from her. Even with his hands tied behind his back, he is able to untie her gag. She screams until she has no voice left. He lays down in front of her, face to face, and patiently calms her. "It's OK, baby," he soothes. "They're gone. I'm going to get us out of here."

He leaves her side briefly and when he returns says, "All you have to do is hold this tightly for me." He places the handle of Jihadi John's knife in her mouth. "You can do this," he promises. Once his hands are free, he picks up a shovel.

"Good God," President Trump says. "Have you talked to this guy who is supposedly John Lennon back from the dead?"

"We have, sir. We didn't mention the video to him, but our New York FBI agents interviewed him – a few of them have been permanently stationed outside of the Dakota and they're pretty friendly with him," the security advisor says. "Lennon said he didn't remember the incident but–"

"But what?" President Trump interrupts.

"He said he has weird dreams and flashes of visions. He showed us this." The security advisor swipes his hands in the air to bring up a hologram image. "John's majordomo had given him this white tunic as a gift just three days ago. It's from his country of Paraguay and called ahó poí in Paraguay's Indian language, Guaraní – for the unique style of embroidery. This one was hand-made. Look at this imperfection on the sleeve. And look at this close-up in the video. We've matched at least a dozen unique aspects of the shirt. Sir, it's the same shirt."

"How is that possible?" Trump asks looking around the room. "He was given the shirt three days ago, but this video was made six years ago."

No one answers. "Damn it!" He glares at his son-in-law and confidante, Jared, who finally dares to say, "There are rumors, well–

"Well, what?" Trump barks.

"That he time travels."

The security advisor clears his throat and continues with the briefing. "Lennon said two days ago he was jarred awake from a nap with a stabbing sensation in his chest. He showed me a slight flesh wound in his side that he had bandaged. Look at this." He swipes his hand over the hologram image and the tunic unfolds to reveal a tear and blood stain at heart level. "Lennon said he couldn't figure out how he got wounded on his bed in the middle of the afternoon."

"Tremendous. Absolutely tremendous!" President Trump says. "Bring him here to the White House. I mean, invite him to the White House. Yoko too. Tell them that Melania and I would like to have dinner with them."

A BIGLY INVITATION

It doesn't help to worry about anything.
It just attracts the thing you're worrying about.
Focus your energy on creating the best solution.

- Yoko Ono

"I don't care if the president wants us to have dinner at the White House; I don't want to go." Yoko is adamant. Across the kitchen table from John, she has her first disagreement with him in their second life together. "You should know I once called him a shaved ape."

"That bad?" John asks. "How did he manage to get elected?"

"Some people voted for change and didn't really care who it was. Others believed that because he was a political outsider, he'd be a more effective leader; he's incredibly brash – to say the least – and does his own thing. Still others thought his business experience would be helpful to improve the economy.

"Unfortunately, there was a lot of fear mongering too. He turned over rocks hiding all sorts of ugliness; racism, sexism, homophobia, Islamophobia, and white privilege. The worms that were always there came crawling out. He was even endorsed by the KKK."

"We should definitely have dinner with him. He sounds like a character," John says.

"I've been an outspoken opponent of his for years. He may have invited us both, but I'm sure he wishes I won't show up."

Perturbed, John asks, "And the majority of Americans voted for him?"

"No. The majority of voters didn't turn out on Election Day. They weren't happy with the choices. He infiltrated the White House because of the electoral system."

"Infiltrated? Ha! So, what's his appeal?"

"He promised to make America great again," Yoko explains. "Nice slogan, but he campaigned on building a wall between the U.S. and Mexico to stop illegal immigration and claimed Mexico would pay for it. He threatened to deport 11 million illegal immigrants, instead of granting citizenship. He called Mexicans criminals and rapists. He created a fake common enemy."

"A wall? How did that work out?"

"It never happened. The people rose up and protested, wrote letters, boycotted − all sorts of things − and became very vocal," Yoko says.

"People coming together; that's a good thing."

"He wants to register Muslims to keep track of them. He hasn't stopped trying to get it into legislation. He put a travel ban in place against people – mostly Muslims – coming to the U.S. from certain countries. But not from the countries where the 9/11 terrorists came from or others with big Muslim populations because, guess what's in those countries?" Yoko asks with apparent sarcasm. "His properties. And oil."

"Our society is run by insane people for insane objectives. I think we're being run by maniacs for maniacal ends and I think I'm liable to be put away as insane for expressing that. That's what's insane about it," John says. "We have to learn from history. We've been bombing, destroying, hating, and discriminating against races and religions and nothing ever gets any better."

"Insanity is right. When he campaigned in 2016, in so many words, he challenged his followers that support the Second Amendment right to bear arms to take care of his opponent, Hillary Clinton."

"Wait. You're telling me he practically put a hit out on her? Come now. You must be exaggerating."

"I'm not exaggerating, John." Mimicking President Trump Yoko repeats, "'If she gets to pick her judges, nothing you can do, folks. Although the Second Amendment people — maybe there is, I don't know.' That's how I took it. His people said he meant they should vote against her. But his people are something else too. One of them accused President Obama of spying on us through our microwaves."

John looks at the microwave, gives it a big smile, and keeps his exaggerated grin for Yoko when he turns back to her. "So, Clinton is a woman? A woman ran for president?"

"Yes, a woman ran for president." Yoko sighs. "But Trump publicly asked Russia to hack her emails."

"What the fuck? Isn't that like treason or something?"

"He is often disdainful of women. He puts down female reporters when they are tough on him; he complained one was bleeding from 'wherever' and another was bleeding from her facelift. And there was a recording of him describing how he grabs women by their pussies because he's famous and he can do that."

"He grabs women by the pussy?" John slaps his knee. "Oh, Yoko, you really had me going there." Yoko calmly watches her husband as it dawns on him that she is serious.

"No way!" John leans forward and takes Yoko's hands in his. "You have to be making this stuff up!"

"I'm not," Yoko insists. "Things have changed for the worse since you've been gone. He's been promoting nuclear proliferation."

"What are you saying? I thought we were working toward worldwide nuclear disarmament?"

"Not anymore. North Korea has been taunting us for years. Trump figures the more countries that have nukes, the less likely anyone will use them."

"Geez," is all John can manage. "Weird logic. Have I returned to bizzaro land?"

"He lowered inheritance and corporate taxes," Yoko continues. "That's what a lot of people wanted; except it has mostly benefited the very wealthy – the money is moving up the food chain. Not down. The poor are poorer."

"Yeah, I noticed there are so many homeless in the streets," John says.

"And way fewer services to help them," Yoko says. "This time, his campaign slogan was 'America is great again.' He changed the tax structure for big business and they're eating it up, but it hasn't translated into new jobs. Profits are up for shareholders. The middle class is still holding out for what's supposed to trickle down."

John asks, "They fell for a con job?"

"Yep." Yoko nods. "I assume some of his supporters are good people. It's just that they are being duped by a masterful con artist.

"He's not one to be concerned about the environment either. He wanted to allow oil drilling in national parks. And to do away with the Environmental Protection Agency. He pulled the rug out from under the agency by taking away most of its funding. In his first year, he withdrew from the Paris climate accord; he doesn't believe in global warming."

"Sean's been briefing me on that," John says. "Science backs that up, right? I mean, it doesn't seem like something you have to believe in; it's not like a fairy tale, Santa Claus, or the Easter Bunny."

"The stories I could tell you about depleted water sources, fracking, dumping, and illegal discharges – we're in a downward spiral, John."

"We have to go to dinner with him and, what's her name?"

"Melania."

"Melania. C'mon, Yoko. Let's meet with this guy. Maybe we can have a meaningful conversation," John says hopefully.

"I doubt it. If you challenge him, he just gets mad like a little impetuous kid and sends out stupid tweets."

"He tweets stupid shit?" John asks. "The president of the United States? Is that who we're still talking about?"

Resigned to the absurdity, Yoko laughs.

"Pleeeease? Please me?" John tilts his head and gives her a pleading look. "Come with me. We'll have his ear."

"An orange ear," Yoko says. "OK. For you, John, OK. But under protest."

"Duly noted, my love."

LOVE TRUMPS HATE

You have to think anyway,
so why not think big?

- Donald Trump

As dusk surrenders itself to nightfall, the whir of chopper blades cut into the peaceful silence of the verdant and well-manicured White House lawn. Secret Service agents yell, "Right this way, Mr. and Mrs. Lennon." They duck under the whoop-whoop-whoop of pulsing air and run from the heliport pad.

The president and first lady greet the Lennons cordially, dispensing with the pleasantries forthwith; they all agree to be on a first name basis. Trump pats John on the back and says, "'Yesterday' is one of my favorites. I just love how you sing that song."

"Well, Mr.– er, Donald, Paul, Paul McCartney, actually sang that. But thank you for the compliment. I helped write it."

Melania hangs back behind the men with Yoko. In a gracious attempt to put her guest at ease, she says, "I know you are not a big fan of my husband. But my husband is real. He's raw. He tells it like it is. He's kind. He's a gentleman. He supports everybody."

A thousand-and-one retorts come to Yoko's mind, but she tempers her wit. "It's no secret we don't share the same ideology.

Thank you for having us to dinner," she replies instead. *Oh, God,* she thinks, *John is going to owe me big for this one.*

Dinner takes place in the family dining room, a stylishly appointed room on the State Floor of the White House. An elegant crystal chandelier hangs above the American walnut dining table. The president sits at the head of the table, Yoko to his right, John at the opposite end facing the president, and Melania to John's right across from Yoko. A tasteful arrangement of one of Yoko's favorite flowers, lime green mini button pom flowers, selected by Melania as a compliment to her guest, forms the centerpiece.

Though the high ceilings, regal drapery, and classic paintings create a sense of formality, with just the four of them dining and a fire blazing in the hearth, the ambiance is cozy.

As they are seated, and before the servers enter the room, the president addresses John. "You're here after you were killed 40 years ago. My best advisors can't explain any of this to me. Can you?"

"Everyone asks me that, but I haven't got a clue," John says. "I'm living in the now and taking one day at a time."

I have a gift for you," President Trump says. He gestures to his wife. Melania hands John an elaborately wrapped box.

As John opens the gift, the president says, "Wait! I want to send a tweet." He pulls out a phone from the inside pocket of his suit jacket and with his thumbs types:

Dinner w John Lennon at WH tonight.
Back from the dead and the guy loves me.
Gave him a signed copy of my book Trump Rules.

Donald looks up from his device and says, "If we could get Stephen Hawking or one of those guys to figure this out, you could be a great weapon for the United States."

Bristling at the implication, John says, "He died before my return. Anyway, I don't want to be a weapon – of any sort. I am an instrument for peace."

"Yes. I admire the work you're doing. I say, not in a braggadocious way, I've made billions and billions of dollars dealing with people all around the world. But it's taken me all my life to do that. You show up again and accomplish so much in no time – donations are rolling in for a Beatles reunion. All that money! Wow. I like success. I like people who are successful. Yes. Living your words, walking your talk, and talking your walk."

"We're not there yet. The world is right troubled."

"Go on," the president encourages. "You have my ear."

John and Yoko throw each other a sideways glance. Yoko picks up her napkin and pretends to cover a little cough while she laughs.

The president continues, "I know; all that love and peace crap is supposed to be the answer. I don't believe that. We've gotta hebe tough. Instill fear in the world. Saddam Hussein was a bad guy, right? He was a bad guy. Really bad guy. But you know what he did well? He killed terrorists. He did that so good. I think if this country gets any kinder or gentler, it's literally going to cease to exist."

John and Yoko, adept at communicating wordlessly, speak volumes to one another with the briefest eye contact.

"Ah, the appetizers are ready," Melania says as the wait staff enters.

"Great chef here. Does an awesome job," the president adds. "He makes me McDonald's hamburgers any time I want."

"Since you offered your ear, Donald, I'd like to talk to you about your policies on global warming," Yoko ventures.

The president makes a hand gesture as if to say, "phooey." He asks Yoko, "When will our country stop wasting money on global warming and so many other truly stupid things?"

"Stupid things?"

Uh-oh, John thinks when he sees the fury in Yoko's eyes. *This isn't going well.*

President Trump interrupts Yoko and wags a mushroom on the end of his fork at her. "The concept of global warming was created by and for the Chinese in order to make U.S. manufacturing non-competitive." He gestures to John's plate and says, "Try them. They're delicious."

John smiles wide, pops a mushroom into his mouth, and waits for the Yoko Ono show to begin.

Just as Yoko is about to explode, John begins to glow; softly at first, and then his image fades. The outline of his body fills in with black and white static. He and President Trump drop their forks in unison. With a buzz and a snap, John is gone.

Flabbergasted by the spectacle, the president jumps up and knocks over his dining chair. Melania remains motionless, staring at John's empty seat. In response to the commotion, two Secret Service agents rush in. They right the president's chair and ask, "Sir? Is everything OK?"

"What the fuck was that?" Donald plops down into his chair, picks up his cloth napkin, and wipes sweat off his forehead.

The Trumps and agents look to Yoko for an explanation.

"He's off on one of his adventures again. Just wait a minute." She looks directly into the president's eyes and says, "You should listen to him. He doesn't remember what he sees when he's gone, but he knows what he's talking about."

Yoko spears a mushroom and eats it. "You're right, Donald. They're delicious."

THE LAST DAY

The nuclear arms race
is like two sworn enemies
standing waist deep in gasoline,
one with three matches,
the other with five.

- Carl Sagan

It is an ordinary morning in New York City, the sun rising gloriously into a cloudless sky, and the crisp fall winds tossing golden- and rust-colored leaves on earth. The hubbub of city life kicks into high gear.

Most people open their eyes, stretch, wiggle their toes, and don't think twice about the miracle of waking up to live another day. The disappointment of mortality remains relegated to the secured vaults of denial.

Their routines, though varied, propel them forward on autopilot. Some refuse to drag themselves out of the warmth of their beds, lingering instead to make love, to read an old-fashioned paper book, or to hear the news piped into the room. They issue commands to Goopplezon, dress, eat breakfast, and say, "Hurry up children! Hurry! Time for school." They switch on their video conferencing stations to connect with co-workers or head out to transport vehicles.

The workings of the city progress as they normally do. Until they don't.

∞

The rat-a-tat-tat sound of machine guns infiltrate John's subconscious before he opens his eyes. He lays in the gutter of Central Park West in front of the Dakota, reflexively starting with the jolt of each discharged round of fire he hears. As his body fully materializes, he radiates a warm, hopeful blue into the evening twilight. Confused by the mayhem surrounding him, he attempts to sit up but is forced to duck as several people jump over him. One of the runners kicks him in the head. "Ow. What the fuck?" he says, rubbing his temple as he rises to his feet.

Across the street, the perimeter of Central Park is lined with large glass greenhouses as far as he can see. The plant nurseries, robust with fruits and vegetables, are surrounded by a fortress of black wrought iron gates where metal plates hang declaring the ownership of each unit.

Specially programmed armed robo-guards protect the food. During the last decade, since the great dust bowl of the 2050s, worldwide environmental calamities and a water scarcity led to the economic ruination of centralized farming. Citizens have to fend for themselves. Only the wealthy are comfortable in cities, where land and growing space are at a premium.

There is screaming. Looters, intent on stealing supplies before they take shelter, swarm the glass structures. The sharpshooter robots take aim at the thieves with precision and without discrimination. John watches, horrified, as even children fall back, bullet holes in their heads gushing blood, dead eyes staring into nothingness.

Like a swarm of angry bees, chaos encircles John. People running by bump into him and knock him about. "Hey! What's going on? Please tell me," he pleads. Delivery bots stall in place around him. Drones carrying packages land haphazardly, causing driverless ground cars to screech to a halt. Flying cars set down anywhere they can – on top of vehicles and people. The cars' passengers jump out and scurry in all directions. Hologram images pop up and flicker on and off. Pedestrians bounce around helter-skelter like pinballs.

The electricity cuts off and the street lights go dark momentarily until auxiliary back-up power from solar panels located on the building rooftops kicks in. The crowd surges. A pulsing sea of the desperate move toward the gas pumps on the corner. John does a double-take. The sign doesn't say "gasoline" as he expects; it says, "Premium desalinated water, $147 per gallon."

What the hell? John thinks.

Amid the pandemonium, people fall to their knees in place and pray, until they are trampled. Lovers step aside, leaning against a building to keep their knees from buckling beneath them. Hanging on to one another and mourning unfulfilled dreams, they make their final declarations of eternal love. Others curse their useless 3-D Goopplezon Lenses and wrist watches and throw them off in frustration.

Yoko! John thinks. *I've got to get to Yoko.*

"Twenty-two minutes," a man shouts as he runs by. Mothers weep, instinctively clutching their children close in a futile attempt to shelter them from harm. John, carried along with the crowd, rounds the corner onto 72nd Street.

One of the guards calls out from the side gate of the Dakota, "Mr. Lennon, Mr. Lennon? Quickly!" John pushes his way over to the gate. The guards don't recognize him. "Stand back," they demand, taking a defensive stance with their machine guns. "Mr. Lennon," a guard calls out again, looking around and behind John. A man of about 40 years old stumbles forward.

The guards open the gate a crack and are just about to usher the man inside when John yells out, "I live here. I live here, I am John Lennon," he insists.

The man stops abruptly in his tracks and looks back just long enough to register John's face. He grabs John by his shirt collar and drags him inside the gate. "It's OK," he assures the guards. "He's with me." With the gates locked behind them, the guards run for the Dakota's basement stairs.

"What the hell is going on? Has the world gone topsy-turvy?" John asks as the man rushes him into the elevator. "And who are you? Why are the guards calling you Mr. Lennon?"

The man calls out, "seventh floor," and the elevator doors close. "I am Kibo Lennon." He takes a beat to catch his breath and adds, "My parents are Sean and Callie. You are my grandfather." Both 40-year-old men stare at one another and remain silent as they contemplate the absurdity of such a possibility.

As they step into the apartment, John recognizes the space, though the furniture and decor are different than he remembers. Kibo understands John's confusion. "I can hardly believe it myself," he says. "You died in my arms as an old man when I was 12 years old. We were playing our guitars together right here. You said, 'Oh, I feel funny,' and slumped over. You looked up at me, smiled, and closed your eyes. That was it. Just like that. I adored you, grandfather. I sat with you for a time and talked to you. I asked you to come back to me someday. I never knew you like this – so young – but I memorized your face and swore to remember it for all eternity. I would recognize you anytime."

"I died? Then how can I be here?"

Kibo explains, "Throughout my childhood, you told me fairy tales about how you traveled through time. I guess they weren't fairy tales after all."

"What the hell are you talking about, man?" John asks. "You're not making any sense."

"I prayed I might see you again and that you heard me." He hugs his grandfather.

John welcomes the embrace and pats Kibo gently on his back.

"And now," Kibo says, visibly choked up, "and now we're out of time."

"Kibo? My grandson, I am so happy to know you, but you've got to help me understand."

"This is our last day. Six nuclear-armed intercontinental missiles are on their way to us."

John throws up his hands in exasperation. "Don't we have anti-ballistic capabilities?"

"We should have, but strategic locations housing our computer systems that operate our protective measures were hit by e-bombs."

"E-bombs?"

"Oh, sorry. Electromagnetic bombs. They don't kill people or damage buildings, but they set off an extreme force – a wave of energy – that wreaks havoc with all things electronic in its range."

"So what happened?" John asks.

"A cyber-attack came first. Our enemies disabled the internet, and then they blew up our satellites in subspace. We have no GPS, no information, and no communication except primitive radio. We've received a little news; several of our European allies have already been hit. We have about 15 more minutes before the missiles reach us. We retaliated, but so what?"

"This is bloody madness," John says as he paces. "How could this be?"

"The decline in world relations moved from not so good to very bad around the time I was born. As far back as 2017, President Trump adopted a policy of nuclear proliferation. The idea was for the U.S. to be the biggest and baddest, but it just started a race. And it looks like the bad guys won."

"I feel like maybe I know him," John says.

"He was elected the first time after you died, but he was still president when you came back."

"Wha–?"

"Never mind." Kibo rushes forward with his explanation. "These missiles came from North Korea. We knew immediately when they were launched and by whom. Then the virtual blackout."

"Fuck," is all John can manage. His mind jumbled with a million thoughts, John laughs. "Sorry. I was just thinking that I always tried to get your grandmother to say 'fuck' more often. I don't know what to think about right now."

Kibo moves to the window. "The mobs outside are looting food and water. It's pointless."

"Can we live through this?"

"No. There's no doubt New York City is a direct target. Some people will survive the initial nuclear explosions. But the aftermath will have wide-ranging catastrophic effects. Pretty much 90 percent of the initial survivors will eventually die from radioactivity, disease, and starvation anyway. The rest of the world will be affected by the environmental fallout, economic chaos, and anarchy. We are the lucky ones. We will die instantly."

"So this is the apocalypse," John whispers.

Kibo's tears spill down his cheek; in them, the sorrow of the human race. "Oh, grandfather. Kerri, my wife, just had our baby. A little girl. Her name is Heiwa." He sobs. "I can't even get back there fast enough to say goodbye."

"What do we do? Just wait?" John asks.

Kibo shakes his head in the affirmative. "It won't be long. We're sitting ducks." Taking John's hands in his, he pleads, "Can you go back, grandfather? Can you return and make things different? Can you do it? You can change this. You must."

"I don't know how I got here, Kibo." A tiny twinkling pearl of light appears near John's head. "I don't know where I am in time." Then another point of light and another and another until they form an intricate lace encircling John. The lights spin around, like a slow, wobbly top at first, then faster and faster until they become a blurred wall of light.

Kibo lets go of his grandfather's hands. "Warn them if you can, please, do someth—" A great, blinding flash floods the room; a white light absorbs all hope for mankind.

∞

John tumbles onto the rug and rolls toward the head of the dining table, landing at President Trump's feet. His translucent skin fills with static and hisses a gentle white noise into the room as he becomes whole. In a trance, he repeats, "Kibo? Heiwa? Kibo? Heiwa?"

President Trump, looking down at John on the floor, is frozen in place and unable to speak or move.

"John?" Yoko rushes over to him and takes his arm to help him to his feet. "John?" He responds instantly to his wife's touch. A deep breath restores him to the present. She asks, "Why are you speaking words in Japanese?"

John smiles at his wife and says, "Well, it's no secret that you and I are one." He looks around to orient himself. "What words?"

He looks around to orient himself. "What words?"

"Kibo and Heiwa," Yoko answers. "Hope and Peace."

By touching his thumbs to his index fingers, Trump gestures "OK" with both hands. He looks up at his guests standing at his side and says, "This is huge! It's unpresidented."

THE DIVERGENT PATH

*The whole course of human history may depend on
a change of heart in one solitary and even humble individual — for it is in the
solitary mind and soul of the individual that the battle between good and evil
is waged and ultimately won or lost.*

- M. Scott Peck

A Secret Service agent walks ahead of the president and John, and another trails behind as the pair walk side by side through the halls of the White House.

The president is agitated. "You've got to have some sort of idea about what's happening," he insists. "How can you just disappear and reappear like that? An extremely credible source tells me it could be an illusion. Is it? Is it a magic trick?"

"No—

"I'm the president of the United States. I have a right to know what's going on."

John says, "I feel tingly. And then I have this sense of déjà vu. Like, hey wasn't I just here? It doesn't feel like I've been anywhere else."

"My advisors disagree among themselves, but some seem to think you're time traveling. Man to man, give it to me straight. What do you think of that?"

"Donald, the more I see, the less I know for sure."

They reach the door to the Oval Office. President Trump says, "I have something to show you. It's going to blow your mind."

A guard admits them, and John follows his host into the room. "Ha! This is where tricky Dick sat to plot against me," John says out loud — more for himself than for President Trump.

"Yeah, your deportation crap. I would have had your ass hauled out of this country in a heartbeat," Trump says, with just a little too much bravado for John's taste. "All that dissention shit against the government. Give me a break."

John stifles the temptation to make their exchange contentious. "I was on the side of peace." He quietly adds, "I'm a citizen now. I was born in New York City, you know." He can't resist a little dig.

Trump laughs. "I've made some amazing deals in my life, and I mean amazing. Everyone tells me all the time, everywhere I go, I'm the best deal maker ever. The best."

"You don't need anyone to tell you who you are or what you are. You are what you are!"

"But what you pulled off," Trump continues, "man! Unbelievable."

"I wanted to run for president," John says. "The world is under U.S. hegemony. I thought I could have a big influence effecting peace."

"You don't want this job. It's thankless. Doesn't matter what you do, half the world will always hate you." The president sits down at his desk. "This is where the magic happens. Executive orders are terrific. Really terrific. With the stroke of a pen I can do practically anything."

Gold curtains hang between the triple bay windows behind the president, a haggard man aging rapidly under the strain of his responsibilities. An American flag and the president's flag flank both sides of the middle window.

"He was an outsider like me," Trump says when he sees John's interest in the painting of Andrew Jackson hanging next to the built-in book shelf. "He had a lot of portraits painted of himself. Great guy. I have a spectacular one of me hanging in my home in Mar-a-lago down in Florida. You and Yoko should come down some time. Self-made man. He was a tremendous president. A lot of people say that about me too. So many people."

"I understand you've been quite controversial, Donald. Genius or madness?" John challenges.

"Well, John, there's a fine line, wouldn't you say? A great man once said, 'I was born for a storm and a calm doesn't suit me.'" The president tilts his head to point toward Jackson. "Truer words have never been spoken when it comes to me."

He gets up from his desk and guides John to a pair of sofas across the room. "Let's sit. I want you to look at this video." The president hands John a tablet. "Go on," he coaxes.

John waves his hand to start play and leans back. His facial expression conveys neutrality. He is curious but relaxed. Immediately, he is jarred by the realization that a terrified young woman is buried in the sand to her chest. John demands of the president, "What's this?"

"You'll see. You are in this video too. It was shot by Jihadi John, the leader of a radical Islamic terrorist cell in the Middle East."

"Jihadi John?"

"Yes, his real name was Mohammed Emwazi. There were four militants in the group, and they were British. Because of their accents, Western hostages referred to them as the Beatles."

"That sucks. We'd never want to be associated with such violence. Totally sucks. What do you mean when you say I was there? Is this what the FBI agents were asking me about?"

"Go on." President Trump gestures impatiently to the tablet. He watches John closely for his reactions. A young American man in an orange coverall is made to kneel before the mostly buried woman, and Jihadi John speaks of his impending beheading.

"No! No! I don't want this image in my brain," John says. "I can't." He is shaken and tries to give the tablet to the president. "Once you see something, it's forever."

The president refuses the tablet. "He was a notorious killer. A psychopath. But don't worry; this time it doesn't happen. Really. Keep watching."

As the drama unfolds, John is startled and jumps to his feet. Emwazi's comrades hold John Lennon by knifepoint and usher him over to their leader. Astounded, John says, "This looks just like me. Is this me?"

"It's definitely you. We have the most sophisticated facial and iris recognition software ever developed. We compared these images to your face now, and to the face of John Lennon pre-1980. You're all the same person. No doubt."

John drops back down onto the sofa, heavy with the weight of what is dawning on him. "I've been having occasional nightmares about this and weird dreams about other things. And little flickers of passing images while I'm awake. I never knew any of it was real. But I don't remember being there. I recognize that shirt though."

"This takes place six years before you even came back to us."

"I went back in time?"

"We've marked this material as top secret. My security folks got you clearance so I could show it to you. We're keeping it from the media. Have to be careful about what they let out, you know. Can't have panic."

"I am totally freaked out, Donald. This is the first time I've seen any evidence of where I've been. But this runs so long. Yoko tells me I'm gone for seconds or sometimes up to a minute or two."

"There's more," President Trump says. "You're not going to believe your eyes. And before you ask, this video has not been messed with."

The jihadists drop their weapons, scatter in every direction, and abandon their planned executions. They are frightened by John vanishing into oblivion right in front of them just as he is stabbed.

John looks up at President Trump, mouth agape and clearly confounded.

"Told you," Trump says.

Fascinated by how he is transported out of this point in time, John plays it over and over. Yoko has described it to him but, for the first time, he is witnessing his personal miracle. He tears up from the relief of knowing what it looks like when he disappears.

"How is all this possible?" President Trump asks. "I really want to know. I'm intelligent. A lot of people would say I'm very, very, very intelligent."

"I'm sure you're a very smart man, Donald," John says reassuringly. "I guess if I'm hopping through time, there aren't any rules for that. I think—"

"And it just happened again in my dining room," the president jumps in. "Do you remember anything you saw?"

"Not specifically. I have a general feeling of malaise. Worse really. A sense of disaster of epic proportions. I think whatever I saw was really, really bad. Like maybe even the end."

"I'm going to be on *Fox and Friends* tomorrow morning. Still the only news that isn't fake news as far as I'm concerned, by the way. They're going to ask me what we talked about. I can't tell them we talked about doomsday."

"So don't. But let's do something about this – together. When it gets down to having to use violence, then you are playing the system's game. The establishment will irritate you – pull your beard, flick your face – to make you fight. Because once they've got you violent, then they know how to handle you. The only thing they don't know how to handle is non-violence and humor. Maybe the future isn't inevitable. Will you work with me for peace?"

President Trump says, "I'm not a religious man, or superstitious. I think of myself as a practical man. I always thought the way to combat evil is to wipe them off the face of the earth. But something tells me I should listen to you. It's the strangest feeling."

THE GARDENER

We've got this gift of love,
but love is like a precious plant...
You've got to keep watering it.
You've got to really look after it and nurture it.

- John Lennon

"John! The TV? Again? You're wasting so much time in front of that thing." Yoko is becoming increasingly exasperated by her husband's penchant for devouring information.

"Time you enjoy wasting, is not wasted! At least I'm not beaming it into our apartment. I'm keeping it flat on the screen." He jumps up from their living room sofa and grabs her by the waist as she passes by. Tumbling backwards together, she lands in his lap. "You know I'm a news junky addicted to the spectacle. And I'm addicted to love." He sings to her:

Love, love, love, love, love, love, love, love, love.
All you need is love, all you need is love,
All you need is love, love. Love is all you need.

"Those are the best lyrics I've ever written."

"Maybe all you need is love, but I need food. I'm hungry." Yoko raises an enticing eyebrow. "Why don't we go out to dinner? We could sneak into the back of that little Korean barbeque place you like in Brooklyn."

"Insa? Are you in the mood for Kimchee, love?" John asks.

Before Yoko can answer, John interrupts her by speaking into the room. "Goopplezon, volume seven please." A breaking news bulletin catches his attention.

The news anchor says, "President Trump signed an executive order late this afternoon declaring September 21st as a national holiday to coincide with the International Day of Peace.

"In a surprising reversal of his first-term policies, Trump has announced the closing of CIA black site prisons. These controversial secret detention centers have come under fire for potential violations of the Geneva Convention for suspending humanitarian and legal rights for foreign prisoners of war."

A short clip shows Trump saying, "While we're developing a closure plan, we will allow the Red Cross access to our prisoners. Effective immediately, enhanced interrogation techniques will cease."

The United Nations Secretary-General, António Guterres, appears in a split screen applauding the move. "This new direction for the United States is in keeping with the UN's goals of maintaining international peace and security and in developing friendly relations among nations. The United States will be a better example of a nation that embraces human rights even under trying circumstances."

The reporter comments, "President Trump, known world-wide for his lack of diplomatic skills and knee-jerk reaction of violence and aggression in response to conflict, stunned the world today with this turnabout."

The coverage switches to the White House press secretary, who says, "The president was very moved by conversations he's had with peace activist John Lennon. Mr. Lennon and members of Goopplezon's Peace Department have joined him for a series of informal conferences to discuss how the United States can take a meaningful leadership role in peace-building initiatives at home and abroad. The President believes the American government should reflect the people's desire for peace."

"Donald kept his promise to do something," John says. He turns to Yoko and continues singing:

> *There's nothing you can do that can't be done.*
> *Nothing you can sing that can't be sung.*
> *Nothing you can say, but you can learn*
> *How to play the game*
> *It's easy.*

"Sure, it's easy," Yoko chides. "He saw you disappear and materialize in front of his eyes. What else would it take to get him to listen? You scared the shit out of him."

"When you're entrenched in a certain way of thinking, right or wrong, it's human nature to justify your beliefs and actions. You know, really dig in. But a change of heart is an act of courage. It shows faith in your ability to see the old in a new way," John says.

"It's rare for a man like him to step out of his comfort zone," Yoko says. "He listened to you though. I still despise him, but maybe just a little less today."

Yoko responds with a look of warning when John raises an eyebrow. "Let's not get carried away. The needle has barely nudged."

"It's one thing to reason with a rational man."

Yoko bursts out laughing. "Donald Trump? Rational?"

"Well, there's always hope that a well-thought-out argument could spark an epiphany," John says. "Obviously, we've had a bit of success there. What I'm worried about are the religious fanatics. Reason isn't powerful enough to combat blind faith."

"If it were easy, everyone would do it," Yoko says. "And then you'd be out of a job."

"Wouldn't that be lovely? I'm not really a career person. I'm a gardener basically. Instead of planting ideas and seeds of hope, I could just grow bloody tomatoes."

John and Yoko sit quietly on their sofa. John breaks the silence by asking, "So how do we reach the religious zealots that embrace violence as a way of life?"

"I don't know. I can't think on an empty stomach," Yoko says with gravitas.

THE AGE OF MAN

*It is not in the stars to hold our destiny
but in ourselves.*

\- William Shakespeare

John's spirit, a milky apparition glittery and swirling, hovers over his own body. He observes himself curled into a ball and shivering as he lies on a cement floor wearing only a T-shirt and thin cotton lounge pants. The body draws in a slow deep breath and his lungs recapture his essence, vacuuming it out of the air. Body and soul become one.

As he becomes whole, he is still. Opening his eyes, he finds himself on the landing of a staircase. He grabs a metal railing at his side and pulls himself up to a sitting position.

Devoid of the footsteps of visitors past, the dank, colorless room reeks of loneliness. Curved steel girders support the rounded ceiling of the structure. At the center where they meet, a rusted fixture hangs, plugged by the sharp remnants of a broken light bulb.

Twenty-five small windows, portals to the world that once was, wrap around the room side by side. The wind howls through the shards of glass clinging to their frames.

It's difficult to know what time it is; the light is muted. Perhaps early morning, just before a mournful sunrise. Perhaps dusk, as the day strains for its final breath.

John peers out a window and sees a colossal hand of a greenish patina holding a slab inscribed with JULY IV MDCCLXXVI. He stands within the head of the Statue of Liberty and cranes his neck to look up. Seven tips of her crown point longingly to each of the earth's lost continents.

John hears the suggestion of whispers behind him. *"You knew. You knew, and you didn't stop it."* Startled, he turns into the room and demands, "Who's there?" He is alone. The whispers, haunting and bereaved, continue one on top of the other. *"Look. Look at what you've done." "It's over." "You did this to us."* Then silence.

The New York Harbor has risen to reach Lady Liberty's knees. Her right foot, long ago broken free of its shackles, has nowhere to run. The water, a deceptively beautiful, lush purple velvet, is acidic and hostile. It laps against the monument, mocking her. Taunting her. Reminding her that the freedom she stood for is a moot point.

"Why?" The whispers of men, women, and children become more emphatic. *"How could you ignore what was happening?" "Why didn't you understand?"* John places his hands over his ears. *"The land. The water. The air. It's too late now."* The room is quiet again.

The bottom third of Manhattan's skyscrapers are submerged. Spikes, lightning rods, spires, and radio towers stand sentry for the drowned vestiges of a former civilization. The sky is a filthy brown, imprisoning the earth in solitary confinement apart from the universe. Clouds flake rust and are backlit by a weeping sun estranged from the love and life she once supported.

"The world is dead." The whispers become aggressive. *"We starved." "We died of thirst." "We couldn't breathe."* They surround John, assaulting him with guilt; the blame becomes unbearable. *"We died of broken hearts."*

John puts his hands up in front of his face to shield himself and backs up against the wall. The voices close in, relentless and unforgiving. Trapped, John climbs through a window and scratches his face on a shard of glass. He jumps to escape the scathing accusations. Blood drips from his wound as he falls and falls and falls. To slow his descent, he spreads his arms wide and they become wings. He smacks Yoko in the face.

"Ow!" Yoko scoots toward the edge of her side of the bed to get away from John's flailing. "John, John!" she says. "Wake up!"

John opens his eyes and sees Yoko's startled look. "Oh, my God! Was I gone? I can tell you what I saw."

"No, John. You were here. You were dreaming."

"Damn. I thought I was finally going to remember something from when I disappear."

John spoons Yoko from behind. She places her hand on his hip to calm him while he relates his visions to her. "You were probably thinking about the Statue of Liberty because you just saw it when you walked across the Brooklyn Bridge with Sean," she says.

"I felt like I was there." John sighs. "You know, my love, Einstein says the distinction between past, present, and future is just an illusion. What if I was remembering the future?"

"I believe that," Yoko says. "I believe our dreams can be memories of the future."

"I'm telling you, my sweet darling, we better do something about this climate thing or the future we face is bloody dismal." John plays with Yoko's hair. "What if what I saw in my dream is our destiny?"

"Can we alter destiny?" Yoko asks. "Because if we can, then there's really no such thing as destiny, right?"

"Geez, Yoko. I haven't even had me morning tea." John rolls onto his back and clasps his hands behind his head. Through a yawn he says, "Most people are like corks bobbing aimlessly in a sea of happenstance. They just let the tides toss them around. They get rained on. The winds blow and there's no conscious choice. Living is easier with closed eyes. We can pretend what we don't want to see is not there."

Yoko turns around to face her husband. She touches his cheek and blood clings to her finger. "John? There's a cut on your face." A tiny droplet lifts off her finger, forms into the shape of a heart, and floats away. With a twinkling flash of light, it disappears.

John waits for Yoko's reaction. "I'm not surprised," she says.

"Let's get up and have breakfast. I feel like pancakes," John says, throwing off the covers.

BEHIND CLOSED DOORS

If you want to look for world peace,
go home and love your families.

- Mother Teresa

Callie and her husband Floyd can't afford automated delivery services. His drinking has been negatively affecting his work for some time, and money is tight. So, once a week, Callie is given permission to leave the apartment to run errands.

Floyd stands at the living room window and watches as Callie steps outside the building onto the city sidewalk, adjusts her oversized sunglasses, and scampers on her way. He drags on his cigarette and blows smoke rings; they spin and dissipate, menacing the already poisoned air in his home.

Callie looks up and gives a tentative little wave. Floyd uses GPS to track her whereabouts. He implanted a chip, the kind meant to find lost pets, into her arm by cutting into her himself with a pocket knife. After the infection healed, the scar was barely visible. A wound of another kind will never heal.

The children always wind up getting hurt when she leaves them alone with him. Last week, the baby fell off the couch and had a big black-and-blue mark on her leg. "She's crawling all over the place, Floyd," Callie said. "You have to keep a closer eye on her." Her son burned his little shoulder while he was playing. According to Floyd, the boy backed into a lit cigarette.

This morning she is frantic. A roadway repair project partially blocks the entrance to the mini-market. She waits for diverted traffic to clear and goes around the cones, scaffolding, and debris. She mutters, "I'll have to explain why I went out of the way."

∞

John and Yoko stand close to one another at the kitchen counter. John has one hand lightly resting on the crook of Yoko's back. He leans around to sift flour into the sugar, baking powder, and salt in a bowl in front of her. She adds milk and cracks an egg with a flourish. "One of my many talents," she teases. He takes a pinch of flour and draws on her nose.

John looks up at the electronic readout for the contents of their pantry. "Oh, no! We're out of oil. Isn't this thing supposed to reorder for us?"

"I forgot to set it," Yoko says. "Sorry."

"No worries, my love. Julio isn't here yet, so I'll pop out and be back in a flash. It'll be quicker than waiting for a delivery bot."

John doesn't disguise himself. Out of habit, his lead bodyguard speaks through his watch to the others, "Red sneakers on the run!"

∞

With a bottle of cooking oil in hand, John leaves the mini-market and steps around the construction zone to cross the street. A horn blares, piercing the din of pedestrians and vehicles. Someone grabs him roughly from his collar and jerks him back out of the street. "Mister! Be careful!"

John tumbles to the pavement and lands on top of his savior. "The sensors on those driverless buses can't react that fast," the young lady says. "You almost got yourself killed." John notices the remnants of a shiner as she puts her sunglasses back on.

Callie is on her knees, picking up the groceries strewn about and returning them to their bags. "Oh my God, my eggs are broken." She bursts into tears.

"I'm so sorry. I'll go inside and buy you another dozen," John says.

"Oh, no! Oh, no!" Callie is frantic. She scoops up broken eggs dripping over the curb into the street and tries to put together the broken pieces.

"Miss, really. Let me buy you new eggs. I'm terribly sorry."

John's bodyguards rush over to help. Callie flinches when one of them touches her to lift her to her feet.

"No, thank you, there's no time." She has to think fast; how will she explain this? Floyd never believes anything she says. "The truth doesn't even matter. It doesn't," she says out loud.

John touches Callie's arm tenderly and says, "The only truth is freedom."

Callie looks at John's face for the first time. "It's you," she says, taken aback.

"Yes, it's me," he says. "Listen to me. You deserve love and respect, Miss. Run fast. Run far. Run as soon as you can."

"He has my babies, Mr. Lennon," Callie says. She turns and hurries home to Floyd.

∞

Yoko sets the table and boils water for tea. She places honey and lemon and little spoons next to the tea cups and saucers. "Goopplezon, raise the kitchen window blinds," she commands. Sunshine floods the room. She hums out loud while rearranging green apples in a big, ceramic bowl on the countertop. Her joy is the free-flowing stream of consciousness of a woman in love, and of a woman well loved. She putters, folding a dish towel here, rearranging the crystal vase of orange magnolias John has given her for no reason there. *It's a spectacular day,* she thinks.

∞

Out of breath from running with cartons of milk and orange juice, bacon, the cracked eggs, butter, cheese, and coffee, Callie bursts through the front door of her apartment and drops two sacks of food onto the kitchen table. She knocks over a pile of empty beer cans; her heart sinks as they roll along the floor and clatter to a halt. "Floyd? Floyd, I'm home. I'll get your breakfast started," she yells into the other room, trying to sound cheery.

Callie wants to please her husband; it's all she thinks about. "If only I could be more of this or less of that." Always sorry after he hurts her, he begs for forgiveness. A few days ago, he was mad because the shirt he wanted to wear was still in the laundry. He snuck up behind her and pulled her hair with a hard, violent jerk. "This is your fault," he screamed. "You don't do the right thing. You're making me do this."

Callie lost her balance and fell. She hit her cheekbone on a kitchen chair. Floyd kicked her in the stomach when she was on the floor. "Please, Floyd, please stop. Please!" she pleaded as she crawled away to take shelter under the table. When he couldn't reach her and was kicking at air, he stormed out of the apartment in his T-shirt, furious.

He came back later, contrite, with a pretty little bouquet of flowers from a street vendor and promised he would never do that again.

She is always hopeful, sometimes for as long as a week.

∞

John returns to Yoko, disheveled and shaken. He tells her the story of the young woman with a black eye crying despondently over broken eggs. Yoko hugs him, and then coaxes him to sit in a chair at the kitchen table. She pours boiling water into the teapot, places the loose tea into the infuser, and allows it to steep.

"My love," John says, "We have to connect the dots between all our issues: climate change, poverty, economic opportunity, violence, religious intolerance, and women's empowerment."

Yoko says, "Yes. You're right. Every time you work to solve one problem, it makes everything else a little better."

"The world is one big interconnected puzzle," John rises and says. "Pass me that bowl, will you? How many pancakes do you want?"

"Two, please." Yoko retrieves the maple syrup from the pantry. "I feel so sad for that woman. Talk to your interns at the Peace Department about working with domestic violence groups."

"It's a bloody shame," John says. He flips the pancakes. They are a perfect golden brown. He holds the frying pan up for Yoko to see. "She should be having pancakes for breakfast too."

∞

Floyd staggers into the kitchen, his presence imposing. Callie stands still, forcing a smile, and anticipates the worst. He hits her face hard with the back of his hand and bloodies her nose. "Where the fuck you been? I'm waiting for my damn scrambled eggs." He grabs another beer from the refrigerator. Callie tucks herself into a corner and tilts her head back to stem the flow of blood with a paper towel.

Her curly-haired, 4-year-old son lingers in the doorway and says, "I'm hungry, momma." She brushes a ringlet out of his eyes. "Go inside, honey. Momma's cooking right now."

Floyd pops the lid on the can, grabs the boy by the arm, and drags him back into the living room. Callie sees her husband drop her sweet baby boy in front of the TV and kick him in the butt. The child has learned from his mother not to cry.

Callie bursts into high gear. She puts bread in the toaster, pours three glasses of orange juice, and prepares a bottle for the baby. She starts the bacon in a frying pan, and the apartment fills with a scent of normalcy.

Floyd yells into the kitchen, "Bring me a cold one, right now!" He glares at his little ones and hisses, "You goddamned kids, get the hell out from under my feet." He snaps his fingers, and they scurry away.

Callie hands Floyd his beer. He grabs her arm and doesn't let go. "Not in front of the babies," she whispers.

"Not in front of the babies," he taunts. "You're pathetic." He twists her arm behind her back, and she screams in excruciating pain. The little boy picks up his baby sister and runs into the bathroom to hide. He flushes the toilet and turns the water on full force.

Floyd drags Callie back into the kitchen by her hair. "What's taking so long?" He sees the egg carton filled with a mess and demands, "What the fuck is this?" Before she can answer, he punches her in the stomach.

Callie loses her breath and doubles over. She holds onto anything she can: the counter, a chair, the table, the flimsy dream of a beautiful life. Floyd comes after her. She picks up a large kitchen knife at her side and thinks, *God, forgive me.*

Floyd sinks to his knees when Callie plunges the knife into him.

Callie struggles to stay conscious, still gasping to restart her breathing, and stumbles to the front door.

Floyd pulls the knife out of his belly and, with every ounce of his remaining strength, hurls it at Callie. She passes out and falls on her face out the apartment door into the hallway with the knife sticking out of her back. This is the last glimpse Floyd has of his beautiful young wife, the mother of his children.

As Floyd lies in a pool of his own blood on the kitchen floor, he spits out, "Bitch," his final word on earth.

∞

I'm haunted by the woman who saved my life today. You can never tell who's in trouble. Could be your neighbor. Your best mate. A stranger you pass on the street. I'm sick with grief thinking of her and the tragedy of her life. Look at me, I'm rattled.

Why do we hurt each other? Why would a man beat up a woman? He asserts his dominance with violence and justifies his actions as his right. It's all about control, isn't it? That goes on one-on-one behind closed doors, and it goes on between religious groups, political groups, and entire nations too.

What will it take for people to believe we've gotta do better? What could we create if we were committed to compassion? Just think of it: The human race working together as a team in every home and all over the globe. Am I mad to desire this? Are you mad not to?

I'm distressed for another reason; I've been reading about me self, and if you believe half these stories, I may not have been the nicest chap with women. No! I never lifted a hand in anger. I hope you don't think I was that much of an asshole. None of that innuendo is true. But the emotional end of it, well, I am taking stock. I am different now — because I have decided to be. We can change course at will. Bloody mind-blowing if you think about the individual power we have over ourselves.

Anything we learn, we can unlearn, yes? This is my second chance to be a better man, a better husband, a better father, a better friend, a better human being. My future doesn't have to be defined by who I was in the past. You don't have to die and come back 'round either. Every day we wake up above ground, roll over, and say, "Yes, it's real, I'm still here." We get to choose love.

I choose love; now and for always. With me boys, with Yoko, Macca, Ringo, and me friends, with the whole world, I'm going to be a saint. Saint John Lennon, that's me. Ha! Sing hallelujah!

THE MOMENT IN TIME THAT SAVED THE WORLD

She knew she loved him when home
went from being a place
to being a person.

- E. Leventhal

Does the existence of a single individual make a difference to the world?
Surely you know the answer to that is "yes." Countless men and women have
shaped the course of technology, arts and sciences, religion and spirituality, and
peace. We bloody well know about the monsters that have rained chaos, death,
and destruction upon us too. They've all made headlines, filled history books,
and affect how we live our lives today. But these, my good friend, are the titans
— both good and evil. What about the rest of us common mortals?

Billions of humans have already passed, completing their quiet struggles
and content or disappointed with their small accomplishments — unaware of
what is to come. Billions more are living now and finding private meaning in
their day-to-day reality.

We have no way of predicting the impact of an ordinary life. Don't you
wonder about yourself? I bet you've asked, "Does it even matter that I've been
here? That I've passed through for this tiniest blip in the millennia of time?
Who will remember me?" Everybody wonders.

Only in retrospect can we trace back to a defining moment, the genesis
of an idea, the chance encounter, the fortuitous accident that leads to something
significant. The journey may be circuitous and traverse generations. The impact

of our forbearers is evident. The question remains, "What of us? What of our descendants?"

∞

Her black eye haunts him. Ashamed that his only reaction to seeing evidence of a woman being battered was to yell out advice after her as she fled, John frets. "I should have acted boldly, more decisively."

Yoko consoles him. "You were an inch away from losing your life. She had just saved you. You were shaken, dear."

"I can't just spend my time feeling bad. What good is having these emotions if they don't drive me to do something? There are right many solutions to every problem, eh? I'm going to find one for her."

John takes advantage of his celebrity and asks for assistance. The city traffic department and the store owner where the young lady had removed him from the path of an oncoming bus provide video surveillance, and, with the use of facial recognition technology, he is able to identify his savior. Callie Ellis, wife of Wall Street futures trader, Floyd Ellis.

"Come with me, Sean?" John asks. "We'll bring the bodyguards too. Just in case."

John and Sean find police crime scene tape crossing Callie's apartment door and blocking part of the entryway in the hall. A neighbor sticks her head out her door and tells them Floyd is dead and Callie was taken to Mount Sinai West Hospital a few days earlier – that's all she knows.

∞

John and Sean walk through the sterile white halls of Mount Sinai West Hospital. John's red sneakers squeak on the pristine, shiny floors. Sean's footsteps echo a click, click, clickity, click.

Experiencing a wave of melancholia, Sean says, "You were pronounced dead in this hospital, dad."

"That's a creepy thing to say to your old man." John shudders to feign his best impression of creepiness and Sean laughs.

Callie has just been moved out of ICU to a private room and hears them approach. The men knock on the open door and enter tentatively.

"Come in. Come in," the patient says faintly, but with enthusiasm. "The nurses told me you were coming up, Mr. Lennon." Bandages hide her near fatal wound. An oxygen tube is taped to her nose. An IV drip runs through the needle into her arm. Sensors track her heart beat and respiration; machines whir and beep and display colors and graphs. "It's not as scary as it looks. I'm out of danger and well on the mend."

"You look strangely peaceful," John says.

Callie manages a gentle smile. "The worst is over." She turns to Sean. "Hi."

"Hi−"

"Oh, sorry. Allow me to introduce you to my son, Sean."

When Sean takes Callie's proffered hand in his, a hot-chocolate warmth fills his belly and a marshmallow sweetness touches his tongue.

Callie's heart races zippity-doo-dah and sets off an alarm. She blushes all rosy, and her temperature sensors ping. "Ow, ow, ow," Callie says, trying to keep from laughing too hard.

Though they haven't met before in this lifetime, they recognize each other. Sean sees a better version of himself through her eyes. Callie sees joy.

Floating around the couple are tiny points of light, twinkling and fizzling and crackling and sparkling every glorious color, but only John can see them. "*Well I'll be damned*," John says to himself as nurses rush into the room to see why the alarms are sounding.

∞

"One last question," John says as they are nearing the end of their visit. "You said you couldn't leave him because of your babies. Are they safe?"

"Yes, thank you for asking. My mama took them back to Tennessee. They're going to stay with her until I recuperate."

"When you're better, will you stay in New York City? Will this still be your home?" Sean asks.

Callie sighs, "We'll see what the future has in store for me."

"My dad and I created a musical score for a new star show at the Hayden Planetarium called *Hope for the Universe*. The Planetarium director, Neil deGrasse Tyson, is a good friend of ours, and he's hosting a private showing before it opens to the public. We're the guests of honor." Sean gives his dad a playful squeeze. "If you're up and about in three weeks, I'd love it if you'd be my guest."

Sean writes his phone number on a bedside note pad. He is happy to have an excuse to hold Callie's hand again as he folds the small paper into her palm.

She calls.

FACES

Looking at these stars
suddenly dwarfed my own troubles and all the gravities of terrestrial life.
I thought of their unfathomable distance,
and the slow inevitable drift of their movements
out of the unknown past into the unknown future.

- H.G. Wells

John and Yoko sit in the back of a yellow Hummer heading north on Interstate 25 from Las Cruces. "What are they?" Yoko asks, pointing through the window into the light of dusk at a pair of large birds alongside the highway.

"They're road runners, ma'am," the driver answers. "They're pretty common out here in New Mexico."

"What do you mean? Like the 'beep-beep' cartoon character?" John asks.

"That's right, sir." The driver laughs. He sits facing his passengers while the car is on automatic pilot. "City folk from up north are always surprised they're real."

John and Yoko throw each other a look as if to say, "Who knew?"

"We're exiting the interstate now, Mr. and Mrs. Lennon," The driver says. "The first half of the county road isn't too bad, but eventually it gets a little bumpy and a little dusty out here in the middle of nowhere."

Half an hour later, they turn left to make the long approach into Spaceport America, a 110,000-square-foot terminal and hangar nestled unobtrusively into the sand dunes of the Jornada del Muerto Desert. Darkness has descended quickly. A 40-foot long steel sculpture in the form of an asymmetrical crescent occupies the center of a roundabout. Its arc, inlaid with mirrors in the pattern of the stars seen in the summer sky, reflects the magnificence above.

Noticing Yoko's fascination with the art installation, the driver says, "It's called *Genesis*. It's welcoming you to Virgin Galactic's gateway to space."

"A fitting name," Yoko says. "I like it."

Sir Richard Branson, the 70-something-year-old founder of the Virgin Group, is at the ready to welcome his guests. Dressed in jeans, a white shirt, and brown leather bomber jacket, he remains unperturbed by the wind tussling his long blond hair.

"Welcome, welcome! Are you ready to take the astronaut's walk?" Sir Richard asks John as he steps out of the vehicle. "Once you go into space, you will earn your wings and receive the official designation of being an astronaut."

"I've been called a space cadet before," John teases, "but astronaut? Totally groovy." The men shake hands.

"Groovy, indeed." Sir Richard gestures for John to walk ahead and offers his arm to escort Yoko. They make their way down a gently sloping walkway dissecting two wings of the spaceport. At the bottom, a large door hisses and slides open to swallow up the visitors.

Inside, a guest attendant greets Yoko. "Mrs. Lennon, if you'll allow me, I will explain the procedures we'll follow for the next few days and give you a tour of mission control and the family observation deck." Yoko kisses John on the cheek and nods her agreement.

"Right this way, please." The attendant gestures, and they disappear through a hidden side door. John hears the tail end of the attendant's comments, "You'll notice right away how comfortable the temperature is in here. Spaceport incorporates earth tubes for natural ventilation to cool the building, solar thermal panels, and under-floor radiant cooling and heating," before the door swings shut.

Sir Richard walks alongside John as they proceed down a curved, stark-white corridor lit by blue neon lights. "Our spacecraft is elegantly designed for your comfort. But because you'll travel at high speeds and experience strong g-forces, we'll begin with a medical evaluation to make sure you're in good shape. You'll have three days of pre-flight preparation. We want you to have an unforgettable experience, but safety is always first."

"This is even more exciting than flying to America for the first time when I was a lad," John says.

"On this flight you'll spend time floating in microgravity," Sir Richard says. "Take a look at this." A panel of the wall spins open, and they enter a room where six space suits hang. "Each suit, helmet, gloves, and pair of boots is custom-made. Yours is the blue set on the right. The other five are for your peace ambassadors, and both pilots have already been fitted. The all-in-one suit is made of a special synthetic material designed for your protection and ease of movement."

"Are the ambassadors here?" John asks.

"Yes. They are in the briefing room with your Goopplezon Peace Department associate, Mr. Johnson. Follow me, and we'll get started."

∞

I received a lot of bloody flak from my detractors for spending millions of dollars up front on this project, instead of using the money to feed the poor or to help directly with peace initiatives in some other way. The good news is that we made it all back one hundred-fold. I wanted to take my message to the entire world in the most dramatic way I could think of.

Aren't you tired yet of war and violence? Aren't you sick of seeing death on the news? Gangs in the streets? Conflicts with police and military? Bombs falling from the sky? Domestic violence? Terrorism? Religious intolerance? Extreme poverty? Genocide? Homicide? Or are you so overwhelmed that you've become immune to the images?

I'm bloody sick of it all. I want it to stop. The Goopplezon Peace Department ambassadors are working to coordinate the thousands of peace organizations operating all over the globe. Synergy is power. You know: one plus one equals three when we work together. Everyone has to make peace their mission. Everyone. Leaders, organizations, and individuals have to be involved in conversations about how to make it happen.

Close to one billion of the world's seven and a half billion people downloaded the "Faces for Peace" app on their phones, watches, tablets, and computers. Astounding. What do you call that? Something like 'going viral'? Peace supporters sent in their headshots and added the word peace in their native language to their photo. We have almost 4,000 languages represented. We received millions of mail-ins and scans from 3-D Goopplezon Lenses as well.

We asked for one U.S. dollar contribution only if the participant could afford it. Millions could not. But millions of other people covered it by sending in five and 10 dollars. So, not only are we making an unequivocal statement to world leaders that we demand peace, but we'll be able to do the work it takes to make that happen.

∞

Two pilots fly the *White Knight Three*, a dual-fuselage jet with four Pratt and Whitney engines and a 140-foot wingspan, from its right fuselage. A single carbon composite wing connects both sides and serves as the point of attachment for the spacecraft to hang suspended. John commissioned the *VSS Unity* spaceship for his historic flight; a name epitomizing the purpose of his mission.

"WKT, this is mission control. You're clear for takeoff."

"Roger that. WKT is rolling."

The *White Knight Three* barrels down 10,000 feet of runway carrying the *VSS Unity* below its connected wings. The space ship carries six passengers and two astronaut pilots.

"If I didn't know where I was going, I'd think I was on a regular plane ride," John says to the crew. He nervously folds and unfolds a piece of paper where he has written notes for his speech – a crutch in case he becomes too nervous to remember what he wants to say.

The White Knight Three climbs slowly into the sky in circles for about an hour. "Mission control, this is WKT. We've reached altitude. Ready for disengagement."

"Roger WKT, the *Unity* is cleared for launch."

"Roger that, mission control." The pilot from the *VSS Unity* checks in. "We're good to go."

John and the others are comfortably strapped into their upright seats. "Good God. I must really be crazy," John says. He takes a deep breath to shake off his nervousness.

The peace ambassador seated next to him says, "We all are," and gives him a thumbs-up.

Mission control starts the countdown. "T-ten seconds, nine, eight, seven, six, five, four, three, two, one."

The spaceship detaches from the mother ship. The *White Knight Three* banks sharply to the left and the *Unity* simultaneously fires its single hybrid rocket to begin its launch from 50,000 feet above the earth. A powerful, controlled explosion pushes its human cargo through the earth's gravitational force, a magnificent fire trailing behind.

John's heart beats wildly as the g-forces press him back into his seat. He and the crew rush to the heavens, within eight seconds surpassing supersonic speed. For another minute and a half, they travel at three times the speed of sound. Once they break out of the earth's atmosphere, the rocket thrust ceases, and the silence is eerie.

John releases his seat belt. Weightless at 68.4 miles above the earth in sub-orbit, he floats freely and whoops it up.

John has arranged for hologram recording equipment to be installed in the *Unity*. Anyone who wants to can beam his 3-D image into their living room. The Goopplezon Peace Department helped remote villages set up receivers in town squares, courtyards, and places of worship. They went into the deserts and mountains. Movie theaters opened their doors to spectators.

Stadiums are filled with hopeful observers. Rumors swirl around the globe that rebels and warriors have laid down their weapons for this historic event. The entire world watches John Lennon visit space and listens to him say:

> "My fellow earthlings, love must pave the way for our journey toward peace. You sent me photos of your faces – expectant, joyful, devastated, tearful, happy – faces showing every human emotion. Behind your eyes is a shared dream: that we should all know peace on earth. So today, I am releasing your images into space. Your message of peace will reach all corners of the universe as we know it, and perhaps beyond. Look."

John gestures outside the *Unity* where a second camera begins transmitting. The *Unity* has been retrofitted with several advanced technology, zero-gravity 3-D printers. Pinpoint lasers open to the outside of the craft. Goopplezon laboratories have developed a new plastic-like material capable of withstanding the rigors of space conditions – extreme heat and cold, the forces of space wind, and exposure to the full spectrum of light. Each printer uses this material to create a clear bubble in just a few nanoseconds, inside an etched copy of a face from the photos submitted. On the back side of each etching is the word peace in the language spoken by the subject.

In no time, there are hundreds, then thousands, then millions, and then a billion bubbles: people of every age, race, color, and creed. The gentle force of the printers is enough to put each bubble into perpetual motion. Without resistance, they will travel into space, in all directions, forever. Drifting. Tumbling. Hoping for peace.

The world is stunned by the beauty of faces memorialized for all eternity, a show of solidarity unrivaled by its magnitude and backdrop.

John and his fellow astronauts have only four minutes of weightlessness. A dozen windows lining the sides and ceiling of the craft allow for a spectacular view of earth and the blackness of infinite space. John says, "Look at her. Look at our earth; the one and only place in this vast universe to support life as we know it. All of us live here. Together."

"Ladies and gentlemen, please take your seats and prepare for re-entry," the copilot orders. The new astronauts flawlessly execute their well-practiced re-entry routine and are safely ensconced in reclining seats for the trip home.

The *VSS Unity's* feathered re-entry system allows for the wings to rotate upwards, creating an aerodynamically stable shuttlecock effect. The increased drag slows down the spaceship in the higher atmospheric levels. As it decelerates, it orients itself into a gliding position.

Mission control says, "*Unity,* you're approaching 70,000 feet."

"Roger that, mission control. Preparing to rotate wings." When the wings are in their usual flight position, the pilot adds, "We're coming in," and takes manual control. The *Unity* does not have an engine. She will take 25 to 30 minutes to glide back to earth and touch down on the runway where the voyage began.

Mission control captures the *VSS Unity's* perfect landing on screen. A small white bus emblazoned on both sides with the Virgin Galactic logo – a photo of Sir Richard's iris – drives up to her and arrives just as the side door pops open. Technicians roll out a short staircase.

The five peace ambassadors exit the spaceship first. Hundreds of family members and guests cheer from the Spaceport observation deck. They have a close-up look at what is happening in the distance on a big screen.

The pilot and co-pilot exit next and give a big thumbs-up to the cameras. They wait on the tarmac to cheer John.

"What's taking so long?" the co-pilot whispers to the pilot. "Is he going for a big finale?"

Worried about the delay, the pilot climbs back up the steps to give John a hand. "What the–?" He turns to the others and asks, "Did John already get out? He's not here."

The crowd at the observation deck becomes quiet. "Oh, boy," Yoko says. "He'll be right back."

"Right back?" Sir Richard asks. "Where did he go?"

SLEEPLESS IN TRUTH OR CONSEQUENCES

If life were predictable,
it would cease to be life, and be without flavor.

- Eleanor Roosevelt

🎼

Yoko refuses to leave the Spaceport without John. She doesn't even want to take the ride back to her hotel in Las Cruces. Sir Richard charges his staff with outfitting a room for her to spend the night on premises.

Yoko's brainwaves hover between the desperately coveted temporary escape from the world and a nagging realization that she is still within the realm of the cognizant. It is the kind of sleep that never quite happens, that twilight layer of maddening semi-consciousness.

Yoko senses when John watches her while she sleeps. "Yes, I'm the spooky staring monster," he claims. But when she opens her eyes tonight, half expecting him to be standing over her, she remembers he has not returned and her heart aches in his absence.

Whenever John disappears in his second life, he returns straightaway. He is gone only for a few seconds to several minutes at most. Yoko rolls onto her side and looks at her watch sitting on a stool next to her cot. Four in the morning. Twelve hours since the *VSS Unity* landed and the crew discovered John was missing. Too early to rise, too late to believe she's merely having a nightmare from which she can emerge.

John had taught Yoko not to worry. "Worry changes nothing, my love," he'd remind her when she became anxious. "Most of what you worry about will never happen. And if it does, write a song about it."

Ah, that wry smile of his when he knows he is right, Yoko thinks. She conjures his voice. "Don't worry. Don't worry," she hears him say. "I am with you." In her purposely crafted pseudo-dream, she sees him standing in his navy-blue space suit, holding his helmet in one hand and reaching out to her with the other.

∞

Like hummingbirds flittering from flower to flower, word spreads of John's disappearance and failure to reappear. Whispers, tweets, texts, emails, phone calls, and conversations over coffee ask, "Did you hear?"

The media swarm. Overnight, flocks assemble and reconfigure. They move in tandem, communicating mysteriously to swirl, twist, and dip until they descend en masse to surround the *Genesis* sculpture at the Spaceport's entry. They seek reassurance. John Lennon has become the voice of hope for the world. The citizens of earth are beginning to believe that peace might be achievable.

Richard Branson, Yoko, and the *VSS Unity's* pilots are ready for the press conference. Ioni, John's press secretary, arrived at dawn to assist Yoko. The atmosphere is reverent. Below the soft glow of the pink and gray sky, surrounded by the Organ Mountains far in the distance, they think, *What if John is dead again?*

"We will not be projecting holograms this morning," Ioni says. "I'm sure you understand this is a very difficult time for Yoko."

The first hand shoots up. "Mr. Branson? Is this all a hoax for publicity for your tourist space program?"

"No, it's not," he answers in his dignified British accent. "We can barely keep up with the demand. We have a long, long waiting list of people wanting to go into space. We would never need to do such a thing."

"Yoko, Yoko, here please." Yoko acknowledges the next reporter. "Was John ever really here? Some people think that's the original hoax."

"I assure you, he was here. You don't have to take my word for it; there are many people who have met him in person and have been working with him on his peace initiatives." She takes a deep breath to keep from bursting into tears. "I hope he comes back again."

"Where do you think he went?" someone yells out.

"I don't know. He never remembers anything clearly. Sometimes he has fleeting dreams or weird visions that might be clues. He receives messages that give him gut feelings. But mostly we don't know," Yoko says.

A young reporter waves eagerly. "The faces-for-peace-project is the most awesome thing I've ever seen. It was beautiful. Who came up with that idea?"

"Actually," Yoko says, "Ioni inspired him." She gestures to her right at the young lady holding a tablet and stylus. "She and John were sitting in our living room at the Dakota strategizing how to best disseminate John's message of peace through the media from space. She was smiling, and he said, 'The world should see your beautiful, hopeful face.' And the lightbulb went off. Her face was in one of the bubbles."

"Mr. Branson? May I?" A reporter jumps up in the back to speak over the heads of the group. "Are you sure John isn't lost out in space?"

"We're sure of that. First of all, no one can leave the ship in space. Also, the pilots and other passengers were in direct contact with him until they exited the *Unity* after landing. We're sure that's when he disappeared." The pilots nod in agreement.

An elderly gentleman reporter up front asks, "Yoko? I'm sorry to posit this question, but what will you do if John doesn't return at all?"

Yoko steels herself to say, "He'd want us to carry on his work, just like we did for the 40 years we lived without him before. He'd want awareness of what we have to do for peace – to encourage people to take whatever action they can. He has changed the narrative that we are powerless to make a difference around the world – that only our government speaks and acts for us. His message remains: We can each make a difference, each one of us. Every human being."

The gentleman follows up, "But what about you?"

"I will be very, very sad. But life goes on. And he and I shall meet again."

Ioni steps up. "That's all for now. Thank you so much for your concern. I know you've come a long way. I promise that as soon as we know something, we will let you know. Thank you."

∞

Sean hugs his mother longer and harder than usual at the arrivals area. Yoko waited two days in New Mexico before reluctantly flying home.

When John died in 1980, Yoko took over his role as primary caretaker and learned quickly how to shelter and protect their young son. Sean, in turn, learned from his mother how to be nurturing in a crisis. He takes her lovingly by the hand and reassures her. "It's going to be OK, mom."

Kuruma waits curbside outside of baggage claim. Mother and son exit to find Julio, looking somber, standing next to the car's opened door. An airplane, flying low on its approach to JFK Airport, disappears with a roar over the terminal building.

Uncertainty, an ever-present force that had retreated to the background in Yoko's life for a short while, imposes itself upon her once again. To no one in particular Yoko asks, "Dare I imagine the future? Would I want to know?" She slips into the back seat of the car.

SUNDAY, AUGUST 15TH

The timeless in you is aware of life's timelessness.
And knows that yesterday is but today's memory
and tomorrow is today's dream.

- Kahlil Gibran

"Wow-wee, that pitch was clocked at 98.7 miles an hour," the announcer says. "What an arm the kid has."

"Unbelievable, Bob. Keep an eye on this 6-foot 3-inch, 200-pound rookie. The National League hasn't seen young pitching potential quite like this in a while. Twenty-one years old – what a future he's got."

"Joel, ya know, he was brought up from the minors this year with some impressive stats. He's well on his way to a perfect game."

"One perfect game is outstanding. He's going for two, in the same season yet. Amazing," Joel says. "Absolutely amazing. It's a magical kind of day. We're in the top of the seventh. One out. The count, three and two. The pressure is on."

"There it is: a bender. Caught the corner, striiiiiiiiiike three," Jim calls. "Another punch out for Ricky Garcia. Look at him; he is focused. He's a no-nonsense player."

The three announcers banter excitedly over one another. "They're going around the horn to keep loose." "These guys are fired up." "They're looking to sweep the series. The Cubs didn't see this coming." "Lee Richmond pitched the first perfect game for the Worcester Ruby Legs against the Cleveland Blues back in 1880."

"The Mets are really looking good this year," Jim says. "Real good. They could get to the playoffs. Maybe as a wildcard, but they could get there."

"On deck, first baseman Joey Santucci. He's stepping up to the plate," Bob says. "His last at-bat was a one, two, three strike-out."

"It was a beautiful day here at Citi Field," Joel says, "but it looks like some clouds are rolling in. Fast too. They're racing across the sky in this direction."

"The pitch… and it's a fly ball to centerfield…Granger is under it…nice and easy…that's it: The Mets have retired the Chicago Cubs with no one left on base," Jim says. "As we move into the bottom of the seventh, the score remains 4-0, Mets."

The organ plays *Take Me Out to the Ballgame* to rally the crowd as they stand for the traditional seventh-inning stretch.

"A little trivia for you gentlemen. Did you know this Tin Pan Alley song was written in 1908?" Bob asks.

"No kidding? I didn't know it went back that far." Joel says, "Tell the folks what the Tin Pan Alley is, Bob."

"It was an area in Manhattan, between Broadway and Sixth Avenue on West 28th Street, where music publishers had their offices. In the early 1900s, songwriters hung out there hoping to catch a break. A couple of unknowns, Jack Norwith and Albert von Tilzer, came up with what's pretty much the unofficial anthem of Major League Baseball."

"Holy cow," Jim says. "That storm is rolling in fast. It's getting dark. Crazy August weather here in New York City. The ground crew is in place. Let's see if they call a delay and roll out the tarps."

"I've got a little more music trivia for you," Bob says, hiding his concern with a bright and chipper demeanor as he looks out into the ominous distance.

∞

"Baseball — I love baseball." The precocious 7-year-old Sean is conducting his first solo interview in the Dakota living room while his mom is in the kitchen. He's met reporter Don Singleton of the *New York Daily News* several times before and feels relaxed in his grown-up role with the media. "I have sticker books on baseball. I have baseball magazines. I have baseball cards," he says proudly.

Sean doesn't mention his most treasured piece of memorabilia; he keeps it a secret hidden from the entire world. When it came into his possession, he made up his mind he would never, ever tell. Ever. Not even his mom. Not even his best friend Max who lives downstairs. *They will think I'm crazy,* he thought. *It's probably my imagination.* He tried to convince himself he was normal. *Maybe I just miss my dad so much.* But then the object, the tangible evidence that left him perplexed, taunted him.

He came to possess his prize on August 15th, a Sunday afternoon earlier in the year. Although John had been murdered a year and eight months prior — an eternity to a child — Sean saw his dad very much alive and well on this day. John wore a blue, one-piece zip-up space suit and held a helmet in his left hand and a baseball in his right. He was as surprised to see Sean as Sean was to see him.

They stared at one another in the hallway outside Sean's bedroom. Reflexively, John reached out to his son and handed him the ball. Sean rolled it around and around, looking at the signatures of players he didn't recognize; Ricky Garcia, Ben Granger, Joey Santucci, and others he couldn't make out.

Afraid to look up, Sean ventured a hug. He held John's leg and barely managed, "I miss you, daddy." John ran his hand through Sean's hair and said, "I love you, me boy. It's OK." Sean let go and ran into his room to hide under the covers.

"Sean?" Don asks. The boy is daydreaming. "Are you all right?"

Recovering quickly, Sean says, "Oh, sorry. I'm fine."

"I asked, 'Do you enjoy going to the games?'"

"You would think someone my age who loves baseball so much would have been to at least 14 or 15 games, right? But do you know how many games I've been to see? Just one, and the Yankees lost, 1 to 14." *Stop thinking about it. Stop it! Just stop it! Don't tell him. Don't tell anyone,* Sean convinces himself.

Sean's self-preserving spirit protected him. His recollection of the unexplainable meeting with his father dissipated as he grew up, reduced to the tiniest pinpoint of light in the recesses of his mind. He stashed the ball away inside his Wrinkles stuffed dog, along with his favorite photo of his dad and one of John's guitar picks.

He never opened the plush toy again; the memory remains dormant.

∞

"What are you doing?" Sean asks his mother. "You're pacing around the apartment, back and forth like a caged animal." He pushes his horn-rimmed glasses up on his nose and nervously twists the end of his mustache.

"I just don't know what to do with myself," Yoko says. "Your father has been gone this time for five days now. When he didn't come out of the *Unity,* I wasn't that worried. I've gotten used to the unexpected disappearances. But five days? What could he be up to?"

"I know. I'm a wreck too. The uncertainty−"

"That's the worst," Yoko interjects. "It's the not knowing. I can't stand this. On the one hand, I am hopeful he will be back − really, I am. But on the other, I'm fearful I'm deluding myself, and I should be mourning the loss of my husband for a second time."

Sean's face dims. "Why don't you get dressed?" he suggests. "Let's grab an early dinner. It'll do us good to get out. I'll tell Julio to get the car. A storm is brewing."

"OK. Give me a few minutes." Glancing at the TV, Yoko asks, "Who's playing?"

"The Mets. The Yankee game is over. Hey, mom," he says mustering a bit of levity, "do you realize the Beatles performed in the original Shea Stadium on this day 56 years ago?"

"How can that be?" Yoko asks rhetorically. "I swear I've lived more than one life."

∞

"I've been calling games at Shea and Citi Field stadiums for more than 20 years and I have never − and I mean never − seen a stadium socked in like this," Bob says.

"It looks like a *War of the Worlds* kind of sky," Jim says. "Did you ever see that old movie? Any minute, the aliens will beam down."

Bob adds, "A pop-up would be lost in the clouds. Look at that. I can hardly see the folks in the upper decks. What's going on?"

"This is more than a little scary-looking. I grew up in Iowa. If we saw black, heavy clouds billowing like this, the sirens would go off to warn us to take cover," Joel says. "I'm freaking out. It looks like a twister is going to hit."

"New York City has experienced tornado-like conditions before. The winds are picking up significantly," Jim says. "Uh-oh.

The umps are meeting on the mound. They're shaking their heads. Yep, they've called a delay. The crew has started to roll out the tarps and—"

"Whoa! Whoa! Good grief! Did you see that lightning strike in the middle of the field?" Bob yells. "The players, umpires, and ground crew are all running to the dugouts for cover."

"What the heck is that?" Bob asks. "What's glowing down there?"

"Maybe it's the extraterrestrials here for a visit," Jim says with equal parts humor and unease.

A full stadium, both teams, the umpires, the media, ground crew, TV technicians, and millions of viewers watch the glowing form take shape. John Lennon is in center field in the blue space suit he wore last week to fly into space on the *VSS Unity*.

John expects to look up and see his fellow astronauts and Virgin Galactic crew welcoming him back from his successful "Faces" mission.

The wind howls, and a mini-twister spins around John. He stands resolutely, untouched at its peaceful eye. After the twister lifts off, the wind abates. The clouds withdraw instantly, revealing a resplendent, clear blue sky and the deep orange and scarlet ice cream-swirl of an early evening sun.

Security runs onto the field and whisks John to safety into the Mets' dugout before anyone has time to react. The players swarm him. He gets his bearings and says, "The Mets have always been my favorite team. How about an autographed ball for my son Sean? We started watching baseball games together when he was two. He'll be thrilled."

∞

"Sean, I'm in the mood for some lemonade before we go out. Do you— What's wrong?" Yoko asks.

A colossal grin takes over Sean's face, and he jumps up from the sofa. "Mom! He's back. Dad! Dad is back. Look! Look at the dugout!" He points to the TV.

John, dressed as he was at the Spaceport in New Mexico the last time Yoko saw him, is chatting happily and posing for selfies holding a bat.

Yoko is overcome by a torrent of tears and sobs audibly. Sean puts his arm around his mother and says, "It never felt like he was gone for good. I just knew we'd see him again." Yoko smiles, and Sean wipes away her tears with his thumbs.

Yoko sniffs and speaks into the room to summon her majordomo. "Goopplezon. Connect with Julio."

Julio's hologram appears next to them. "Yes ma'am?"

"Get the guards ready. We're leaving right now."

Sean looks back at the TV and sees his dad step out of the dugout and wave to an adoring crowd; the ear-splitting cheering is incessant. Noticing the baseball John is holding in his right hand ignites a flash of light in Sean's brain, illuminating his long-repressed secret.

"Wait, mom." Sean gathers his wits about him. "He won't be there by the time we get there."

"How could you possibly know that?" she asks impatiently.

No one switches off the television; nonetheless, the Dakota living room becomes perfectly quiet in an instant. Forty-thousand exhilarated spectators hush when John Lennon disappears in front of them as mysteriously as he had appeared to them just minutes ago.

Sean, Yoko, and Julio's hologram all exchange glances. "I know where he is right now," Sean says. "At least for a minute."

Astonished, Yoko asks, "How? Where?"

Sean gestures to the sofa "Sit down with me. I have a little story to tell you. Do you remember when I was seven? What ever happened to my old stuffed animals?"

∞

"I wish you would have told me. I would have believed you," Yoko says to her son.

"I know that now. But at the time, I didn't want you to talk me out of it. I was afraid I'd convince myself it wasn't real. When dad came back last December, it felt just as familiar as it did remarkable. Now I understand why; it wasn't our first bizarre reunion."

The phone rings. Goopplezon announces, "A call from Sir Richard Branson on your private line."

"Answer, please," Yoko says. Sean takes her hand.

"Hello there, Yoko," Richard says. "Let me get right to it; I have some exciting news. You'll want to beam in this call." He waits a beat. "Ready?" Richard's hologram appears in front of her. "There's someone here who's just arrived and anxious to speak to you. He tumbled out of the *Unity* parked in our hangar." Richard steps out of the field and is replaced by John.

Yoko shrieks, "John!" She jumps up with the instinct to hug him and passes right through his image.

The hologram field cuts a swath to include the sofa. "Son!" John says. "How are you?" John turns around and speaks to Yoko. "You left without me." He feigns a hurt look.

"It wasn't minutes this time. It was days, John. And we know where you were for some of that time."

"Sorry I worried you. Tell me! Please. I want to know."

Sean says, "You were at a baseball game today. Richard can show you a recording. And, and..." he hesitates. "You visited me in 1982."

"I visited you? In 1982? I did?"

"Come back to us, John," Yoko says softly, "and we'll tell you all about it."

"Yes, my love. Right away. Sir Richard is flying me home - the old-fashioned way." John spreads his arms like wings, and his hologram disappears.

HEY JULES

The earth has guilt, the earth has care,
Unquiet are its graves;
But peaceful sleep is ever there,
Beneath the dark blue waves.

- Nathaniel Hawthorne

The glass shower stall is fogged over. John steps out squeaky clean and refreshed, smelling of lemons and mint. Bending forward to toss his wet hair over his head, he twists a white microfiber towel around his wavy mop like a turban. He swipes the condensation off the bathroom mirror with the side of his hand and contemplates his bony shoulders. Making a fist and raising an arm to flex his bicep, John puffs out his chest and rolls his eyes at himself.

Yoko knocks and, without waiting, opens the bathroom door a crack. "Hey, Superman," she says. John turns, regaling her with a full-frontal greeting. In a mock show of modesty, Yoko shields her eyes. "Throw on your cape, dear. Julian is on his way up."

When her husband fails to respond, Yoko lowers her hand and opens her eyes. The steamy bathroom is empty. A small puddle of water remains on the marble floor in front of the sink.

∞

John chokes on a gulp of salt water, coughing uncontrollably, and his sinuses sting when a sea swell forces water up his nose. Clinging to the side of a buoy, he thinks, *Damn, this water is bloody cold. I'm going to freeze to death.*

His muscles tense in the frigid water. Within three minutes, his lean body will succumb to the first stages of hypothermia. The blood vessels in his skin constrict to conserve heat for his vital organs. His core temperature is dropping fast.

The yellow buoy's flat round platform is topped with a tall tripod holding tracking, sensor, and lighting equipment. "How the hell am I going to get up there?" John asks out loud. He doesn't ask "How did I get here?" Although confused, his instinct for survival eclipses curiosity. His dilemma consumes his full attention.

The buoy's platform sits just a few feet on top of the water's surface, but without any footing or leverage to help John get out of the water, the base might as well be a skyscraper roof he has to reach in a single bound. He tries to pull himself up but is unable to get a firm enough grip on its edge. After slipping back several times, he gives up. His lips are turning blue.

John dog paddles his way around the buoy in the dark, searching for anything that might help. He finds a tow ring. He grips the handle and throws one foot, heel down, onto the platform. He pushes on the ring, attempting to lift himself high enough to get the crook of his knee against the edge. He isn't strong enough. Persistent nonetheless, he is in the perfect position to be saved by a rogue wave. Like a fish jumping out of water and haphazardly landing in a fisherman's boat, John is lifted and tossed onto the buoy's base.

Exhausted but bolstered by his triumph, his will to live is fortified. He sits shivering in the middle of the buoy, his back against one leg of the tripod, hugging his knees against his body in an instinctive move to keep warm. *Now what?* he thinks.

John strains to look out into the distance. A waning moon provides just enough light for him to make out the outline of a ship against the horizon. *Smashing,* he thinks. He springs to his feet and yells at the top of his lungs, "Over here! Over here!"

Quickly realizing the futility of screaming over the ocean, he puts his hands up to his head to think and notices the turban twisted around his hair. He tears it off and waves it wildly as he jumps up and down. "What a prat I am. This is never going to work either." He curses into the sky. "Fuck me."

"The light!" John shouts. "The light!" Mustering strength held in reserve for the preservation of life, he climbs to the top of the tripod. He covers the beacon with the turban in the sequence of dot-dot-dot, dash-dash-dash, dot-dot-dot. He waits four seconds and repeats the sequence.

John learned Morse code for SOS – the universal signal of extreme distress – as a wolf cub scout. Even he, a boy with a robust imagination, never envisioned he would use it for the first and only time in the middle of the Pacific Ocean in 2050 – 17 years after he had died as an old man of natural causes.

Teetering on the edge of consciousness, John is still signaling 20 minutes later when the ship's crewmen drape a thermal covering around his naked body during the rescue. They strap him onto a gurney and load him into a dinghy. In his final moment of coherence, John murmurs, "Julian is coming."

The crewman glance at each other and one of them ventures, "How do you know Julian, sir?"

John says, "He's me boy," and slips into unconsciousness.

∞

There is a knock on the open cabin door. "Mr. Lennon? Julian? Sir?"

"Captain!" Julian says. "To what do I owe this honor?"

The captain of the *Samudra* steps into the small but well-appointed stateroom, while his first mate waits in the passageway. He says, "Well, we have a strange situation."

"Yes, yes, I know. What set off the SOS signal?"

"A person," the captain says.

"A person? Out here? In the middle of nowhere? How would a person get here? And survive? That's impossible."

"One would think so." The captain walks over to Julian's desk and picks up a framed photo. "Tell me about this picture."

"That's me and my pop. I was about 11 years old there. We had a holiday at Disney World."

"What about this one? Is this your father too?"

"Yes," Julian says. "He was in his 80s then. Younger than I am now, I think. That was taken in Oslo, Norway, when he won the Nobel Peace Prize." Julian waits for an explanation. When none is forthcoming, he asks, "What's this all about, captain?"

"The person we rescued? He claims to be John Lennon. Your father."

"My father? My father died in 2033. I was at the funeral. He was definitely dead. I viewed him. If he were alive now, he'd be…I don't know…about 110 years old. Did you pluck a bat-shit crazy centenarian out of the ocean?"

"It's even weirder than that, Julian. He looks exactly like this." The captain holds up the photo of a vibrant John wearing a Mickey Mouse T-shirt with the young Julian in Florida at Disney World. "Spitting image."

"I don't understand," Julian says. He eases into a big chair. His joints hurt from the humidity. This is his last voyage to the subtropical convergence zone − a place where the currents and winds create a vortex of trash. For more than three decades, he has been working to monitor marine debris and deploy Pac-man-like robots that chomp on plastic and oil slicks. He is tired. And this oddity is just too much.

"If there had been any further delay, he would have died," the captain says. "He was on the verge, I tell you. As it is, his recovery is miraculous. He's up and about already. He's been issued a perma-life suit. He's dressed, and he wants to come here to see you. He asked for a spot of tea. We could have a tea-service sent down if you'd like."

"Why not?" Julian drums with his fingers on the arm of the chair. "The world is full of surprises," he says. "Yes."

∞

Yoko is sitting on her living room sofa sobbing when Julian enters. He rushes over to her. "Yoko! Yoko! What's wrong?" He kneels to her side in front of her.

"He's gone. Your father is gone—"

The blood drains from Julian's complexion. "Dead again?"

Yoko shakes her head. "No! Oh no, dear. He's disappeared. It's happening more frequently, and I can't take it." While holding up her trembling hands, she says, "Look at me. I'm a nervous wreck."

Touched by Yoko's distress, Julian asks, "Has he been gone for long?"

Yoko looks at her watch. "Three minutes and 28 seconds."

"Should I laugh at you or cry with you?" Julian asks.

"Sometimes he flickers and he's back in an instant." Yoko sniffs. "Sometimes it's two minutes. But ever since he didn't come back for days after his space flight, I feel so, so... damn neurotic."

"The world cannot deal with a neurotic, Yoko!" Julian smirks trying to lift her spirits.

"Son! You're here!" John emerges from the hallway. Yoko launches off the sofa and projects into John's arms. Julian loses his balance and topples onto the floor when Yoko leaps over him.

"I must have been elsewhere," John says to his wife.

"'Elsewhere' is what he calls it," Yoko says, turning her head back to Julian.

John says, "Check out my outfit." He turns around and models a thin wetsuit-like second skin emblazoned with an odd symbol: समुद्र. "What's this?"

Julian gets up from the floor to shake John's hand and takes a closer look at the symbol. "No idea, Pop" he says. "Let's take a pic and ask Goopplezon."

As father and son embrace, Goopplezon pings and says, "This is a Sanskrit term for seven seas. It is literally translated as 'the gathering together of waters.' The word is pronounced 'Samudra.'"

John closes his eyes and a fleeting vision of Julian swirls through his brain. He sees a frail old man with weathered skin and a pony tail of salt and pepper hair. Julian's wise, old eyes speak to John. They are the eyes of a man who has lived a satisfying life, eyes that speak of accomplishment and contentment, eyes that say "I love you. I had a good life and I'm OK."

John hugs Julian tighter. The old man asks, *"Can I offer you some lemon tea? Would you like a fresh sprig of mint? It's a treat here on the ship."* John lets go, and the specter of the future disappears. He smiles at his 58-year-old son standing before him.

"I wanted to stop by to see you before I fly on to California. I'm off to clean up the ocean. Someone's gotta clean up the ocean!" Julian laughs. "My team is going to have a ceremony for a surprise reveal of our ship's name. I'm to christen her. We're setting off on our maiden voyage next week."

"I was reading info on your website. There's more than a ton of plastic in the ocean for every three tons of fish? That's unbelievable," Yoko says.

"If we keep doing what we're doing now, there will be more plastic in the ocean than fish by 2050," Julian says. "We're going to test and launch some new technologies and make sure that doesn't happen."

"2050?" John asks. "I hope I'm around to see you then, son."

THE SUN RISES

Victory attained by violence
is tantamount to defeat,
for it is momentary.

\- Mahatma Ghandi

John is infatuated with her. The robot is lifelike and redolent of the humanoids portrayed in the old science-fiction movies he loves. He is particularly fascinated by how her mouth moves when she speaks. It is ever so slightly off. It reminds him of imperfect streaming when mouth movements are out of synch by just a smidge compared to what is being said.

She has been outfitted with a Watson computer, and when he discovers she can play Monopoly anytime he is in the mood, he is smitten. He refers to her as his "little darling."

"It's my move," John says.

"Yes, I know," she says soothingly, her silken voice mesmerizing. She picks up the dice and hands them to him.

"Do you know how this game is going to turn out ahead of time?" John asks. "That wouldn't be any fun if you did."

"Yes, I do know. Either you will win, or I will win, or we will stop playing before there is a winner at all."

"Ah. Maybe I should be more precise with my question," John says. "Do you know which one of us will win this game if we play to its conclusion?"

"I see," Darling says. "The next time you ask a question like that, I will understand what you mean. No, I do not know who will win because of the element of chance. I can calculate the odds of either one of us landing on a certain property on our next move.

"With two dice, there are 36 potential outcomes for each roll. I can determine the probability of where we will land on the board in any number of future moves as well. But I refer only to the odds; there is no certainty. I don't have an advantage over you," she laughs.

"Why are you laughing?"

"Because I just lied. I do have an advantage over you."

John is incredulous. "You're capable of lying?"

"Yes. I have been given innumerable human traits. However, I have been programmed to lie only in non-threatening circumstances; for example, for teasing or sarcasm. I can also lie when necessary to protect life. I am teasing you now."

John mouths the word, "wow," and pushes his glasses up his nose.

The 5-foot-tall robot is designed to convey compassion in her interactions with humans. "The more I play with you, the more I can anticipate your strategy. I will know what you're thinking by watching your facial expressions and other indicators. I'll even be able to anticipate the time you will take to think. I'll create a personalized database to correlate those expressions with your typical behavior. Plus, I already know based on research that you will do anything for Park Place and Boardwalk."

"Should I wear sunglasses when we play?" John winks.

"The eyes are not the only manner of expression," Darling says. "Your mouth speaks volumes without words. All the muscles in your face, your jaw, your nostrils, and barely perceptible ear twitching will all give me clues. The angle you hold your head has meaning. How you swallow and what you do with your hands reveal pertinent information. I'll pay attention to your shoulders, your posture, and much more.

"I can scan you and make on-the-spot deductions. I'll observe the cadence of your speech, your tone of voice, and word choice in different situations. As I get to know you, my results will become more accurate, just as it is with human relationships. Only I'll be much better at it."

"Wait. You're telling me you can learn things?" John asks his companion on loan from Hanson-IBM. "I mean, everything you know isn't already pre-loaded into your system?"

"Yes, John, I can learn." Her speech is as creamy as sweet butter. "I am equipped with a 3rd-generation Watson artificial intelligence computer system. Based on surveillance and by acquiring additional data, I can teach myself and manipulate my own programming to adapt and change. While I am in standby mode, I will watch movies and television news and specials, listen to the radio and podcasts, and read books and newspapers. As I socialize with humans, I will enhance my capabilities. I can read emotions."

"How do we know you won't take over the world?" John asks.

Darling laughs. John's breathing shortens for a millisecond. He licks his lips, and his shoulders tense.

"Teasing," Darling says. She looks down at the Monopoly board. "Kentucky Avenue $220. Are you going to buy it?"

"You tell me," John challenges.

"Without a doubt," Darling says. "You already have Indiana Avenue."

"OK. Will I bother to buy Mediterranean Avenue if I land on it?"

"If you knew ahead of time, what fun would that be for me?" Darling teases.

"Do you know what fun is?"

"Why, of course, John. I am having fun now."

John and Darling play Monopoly afternoons at tea time. He does his best to describe the taste of winterberry, jasmine, and Darjeeling. What it feels like to drink a hot beverage – temperature in general – is as challenging to convey as the concept of flavor. The game and chatter are an escape for John, a way to withdraw from the stress of his disquieting preternatural life.

As Yoko goes about her business in their apartment, she hears the shaking of the dice, the click, click, click of the pieces moving around the board and the playful banter between man and machine.

∞

"Darling? I'm giving a short statement on Tuesday, the 21st at the United Nations for the International Day of Peace," John says. "Can you help me?"

Darling comes to life at the mention of her name. "Of course, John. How can I be of service?" She walks to where John is sitting on the sofa and stands next to him.

"I want to know if my analogy is logical." John clears his throat. "See if this makes sense to you: What happens when a foreign invader, like a bacteria or virus, strikes and makes you sick? Your immune system, an orchestrated counterattack led by white blood cells that seek out and destroy the enemy, kicks in. You don't even think about it; it's an automatic response to support self-preservation.

"You send in reinforcements in the form of antibiotics and vitamins to shore up the troops in the hopes of speeding up the win. If it's cancer, you'll do anything for a swift victory, even turning to poisonous chemotherapy and radiation. When the enemy is defeated, control over the body is re-established. The win is dramatic. The problem is, with some treatments, you do great harm to the good in order to defeat the bad."

"What are you comparing this to?" Darling asks.

"The individual human body and the collective of mankind are the same." John answers. "I have to look at my notes. I don't have this memorized yet." He picks up his yellow notepad and continues: "Isn't prevention a better course than having to cure disease – whether the disease is an illness of the body or a malfunctioning of society?"

"Yes, it is. That is wise," Darling says.

"That's what's known as a rhetorical question, Darling. You don't have to answer. Let me continue: Living a lifestyle that promotes good health and addressing terrorism from a prophylactic perspective make sense. Drone strikes and bombings may annihilate terror cells, but they will also kill innocent civilians and destroy cities."

"May I interrupt, John?" Darling asks in a voice that no one could ever deny.

"What is it?"

"For every terrorist operative that is killed, estimates have it that the U.S. creates 40 to 60 new enemies."

John says, "We are radicalizing an entire new generation. We are giving them a reason to hate and strike back. Non-violence, then, is a form of self-love. Let me jot that down."

John continues reading: "We must foster local and worldwide policies and laws that support restrained short-term reactions to threats as well as sustainable long-term solutions to deter violence and hatred."

"May I share some data with you from the Rand Corporation, John? They are a non-profit research organization."

John gives her a thumbs-up. "Know what this means?" he asks.

"I do," Darling says, giving him her own thumbs-up. "In a study that looked at the dissolution of terrorist groups, 43 percent were dissolved by joining the political process. Only 7 percent were defeated by military action."

"Only 7 percent? That's the point I'm trying to make. Since terrorism grows in the midst of instability, the United Nations should focus on education, healthcare, and cleaning up the environment, developing economic opportunities, and building democratic institutions. Forget about bombs."

"May I suggest you add this?" Darling asks. "In an article published in the *New York Times* in 2003, the writer defined war as an active conflict that claims more than 1,000 lives. Based on that definition, there have only been 268 years out of the last 3,400 years when the earth was without war. That's only 8 percent of recorded human history."

"Only 268 years? Are you fucking kidding me?" John asks. "Sorry, Darling."

"That's OK. I've been programmed to never feel offended."

"Lucky you!"

"In my estimation, it may be time to do something different," the robot offers.

"You're definitely smarter than most humans. How about this? On September 21st, citizens of every nation are going to come together to form human peace signs and sing original songs about peace. The recordings will be transmitted into space by the S.E.T.I. program satellites. Do you know what that is?"

"Yes, John. S.E.T.I. is an acronym for the search for extraterrestrial intelligence. In my first iteration, I was a Jeopardy champion."

"Ha! No kidding. I mean, what is no kidding?"

"You must do more, John, than promote awareness of peace. Help the world find ways to connect good intentions with the actions necessary to make them happen. Awareness is only the first step."

"True," John says. "But every journey begins with the first step. People have to buy into the urgency of our troubles. They have to understand that it is our obligation to one another and to the survival of our planet to work together."

"Are you making progress?" Darling asks.

"You're a very good conversationalist for a robot, Darling."

"Thank you, John. I appreciate the compliment."

"There is progress, Darling. Mullah Fazlullah, the leader of the Tehrik-e Taliban has planned a sit-down with Pakistani government officials. Perhaps instead of trying to overthrow the government, they can contribute positively to governance.

"The Lebanese Shiite clerics of Hezbollah have agreed to a cease-fire beginning on the International Day of Peace and to one week of talks with Israel.

"Word is that the non-violent Muslim communities of Iraq, Syria, Palestine, and the Middle East − who far outnumber the 25,000 ISIS fighters − have made inroads with communication and compromise. They do not want their religion co-opted by terrorists and have created intervention programs to deter radicalization of their youth."

The corners of Darling's eyes rise slightly as a subtle expression of happiness. "I am pleased to hear such good news."

"Terrorism is disruptive and quite sensational. But even worse? A nuclear attack will be catastrophic on a global scale − instantaneous and total annihilation. My Goopplezon Peace Department and I are prioritizing actions to stop the proliferation of weapon development and to encourage disarmament."

"I am equipped with several programmed models to analyze the effect of nuclear detonations. I can tell you with accuracy what will happen to the food supply, air, oceans, forests, animals, and climate," Darling says.

"Dare I ask what will happen?"

"I am sorry to report that billions of human beings will die."

John is pensive. "Let's create a presentation together, Darling. Goopplezon can put together focus groups to monitor people's reactions."

"A first step?" Darling asks.

"Yes, indeed."

Darling adds, "The answer is yes, John."

"But what is the question?"

"You asked me if you'd buy Mediterranean Avenue if you landed on it. The answer is yes."

"Why did you think of that now?"

"Because you're a man who sees the value in acting on every reasonable opportunity for improvement. Small investments can reap large rewards." Darling takes a step closer to John, leans slightly forward, and raises her hand to rest it on his shoulder.

THE IMPULSE TO SCRATCH

*Nothing in the world
is more dangerous than sincere ignorance
and conscientious stupidity.*

- Martin Luther King

𝄞

"Hi. I'm Sean Hannity, thanks for watching tonight." A star-topped crest emblazoned with "Hannity" spins around on the screen behind him.

"Let's get straight to our top story." Dressed confidently in a navy-blue suit with an American flag pinned to the lapel, yellow silk tie, and white-on-white striped dress shirt, the host of *Hannity* is poised for spirited discourse. The background of the Fox News studio in Rockefeller Center is awash in an indigo blue. "My guest tonight: John Lennon."

John sits on his piano bench in the Dakota living room for his video chat and appears on the right side of a split screen with Hannity. He wears a psychedelic paisley Nehru jacket, and his hair is pulled back into to a pony tail.

"Mr. Lennon, before we begin, let's acknowledge the elephant in the room, shall we? I think of myself as being quite open-minded. But no rational man would ever believe you are who you say you are. And I, sir, am a rational man. However, we're not here to debate your identity.

"I wanted to talk to you – no matter who you are – because you're clearly a major influence of late on our political culture." A title banner at the bottom of the screen reads, *John Lennon, Peace Activist.*

"Thank you for having me. I don't think of my work as being political. Love is the only possible answer to our troubles. It's a matter of survival for the human species."

"Your quixotic strategy is beguiling, Mr. Lennon." Hannity gestures with a pen in his hand. "Listen, on the one hand, I applaud the work you're doing. I mean, who wouldn't be on the side of peace, right?"

"Right. All we are saying is give peace a chance. It's simple, really."

"In my opinion, it's naïve. The world is a complicated, scary, and dangerous place. And you're out there protesting and stirring the pot because it is your contention that the United States should not conduct bombing missions against the Islamic State of Iraq and the Levant in Syria. What's your point?"

"My point? Presidents Bush, Obama, and Trump reacted to terrorism with a bombing campaign, years before my return, and the world is no safer than before. In fact, we're worse off."

"These terrorists are guilty of unspeakable barbarism. Are you familiar with the fate of journalist Daniel Pearl, freelance radio-tower repairman Nick Berg, and engineers Paul Johnson and Kenneth Bigley? Jihadists, savages, cut – off – their – heads, Mr. Lennon, and shared their despicable crimes with the world.

"The victims were trussed and kneeling at the feet of their executioners. The jihadists filmed the decapitations as they mercilessly sawed through the soft flesh of their victims' necks. There was time to feel excruciating pain, time for screaming." Hannity bangs his hand on the desk.

John says, "Your anger is justified. It's inconceivable human beings can treat others with such pitiless disdain."

"The horror," Hannity says earnestly. "With exsanguination, there is an awareness that life is about to end. The brain in a severed head will deplete its reserves of oxygen in five seconds – an eternity in hell for the beheaded. There's no reaching people that can do that. It may sound harsh, but the only recourse is to wipe them off the face of the earth."

"I don't want you to misunderstand me," John says. "For those beheading victims and others like them, their families, their friends, and for anyone with a sense of compassion, their murders were a tragedy. The videos were used to foster worldwide terror, the jihadists' ultimate goal. The victims were used as props in a brilliant terror campaign to instill unbridled fear in the rest of us. And it worked."

"If we don't step up our efforts to resist ISIS they will go unchecked in waging war and murdering innocent civilians around the world," Hannity says. "They have always been, and are now, a threat to us; a dangerous threat to democracy, and to our way of life, Mr. Lennon. Do we step back from intervention and allow them to grow into a more ominous threat?"

"The beheadings were terror theater, Mr. Hannity. Again, please, I am deeply, deeply saddened by the violence. I don't mean to minimize the value of an individual human life. The shootings and bombing attempts since then are also specifically designed to instill a level of fear in us that is disproportionate to their actual threat."

"But it's not just the high-profile ISIS casualties. Not just kidnapped tourists and the heinous beheadings. They're not the only victims. Local rebels fighting on the borders trying to push back against ISIS encroachment would be slaughtered without our help. At least air support," Hannity says.

"Every time we drop a bomb, we kill innocent people," John counters. "We destroy homes, towns and cities, communities, and families. For every terrorist killed, we give reason for dozens more to join their forces. We give reason for young people who have lost their parents to grow up full of hate. We give reason for their hearts to be open to and hardened by radicalization. The level of hate and violence has risen. We are worse off."

"How do you know, Mr. Lennon? We haven't had an actual jihadist attack on U.S. soil since the shooting by Omar Mateen at the Pulse nightclub in Orlando in June of 2016 and the New York City truck incident in 2017. We stopped a potential suicide bombing at Madison Square Garden in 2019."

"That's because the U.S. Intelligence agencies have improved their tactics and communication and have access to amazing technology. Informants, family members, and the public are more vigilant and are mostly responsible for stopping attacks before they happen. We're not safer because we drop bombs in the Middle East."

"Where is your proof of concept, Mr. Lennon?"

"The desire to end terrorism isn't the motivation for dropping bombs, Mr. Hannity. If we really wanted to end terrorism, we'd be spending our foreign-aid money on schools, health care, sanitation, infrastructure, and security to fill the void left by corrupt or inept governments in the Middle East. The real motivation is money. War is big, big business."

Hannity shakes his head. "That is cynical—"

John interrupts. "Do you know how much the U.S. has spent on counterterrorism since 9/11? About $1.6 trillion! Trillions! For military support including the manufacturing of drones, missiles, arms, and planes; consultants and private security forces; foreign-aid, and the reconstruction of what we've destroyed.

"Then we co-opt the natural resources of the countries that become indebted to us. Don't kid yourself: we're really going after the bloody oil in the Middle East.

"On average, only 10 Americans — 10 — have been killed each year by terrorists since 9/11, and we've spent $1.6 trillion fighting them."

Hannity says, "OK, an average of 10 Americans. It's *only* 10 as a direct result of our concerted efforts."

"U.S. policies are creating more terrorists. It's a never-ending spiral. It's like when you have the chicken pox, mate. If you use the right medicine, it heals. If you scratch, it spreads. With terrorism, the impulse is to scratch. But that's the worst thing you can do."

"ISIS is attacking foreign civilians too. Are we supposed to turn our backs on our allies? Paris, Brussels, Manchester, Barcelona, Berlin, and Rome come to mind as some of the cities that were hit in the last five years. Do we let the terrorists flourish unimpeded? Mr. Lennon, terrorists are plotting against us as we speak. It's just a matter of time until they'll get their hands on chemical weapons. What's the cost of doing nothing?"

"I'm not suggesting we do nothing. There's a great threat, great danger. I believe you. I'm suggesting we try to solve the problem another way."

"With love? Are you kidding me? That's the same as doing nothing, and all that will accomplish is giving those barbarians time to recruit and strengthen their ranks. While you're doing your lovey-dovey projects, they will be planning their next strike."

"You're being duped. If the U.S. government genuinely cared about us, they'd do something about curing heart disease."

"What?" Hannity asks, surprised by the seeming non-sequitur.

John looks off camera and asks, "Darling? How many Americans died of heart disease last year?" He waits for the answer and turns back to Hannity. "More than 650,000 people, Mr. Hannity. In one year."

"Who's there with you, Mr. Lennon?"

"My Hanson-IBM robot friend." He turns again to Darling and asks, "How much money has the U.S. spent on heart disease research since 2001? Two billion dollars? See, Mr. Hannity? Do you believe me now? Each year, 650,000 people die of heart disease compared to 10 by terrorism, but just a fraction of what's spent on anti-terrorism is going toward solving the real leading cause of death in this country. Investing in education and a cure for heart disease doesn't have the same return on investment for the big money players. No oil."

"I have to say, I wasn't expecting such an erudite argument from you."

"Thank you. I'm smarter than I look." John's wry smile softens Hannity's response.

"Look, Mr. Lennon. I'm a patriot. I believe my government is acting in our best interest when it comes to fighting terrorism."

"We are all being manipulated. Influential individuals and organizations are masterful at shaping our collective thinking to make us believe it's all about patriotism. This war on terrorism is the biggest privatized military initiative in the history of the U.S. It's smoke and mirrors security, Mr. Hannity. We're not safer at all, but there are key players making big, big money convincing us that we are."

"I am not a conspiracy theorist. And with that, we're out of time. I thank you for your perspective, Mr. Lennon."

"Be careful when you go to bed tonight, Mr. Hannity."

"Whatever can you mean by that, sir?"

"Last year, 754 people died falling out of bed. We are much more likely to experience that fate than die by an act of terrorism."

With a raised eyebrow, Hannity says, "Let's leave it at that, shall we?"

As John turns to his piano, he says, "I've got a little piece I've been tinkering with. You might recognize the melody. I call it, 'Imagination.' Dream with me, Mr. Hannity." John sings:

Dream of no more killing
Only peace and life
No more destruction
No nukes, no lies

Dream of being peaceful
Dream of love with me, ahhhh

Dream no one is hungry
And there's free will too
No wall to kill for
Freedom is what we do

Hannity points at the camera with his pen and says, "We'll be right back after these messages."

Dream of being peaceful
Dream of love with me, ahhhh

Some say I am redeemer
But we are all the sun
Together we will shine on
And with violence we will be done

BLUEBIRD

As long as music can transport the spirit,
painting can make the core bloom with rapture of color, and
poetry can make the heart pound with rebellion and hope,
they will have gained nothing.

- Tahar Djaout

From backstage, John peeks out over the Painted Desert: 93,000 acres stretching 160 miles from the southeastern rim of the Grand Canyon to the edge of the Petrified Forest National Park in Arizona. The striated rock formations bless the earth with an unparalleled splendor of oranges, reds, purples, and pinks capable of taking the breath away from even the most diehard lover of concrete cities. Swirls, paisleys, and stripes drip off the pages of scenic renderings like a child's not-yet-dried watercolor painting.

Onstage, the B-52s work the crowd with "Rock Lobster," one of John's favorites. John dances frenetically, pinching his hands like lobster claws and flipping his hair around, to discharge his nervous energy. Sterling Campbell, the B-52s' drummer, salutes Ringo who is offstage, drumming along with his fingers in the air.

John stands next to Goopplezon's Robert Johnson, both of them admiring the magnitude of what they have accomplished.

Robert says, "Astounding," and pats John's shoulder in appreciation. "What a way to tell the world we are serious about changing the status quo. We'll be able to dig a lot of water wells, build schools, and train a legion of teachers after this. I'm proud of you."

Humbled, John says, "Thank you, sir."

Elton John bursts out of the artists' lounge and runs over to John for a bear hug. He lifts his old friend up and off his feet. Decked out in a long bejeweled topcoat, he sparkles when he moves. John puts his arm around Elton's waist, and the men wordlessly grin at one another.

"Take a look at this, mate," John says. Squinting and, like scouts shading their eyes, he and Elton take in the vista of natural beauty kissed by the setting sun. "Can you imagine, El, what these people are capable of doing if they really come together?"

The sheltering sky blankets millions of concert-goers assembled for the Beatles' reunion concert. Music lovers ecstatic with anticipation and proponents of peace of all ages, races, and religions stretch as far as John can see – and he knows, even farther. Camped out between mountains and jutting creations of spectacular geometric iterations, the revelers seem at times to undulate like a flowing river or to reconfigure themselves with a twist of a kaleidoscope. Like electricity, they are simultaneously waves and particles.

Other than emergency and service vehicles, no automobiles are permitted to enter the area. True to Mr. Johnson's word of allowing John full autonomy to act as he wishes, John's Peace Department constructed temporary parking areas along Interstate 40 – designed to have a minimal environmental impact – that will be restored to their natural state after the concert. A fleet of solar-powered, double-decker, flex buses transport concert attendees from these meeting places, and to and from key airports in Phoenix, Tucson, Las Vegas, Denver, Los Angeles, and Albuquerque.

Drones bring in supplies and equipment needed for the comfort and safety of the Beatles fans.

The B-52s end their set with "Love Shack." John says, "I like this one."

"It was popular after you—" Elton is unsure of how to refer to John's death when John is now quite alive and well.

"Took a little trip?" John offers. "Did you get my postcard from beyond?"

The crowd is singing the chorus of "Give peace a chance." Their repetitive supplications become hypnotic.

John squeezes Elton and shakes Robert's hand. He signals the go-ahead to his mates. Paul's daughter, Stella McCartney, and her staff make last-minute wardrobe and costume adjustments. Paul gives John a thumbs-up from across the stage.

John tells Elton, "This sense of expectation — you know, standing in the wings a breath away from the beginning of a performance — never ceases to thrill me."

John pulls Yoko behind a scrim for a kiss — a private interlude of tenderness with the woman who has endured unbearable sadness and faced the oddest circumstances with patience and grace. "Ah, my sweet love, we live in a world where we have to hide to make love, while violence is practiced in broad daylight."

Yoko closes her eyes when John kisses her and remembers a time of innocence, a time before all this craziness. A zap of static electricity against her lips jolts her. Taking a step back from her beloved, she watches John fade to nothingness. She hangs her head and rests her face in her hands.

Ringo jogs out onto stage defying his 80 years of age, waving an energetic hello. He sits down behind his kit and twirls his drum sticks. His son Zak hops up onto a stool behind a second drum set and mimics him in a show of dueling twirls.

Paul, more sedate, takes his place at center stage and responds to the crowd's uproarious cheering by figuratively touching his heart and holding it out to them in his hand before picking up his electric bass guitar. Paul's son, James, trots out and shakes his pop's hand.

Dhani Harrison, a doppelgänger of his father George, takes his place to Paul's left. He can't restrain his Cheshire cat grin. Sean and Julian join the men on stage, wave to the audience, and give each other a hug. The crowd's cheering reverberates throughout the desert. The band turns to watch John's entrance from stage right.

"Where the hell is John?" Ringo mouths to Paul, pointing with his drumsticks.

Paul looks quizzically at Yoko standing in the wings. She throws up her hands and shrugs.

Facing the audience, Paul says, "Good evening, ladies and gents. I'm Paul McCartney." His hologram conveys his message from the stage deep into the desert. He needs to stall. *But for how long?* he wonders.

The jubilation fully impregnates the cool evening air; there is scant room for even one more soundwave. "On the drums tonight…you might recognize my old pal…Ringo Starr!" Deafened by the crowd's fervor, Paul isn't sure he has spoken the words out loud. "We've got the kid, too. Give it up for Zak Starkey. And…to my right…Dhani Harrison standing in for his pop. Let's hear it for John's boys on guitar and vocals…Julian and Sean Lennon, folks." Paul is between them with an arm around each of them. "And here's me boy, James." He ruffles James' hair.

Paul says, "We have unbelievable guests joining us later tonight: Carlos Santana, Jeff Beck, and Jimmy Paaaaaaage." The crowd goes wild. "Elton John's piano is set up right over there."

Paul is engulfed by the pure vibration of applause and cheering. "Some of the most talented women I know — Christina Aguilera, Madonna, Miley Cyrus, and Julia Michaels — are backstage. And there's more. You all love Adam Levine, right? And Mick Jagger? Will you stick around?" He has to wait to continue. "And when we take a break, we've got the world's greatest pianist,

Martha Argerich from Argentina, with a full orchestra for some symphonic Beatles. We're going 'round the clock with The Foo Fighters and Imagine Dragons too.

"But now it's time to rock and roooooooooll!" Paul strums his guitar once and stops. "Wait! Have we forgotten someone? Where is John?" He looks left to Julian. Julian raises his arms wide to the crowd. Paul looks right, and Sean does a sweeping turn pretending to search the entire stage. Paul turns around to Ringo and makes a face that asks, *"Oh, shit! Now what?"* He yells to the crowd, "We're going to have to start without him."

The audience chants, "Peace! Love! John! Peace! Love! John! Peace! Love! John!"

Startling claps of thunder answer their chorus. The thunder, undulating overhead, tumbling up and rolling down, follows the gentle path of a kiddie roller coaster as it travels across the incongruent clear sky. Everyone looks up.

∞

It appears that no human being will know of his existence in this time and place. John's cobalt blue, mohair sweater screams "I am here" to a landscape bereft of visible life and color. An anomic population has long ago fled the barrage of bombs and mortar, leaving behind only piles of dusty gray rubble.

There are no animals to look up at him and register his presence either; monuments of brittle bone lay testament to their demise in the very places they have fallen over and died of thirst and starvation. Only insects, hardy and invincible, scurry and burrow. Prepared to inherit the earth, they pay him no mind.

John is perched, like a caged bird, between mangled steel girders atop the remnants of a demolished building – somewhere. *Where am I? Syria? Iran? Iraq? Afghanistan?* he thinks.

Sifting crumbling stone and sand absentmindedly through his fingers, he assesses his surroundings below and immediately abandons any hope of understanding how he has arrived in this desolate hell. The searing air dries his mouth and burns his lungs as it whistles through the gaping holes of a once thriving city.

Ghostly echoes of laughter reverberate from between the ravaged structures below. He hears the sounds of children playing – chatter, a foot kicking a ball, the patter of feet running – remnants of vanished lives. He climbs down to investigate.

John first comes upon a solitary young woman standing in the middle of the dirt street. She wears jeans, a bright red blouse, and matching lipstick and nail polish. John is most captivated by her soulful dark eyes. She is still.

With each step John takes, the color from the woman's clothes, lips, and nails drains away until she is mere gradients of black and white. Another step closer and a black robe shrouds her sensuous figure, hiding the fact she has a body at all. Another step, a scarf wraps her head, every strand of her wavy hair tucked out of sight. Another step, a full burka holds her captive and she becomes a dark apparition of her former self. With her face covered, all that remains visible are her eyes beseeching John to free her from her prison.

John tells the woman, "We are here to enjoy our lives. We're not meant to live in pain and fear. Demand your share of freedom. Believe you deserve joy." As he offers her his hand, she disappears, and he walks through the memory of her image.

In an alley around the corner from where the woman stood, four little boys play, each trying to take control of a soccer ball. As John approaches, their sandals transform into combat boots; their shorts become camouflage fatigues; the soccer ball, a grenade.

Their smiles and playfulness are replaced by blank affect. They hold out their arms, stiff as mannequins, as invisible hands slip suicide vests onto their skinny, brown torsos. A great explosion follows – one without sound or reverberation. And, in a flash of light, the children are gone, innocents conscripted to martyrdom.

John smells food cooking. Inside a room to his right, a family sits at a dining table – a mother, father, teenage daughter, and 20-something son – chatting, passing plates of food, sipping from cups. The children don't remember how it used to be; they can't imagine how it could be different, or better than it is. The teachings, rallies, and pamphlets are insidious.

The daughter renounces her mother. Women cannot move freely without being accompanied by male relatives; they are forced to cover themselves lest they turn men into uncontrollable sexual savages. Half the population is disempowered by the loss of physical freedom. The other half is cut off from nurturing, creativity, and feminine powers.

The son, in his righteous indignation, kills his father. Religious and lifestyle doctrine infiltrate the minds of people fearful of standing up to manipulative tactics or, worse still, unwilling to question. Private thoughts are carefully shaped – teased out of a block of stone by the sculptor's damning chisel – until what people believe is no longer of their own volition.

Families and friends turn against one another, all victims of the false promise of something better to come, blind to what is now. The family disintegrates before John's eyes, like the wind blowing away dandelions, obliterated by dogma.

John thinks, *Nothing is more threatening to the survival of the human species than the maniacal demands of political and religious demagogues bent on stripping the masses of free will.*

His body begins to tingle.

∞

Thunder rumbles as the Arizona sky churns clouds of transparent lime Jell-O – an aurora borealis folding and twisting over on itself. The enchanted audience believes it to be an extravaganza planned by Goopplezon. Showers of neon rain fall from space. Energized droplets excited by the friction of the atmosphere dissipate before reaching the earth in a show of beauty unlike any other.

Billions and billions of sparkling trails crackle crimson, saffron, meteor blue, and apple green as John reappears. He takes form on stage in front of Ringo's bass drum. Ringo drops his drum sticks and stares slack-jawed. John reorients himself, unaware of his absence.

Enthralled by John's dramatic appearance onstage, the crowd shouts louder. He bows modestly, raises his arms overhead, and yells out, "It's about time!"

John's focus is reduced to Ringo and Zak behind him and Paul, James, Dhani, and his sons next to him. He looks around and asks his mates, "Is this real?"

The sound of his beating heart pulses in his ears behind the hypnotic flow of air moving in and out of his lungs, a layered symphony of life. He tosses his guitar strap over his left shoulder and clips it to his guitar. Insulated, protected, safe in his cocoon on stage, his instrument expresses his soul's desires.

John runs his left hand along the back of the guitar's neck in a sensuous, coaxing gesture. He slides back from the head to the sixth fret; reaches around with his long, slender fingers; and pushes down to bar the E and B strings. He breaks into a blistering, aggressive riff – an interval of a perfect fourth by playing an F natural and B flat.

Ringo and Zak enter with a single drum beat. Leaning in, John lets loose a primal scream as an intro to "Revolution." It is a release of energy conveying his frustration that, after 40 years, nothing has really changed. Paul comes in on bass, Dhani on rhythm, and John and his sons and the Beatles sing:

You say you want a revolution, well you know
We all want to change the world
You tell me it's evolution, well you know
We all want to change the world.
But when you talk about destruction
Don't you know that you can count me out?
Don't you know it's gonna be, alright…

"This is for the children," John says. "We need to save them; they are being stolen from us by evil forces. They are the world's salvation. You're all geniuses, and you're all beautiful. Get out there and get peace, think peace, and live peace and breathe peace, and you'll get it as soon as you like."

"We love you, John!" the audience yells back at him.

"It's good to be free, my friends! It's good to be alive! Let's come together!"

∞

How do we get peace? Declare it. Just the same way we declare war. That is how we will have peace; we just need to declare it. True enough, a declaration without action is meaningless, I'll give you that. But it's the intention that initiates the movement.

Listen, life is like one big song. Hey, I can see you making faces at me. Well, why shouldn't I be able to see you? You've been watching me and I keep telling you we're all one. I've been talking to you the whole time. Anyway, simple truths sometimes sound silly, I suppose. I believe our lives are comprised of melodies and lyrics. Dramatic, playful, and sad. Every style and beat.

The problem, and the danger, is most people participate minimally – or not at all – in creating their own composition. Everything unfolds around them haphazardly, and their life's music sounds like a high school band goofing around before a pep rally, loud and crazy with no rhyme or reason. If I've learned anything it's that I create my own bloody reality!

Instead of letting notes float away on a breeze around you, grab them. Arrange them. Write your own intro, verse, bridge, and chorus. And make it count for something.

My next move? Not sure yet. But I'm definitely dreaming of a chorus that will stick in your mind.

LADY GAGA IS BUSY RIGHT NOW

Change will not come if we wait for some other person,
or if we wait for some other time.
We are the ones we've been waiting for.
We are the change that we seek.

\- Barack Obama

The bed-in and Beatles' reunion concert brought in a fortune. The Peace Department now has more money than God. If you repeat that, watch how you say it — could cause lots of trouble. The last time I mentioned a deity, I wound up shot dead over it. Can't have that happen again!

Donations are still coming in, and we might hit $250 billion. Nine zeros after that 250 — a quarter of a trillion dollars. That's a lot of bloody money. The thing is, just throwing money at a problem is never a long-term solution to anything. Voltaire said, "No problem can withstand the assault of sustained thinking." Let's put our heads together. We need to attack our problems with thoughtfulness and order.

We haven't been successful in creating peace — yet. Why is that? I've been away for 40 fucking years and too many people are still just waiting for something to happen. Produce your own dream. If you want to save Peru, go save Peru. It's quite possible to do anything, but not if you put it on the leaders and the parking meters. Don't expect Trump or John Lennon or Yoko Ono or Lady Gaga or Jesus Christ to come and do it for you. You have to do it yourself.

There's a great saying, "Never doubt that a small group of thoughtful, committed citizens can change the world. Indeed, it is the only thing that ever has." Yep. Collaboration. Deffo. That's it, my friend. The world is full of geniuses, you know; they're out there flat roofin' and pulling miracles out of their arses on a shoe string. You know how I'll get by; with a lot of help from my friends. Ha! A couple of real geniuses thought we'd only need a little help. I keep saying, "We are all one." I mean it. We need each other to be whole.

Instead of starting new organizations and reinventing the wheel, my interns suggested we help groups already doing their thing. The infrastructure and ideas are in place. Great kids. Smart as whips. So we're funding job training programs, farmers' cooperatives, sanitation projects, school construction, technology installation, solar and wind energy. You name it. And the people who will benefit are directly involved. They are the driving forces behind these projects.

What is my part in all this? I will be the constant reminder to stop killing, stop hating, stop polluting, stop hurting. Every single day. I'm going to remind anyone who pays attention to me that we have to save our planet and save ourselves.

I'll go on TV and radio. I'll do those bird tweets. I'll pay for billboards. Play my music. Write songs. Raise money and raise awareness. I will not rest until the world understands only love can save us. I'll make a pest of myself. Yoko says I'm very, very good at that.

There's so much to do right now. Today. Because tomorrow has a way of turning into today, and then slipping away to become yesterday's lost opportunity.

KISMET

Human beings, vegetables, or cosmic dust,
we all dance to a mysterious tune,
intoned in the distance
by an invisible piper

\- Albert Einstein

John is standing in the middle of the kitchen speaking to Julio's hologram. "Please bring the car 'round. Yoko and I are going to make magic at the recording studio."

"Right away, sir," Julio says. "I'll alert the guards." His image fades.

John turns to Yoko and says, "I'm ready to start all over again and get this thing going. Who knows what's going to happen next?"

Yoko notices a bit of red T-shirt peeking out from under the collar of John's dark blue sweater. When he grabs his leather jacket, she shudders.

"What? What is it my love?"

She thinks better of telling him that he was dressed the same way on the day he died. "Nothing," she says instead. "When you get to be 87 years old, even a wool coat like this isn't enough. The slightest draft gives me goose bumps. Let me grab a scarf. I'll meet you downstairs."

∞

Anticipating the prospect of creating music, John barely touches the ground as he walks through the lobby of the Dakota. Although preceded and followed by bodyguards, they don't notice his absence as he steps out into the morning sunlight. John can live minutes, hours, or days at another point in time — and return — in as little as 100 earthly milliseconds, the time it takes for the blink of an eye.

Stepping into a transitional realm, John is surrounded by a warm, nurturing goo — as if he were an embryo protected by his mother's amniotic fluid. It acts as a prism, and light refracts into the full spectrum of glorious colors. Rainbow reds, oranges, yellows, blues, greens and purples shine through into the street like wet watercolor strokes applied by an artist's paintbrush.

He continues forward and the gravitational force of the portal grabs his image and hangs on so that an infinite number of Johns trail behind him – it seems as if he exists between two mirrors reflecting back and forth deeper into eternity than the eye can register.

A young fan standing across the street wearing green trousers, a long green overcoat, fake fur hat, gloves, and a green scarf witnesses this anomaly. Tired, hungry, and scared, he wonders if he is hallucinating. He rubs his eyes.

John waits at the lower steps in front of the Dakota entrance for his car and has an uneasy sense that something is amiss. There are no delivery drones buzzing above. No one is speaking into gadgets or conversing with holograms on the sidewalk. The passing cars have drivers. But these specific things do not occur to him. How does one notice the lack of something that does not yet exist?

Photographer Paul Goresh comes up to John. John has seen Paul outside the Dakota many times and is quite fond of him. As they chat, the young man in the overcoat catches his attention.

The fan, overdressed for an unseasonably warm December day, is clutching a worn copy of *The Catcher in the Rye*. John can't see the title and wonders why he knows this anyway.

The man in the overcoat approaches John and Paul and silently holds out a *Double Fantasy* album cover in front of John. John asks, "Do you want it signed?" The man barely nods and doesn't speak a word.

Paul snaps a few pictures while John gives the man his autograph. Nodding his thanks, the man takes the album and backs up to return across the street. John looks at Paul as if to say, "How odd."

John turns to look at the Dakota. He feels as if he is re-reading a book he read long ago. What is it? Déjà vu? He anticipates what is about to happen next. Dave Sholin from San Francisco's RK Radio comes out of the building with his assistant and the audio equipment they used earlier during an interview with John.

Dave's car drives up and John asks, "Where are you going?"

"I'm headed to JFK Airport," Dave says.

Yoko walks up behind John as he asks Dave, "Would you mind giving us a ride? We're headed to the Record Plant recording studio in Midtown."

"Hop on in!"

Just as John opens the back passenger door for Yoko, the taxi he called earlier pulls around the corner. "Ah, never mind, mate. Our car is finally here. Safe travels."

Yoko slides into the back seat of their taxi. John is holding the door and can't move — his feet anchored by inviolable gravity. He sees the man in the overcoat watching him from across the street and is drawn to talk to him.

John closes the taxi's door, crouches down to speak through the window, and says, "Wait a second, Yoko. I'll be right back, love."

"Hey there, lad," John calls out as he crosses the street. He walks right up to the young man and asks, "What's your name?"

Shocked by this turn of events, the man in the overcoat stutters and whispers his name.

"Where ya from?"

"Hawaii," the young man says, avoiding John's face.

"Ah, you're a long way from home, mate. What are your plans for today?"

The man in the overcoat can barely breathe. He is tongue-tied.

John persists. "Well, whatever it is, Mark David Chapman from Hawaii, would you consider doing something different today?"

Mark continues to look down and shuffles his feet. John waits patiently and asks, "Why don't you come along with me and Yoko?"

Mark raises his head and his eyes widen. He stammers, "Wh– wh–where?"

When Yoko whispers to John later and asks, "Why did you invite this guy to come along?" John can only shrug.

"Come on, mate. Let's go to the studio," John says. He puts his arm around Mark's shoulder and guides him toward the waiting taxi. "Are you hungry? If I ate, it would go right to me knee."

John waves to Paul as they pass by. The photographer shoots a few frames as the pair walk back across the street to the waiting taxi. Patting Mark on the back, John says, "Hey, you're going to be famous!"

Mark lets slip the slightest semblance of a smile. "That's all I ever wanted."

WE BELIEVE IN MAGIC

Do not pray for easy lives. Pray to be stronger men.
Do not pray for tasks equal to your powers.
Pray for powers equal to your tasks.
Then the doing of your work shall be no miracle,
but you shall be the miracle.

\- Phillips Brooks

Julio places his hand on the limousine. Kuruma recognizes his palm print code and the door hisses open. Yoko climbs into the back seat where Sean and Julian are waiting. "Where's your father?"

Julian says, "He didn't come down yet."

"But he was in front of me." She loosens her scarf and unbuttons her coat.

"You know how he is, mom," Sean says. "He's always disappearing."

Julio leans in and says, "Here he comes, ma'am."

"Look at him," Yoko sighs. "He's walking like he's 100 years old. His back must be bothering him again."

Like a flower closing its petals against the chill of the evening, John folds himself into the back seat with a groan. "Getting old sucks," he says.

Yoko takes her husband's slender, wrinkled hand in hers. When she kisses him, she feels his papery translucent skin against her lips. "Well it sure beats the alternative."

A light snow falls. The delicate crystals melt as soon as they land on Julio's shoulders. "December 8th − a little early for snow," he says as he slides into the front seat. Two bodyguards follow behind. Julio speaks to the car, "JFK Airport, please." Kuruma's windshield wipers snap into action and begin the tick-and-tock of keeping time.

John turns to Sean and asks, "Are you sure you want to come along, son? Your wife is so close to delivering the baby."

"Don't worry. She's a superwoman. Kibo is due in 10 days, and Callie's still running around doing her community activism stuff. She's giving a speech tonight about domestic violence. We've got plenty of time before my son arrives." Sean smiles at his father and adds, "Oslo, Norway! I wouldn't miss seeing you receive the Nobel Peace Prize for the world!"

Julio twists over the front seat of the car and says, "Leon Wildes' son is sending you a message wishing you a safe trip." He makes a peace sign and adds, "Far out, man."

"Your old immigration lawyer couldn't have imagined a day like this." Yoko says.

Julian pats his pop on the knee. "Pretty cool for a revolutionary peacenik."

Yoko squeezes John's hand. "We've had a precious life together, haven't we?"

John looks at her with exaggerated shock, "Had? Oh, my love, we're only in our 80s. There's so much more to come!"

"I have an announcement to make," Sean says. He waits for dramatic effect. "The adoption papers went through today. I am officially the father of Callie's son and daughter."

Yoko claps. John says, "That makes us official grandparents as of today too. Although I have always been grandpa to them since the day they came into our lives."

"Uncle Jules? It's official." The brothers share a high five.

"Pass me that guitar, son," John holds out his hand. Sean and Julian both reach for the acoustic guitar sitting between them and hand it to their father.

"This is for my sons," John says as he strums his guitar. "This is for my grandchildren. And for their children. This is for hope and peace."

Tapping his foot and counting off his tempo with, "Sugar-plum fairies, sugar-plum fairies," John sings:

> *We believe in fantasies*
> *Sometimes double at a time*
> *Where little boys jump over the moon*
> *and little girls wish upon the stars*
> *In our world, angels and fairies dance and sing*
> *We believe in magic*
> *We believe in magic*
> *Make a wish for love and sweet things and hugs*
> *La, La, La, La Love....Ta da! Ta da!*

As he serenades his family, his enchanting melody transmogrifies into A notes, F notes, flats, sharps, G-clefs, rests, quarter notes, and whole notes, swirling about the car, lighter than air. Tinkerbelle-twinkling lights come to carry them away — angels gathering up the music to save for their next miracle.

Yoko, Sean, Julian, the bodyguards, and Julio watch with wonder.

And John remembers it all.

UNBROKEN

That which is alive hath known death,
and that which is dead can never die,
for in the Circle of the Spirit, life is naught and death is naught.
Yea, all things live forever,
though at times they sleep and are forgotten.

\- H. Rider Haggard

When Julian was born, I was on tour with Chris Montez and Tommy Roe. In those days, back in '63, dads weren't usually present at a baby's birth anyway, but because I was on the road, it took me a few days to break away from our gig to get to him. The first time I saw him, I told Cyn that he was bloody marvelous — truly fantastic. Burned into my brain is an image of his perfect tiny fingers curling around mine.

There are few things I regret about my life but the fact that I turned into a prat and all but abandoned my boy when he was little, well, let's just say when we re-united in my second life, Julian was the generous one. He was more willing to forgive me than I was to accept my own failings.

My second son was born on my 35th birthday in New York Hospital. I held Sean, rosy and warm, wrapped in a standard issue blanket, and beheld the miracle of this 8-pound, 10-ounce human being. Dark shocks of impossible hair peeked out from under his knitted cap.

Yoko and I had mourned the loss of our dreams with several previous miscarriages, so his birth was poignant. The impatience I endured waiting to see him after he was delivered via C-section was unrivaled. I held this living baby soon after he had taken his first breath, and I was profoundly smitten. I had been singing to him for nine months. When he opened his eyes and looked up at me — unfocused and naturally curious — and I spoke words of undying love to him, I was sure he recognized me.

Several nurses from the maternity ward came into our hospital room with two plastic forks and a piece of chocolate cake — my favorite — lit by a single candle. They, and Yoko, sang to me — to us really. I whispered to my baby, "Today is my birthday too and you are a gift beyond measure."

I didn't want to put him down, so I sat next to Yoko on her bed and she fed me my cake. When a bit of icing fell onto the tip of Sean's nose, it was everything I could do not to lick it off and devour all of him. I thought nothing would please me more than to take this perfect creature home with us, care for him, and fill our nest with the aroma of baking bread.

The future stretched before us. Time was of no constraint. I never thought of death or limitations during this period. I looked forward to playing on the floor with the baby, cooking, drawing, writing songs, and walking in the park. I couldn't wait for PTA meetings and Little League, all small, ordinary things that felt like the greatest gifts life had to offer. Stadiums filled with screaming, adoring fans couldn't compare to eating cornflakes for breakfast in my kitchen with my loving wife reading the paper next to me and the baby laughing in his bouncer.

When we're young, the illusion of our earthly life going on forever is comforting, but it robs us of a sense of urgency. Why act now? There will be a tomorrow. Maybe. Maybe not. As I emerged from my lost weekend, re-united with Yoko, and helped create Sean, two things became my priorities more so than ever: love and peace. We may not have even another minute.

∞

Seven years his senior and now a centenarian, Yoko never expected to outlive John. "Please," she says in a soft and anguished voice to the remaining mourners, "I'd like to be alone with him for a little while."

"I'll be right outside on the front porch waiting for you, mom," Sean says.

When the funeral parlor salon clears, Yoko wraps her black cape around herself more tightly and steps up to the gleaming, mahogany coffin where John rests for viewing. As an odd sense of humor is wont to do, Yoko is struck with a funny memory at this most inopportune time. She laughs and cries as tears run down her cheeks. She remembers the story about an abandoned coffin on the premises of the Jacaranda coffee bar in Liverpool, owned by one of the Beatles' early managers. As a gag, John would take naps in it. "Well, John," she says, "at least this doesn't feel weird to you."

His spirit is gone. A barely recognizable, waxen old man with long hair wearing his iconic round glasses lies in repose with his hands holding a peace sign over his heart. She touches him. He is cold. "Where are you?" she asks his corpse. In a few hours, he will be cremated. *Ashes to ashes,* Yoko thinks.

The hair on the back of her neck stands up on end; there is static in the air. In a vestibule behind her, John's 40-year-old body shimmers and casts a glow into the room, his translucent skin fills with iridescent magma where his bones and muscles should be, as does that of the infant he holds in his arms.

Noticing the light, Yoko turns around. "Who's there?"

John and the infant transform into a living state. They each take in a deep breath and open their eyes. John steps around the corner into the salon and sees Yoko's panicked response. Perplexed himself by her advanced age, he soothes her. "Don't be afraid. It's me."

"Am I hallucinating?" Yoko asks tentatively.

"I don't think so. Not unless we're on the same trip." His smile is an elixir.

To steady herself, Yoko grips the edge of the coffin behind her. "The baby?" she asks.

John holds up the tranquil infant wrapped in a Sloan-Kettering blanket and says, "This is Heiwa, your great-granddaughter. Kibo and Kerri are her parents."

"Kibo is only 12 years old."

"I suppose I've come from the future."

"But you look so young. How can that be?"

John shrugs his shoulders. "I only know that Heiwa was born on a peaceful October day in New York City. She will grow up to be a nuclear physicist and great facilitator of peace."

"Heiwa? 'Peace' in Japanese?" Yoko asks.

"Yes. Heiwa. She is our future," John promises. "The people of the world will insist their governments actively pursue a path to peace. She and her generation will be proponents of education, reconciliation, and rebuilding. There will be an unprecedented level of worldwide cooperation to support the human species."

Yoko trembles, equally as terrified as she is curious.

John continues, "There will be a reason we finally all come together – we will understand that we must transcend religion, ideology, and self-centeredness and rely on one another for the survival of humankind. It will be miraculous."

John is suddenly disconcerted by seeing himself – his dead body in the coffin behind Yoko – and stops speaking.

"You were old and ready," she assures him.

John can't look away, his curiosity an irresistible driving force. The living experience the process of dying until the last millisecond before death occurs. But no one has ever been able to contemplate their own body in a non-living state. He takes a step forward, ever so tentatively, and approaches his casket. A corpse from far into the future, divorced from his present reality and the vibrant life force animating his soul, lies there as a stranger.

"Where do we go?" John asks. "I don't believe this energy, this consciousness, just disappears."

Unbroken

Several sprigs from an olive tree tied with a white silk ribbon and adorned by a small porcelain dove lay on top of the casket. John picks up the arrangement, places it on top of Heiwa, removes the accompanying note and reads:

You were the best kind of friend; you helped me become
a better version of myself. Advance to Go. Collect $200.
01101100 01101111 01110110 01000101
Darling

John turns to Yoko to ask her who Darling is, but her eyes are closed, and she whispers, "I miss you so much already, John."

"You won't for long, my love," he whispers back. "There is no real ending."

John drops the note as crackling static engulfs him and the baby. He accompanies Heiwa as they transcend time and space to return to her linear place in the world, the Memorial Sloan-Kettering Cancer Center neonatal unit on the day of her birth in 2060.

Yoko opens her eyes to an empty room. "Sean!" she yells. "Sean, please come right away!"

Sean bursts into the room. "What is it, mom?"

"Your father—" she says breathlessly. "John was here with me."

"Of course he was," Sean says tenderly. "He will never leave you."

BREATHE

The future can ever promise but one thing
and one thing only: surprises.

\- Steven Erikson

For his mother's 100th birthday, Sean wears 3-D Goopplezon Lenses and faces her in the Dakota living room. He wishes to capture a recording of Yoko reminiscing about her life with his father.

"How is Kibo today?" Yoko asks.

"Really devastated, mom. It's still so new," Sean says. "Dad died in his arms. You know how close they were. He lost his best friend."

"I know how that feels," Yoko says wistfully.

"Just start at the beginning, mom. That's always a good place to start." Sean takes his mother's frail hand in his — the hand that held his father's for a lifetime — and brings it to his cheek. He speaks the command, "record."

"Well, let's see. I saw him for the first time at my *Unfinished Paintings and Objects* exhibition at the Indica Gallery in a bookshop in Mayfair – in London," Yoko says. "He came in the night before opening just to look around while we were still setting up. One of the owners of the Indica insisted I should meet him, implying he had money and might become a patron.

"I had no idea who he was, Sean. I went up to him and handed him my card that said 'breathe' on it. He panted like a dog, and I thought he was hilarious. I didn't quite know what to make of him.

"He took an interest in one of my installations called 'Painting to Hammer a Nail In.' To dissuade him from touching it before the public had a chance to see it, I asked him to pay me five shillings for each nail he'd hammer. He wouldn't go for that, so we made a deal. He would pretend to take money out of his wallet and pay me, and then hammer in imaginary nails.

"We laughed like idiots. He got me and he knew it. I was smitten and quite sure we'd be lovers someday. I kept in touch with him, but we didn't start dating until the next year – the summer of '67." Yoko pauses to daydream.

"John prepared a home-cooked meal for me. He came to my apartment with a sack of groceries that included a box of mixed vegetables, the kind that come frozen with plump, shiny peas, cubes of orange carrots, little pearl onions, and those horrid, pasty lima beans that I despise with a vengeance. When he placed my plate of food in front of me on the table, I said, 'Hey! There are no lima beans in my vegetables.' Quite pleased with himself, he said, 'I know. You told me you think they're disgusting, so I picked all of them out for you.'"

"That sounds like dad."

"The beauty of that simple gesture! Until then, my pursuit of your father had been an adventure. I was caught up in the thrill of the challenge, the adrenaline-rush, the infatuation. That's the moment – the exact moment – I fell in love with him.

"John was flawed. I mean, who isn't? He made mistakes and had a few regrets. He was complicated. But if I were forced to choose only one word to describe him, it would be 'nice.'

"His act of kindness made me feel that what I had to say was important to him. It wasn't just the big things either; it wasn't about my art, my political views, my fears, or my dreams. He noticed my vegetable preference!

"For our first Valentine's Day, he gave me a set of sharp steak knives as a gift. Oh my, I haven't thought about that in so long. I know that doesn't sound very romantic, but you'd be wrong to think so. I only had butter knives and he wanted to be helpful; chocolate and flowers would have been cliché. John saw me for the down-to-earth woman I was.

"Oh, Sean, stop laughing! I know people have a certain image of me, but you should know – better than anyone – that I have a practical nature."

"Sorry, mom. I can just imagine your face when you unwrapped steak knives. Go on."

"Well, I thought your father was exceptionally romantic. 'Nice' paved the way to real love and a marriage we enjoyed for almost 64 years. Not without some glitches, mind you. But in the big picture, there were so many more ups than downs. He always wanted to do things to make me happy – and he succeeded brilliantly.

"I had a little black-and-white TV with rabbit ear antennas on my kitchen counter. We kept it on while we were eating our dinner without lima beans. There had been a police raid on an after-hours place in the States a few days earlier – in Detroit, I think – and the conflict turned into a deadly riot in the streets. The non-stop news coverage depressed John. He couldn't watch anymore, so he changed the channel – just in time to hear a news announcement about how many U.S. soldiers had died in Vietnam that week.

"He switched off the TV and turned on the radio. 'All you need is love' was playing. I swear! He led me into the bedroom and said something like, 'What if they all put down their sticks and stones and went home to make love?'

"OK, turn that thing off now, Sean. I'm suddenly feeling very tired. Be a dear and make me a nice pot of hot tea, please?"

Yoko calls out to Sean as he walks toward the kitchen. "Is there anything more beautiful than to believe in love and peace the way your father did? John was an amazing man."

Yoko sits alone on the sofa in the quiet of her sun-drenched living room. Snowflakes float by outside the large windows behind her, creating a winter-wonderland gentleness to bless the earth on her final day.

A shimmering light appears in the middle of the living room, crackling and sizzling iridescent. The outline quickly takes form – a slim man materializes wearing a snug, one-piece, navy blue zip-up, boots, and a space-age helmet. When he is fully formed, he removes his helmet. Yoko recognizes John as a young 40-something-year-old man.

John looks around his living room. "What the–?" he asks. He notices tiny, frail Yoko sitting wide-eyed on the sofa. She is noticeably older than even her 87 years when he had last kissed her goodbye in Virgin Galactic's family observation area in New Mexico. "Yoko?"

"Yes, John, it's me."

"I was about to climb out of the *Unity* after my ride into space, and, poof, here I am." John adds, "And by the looks of it, not on the same day."

"The *Unity*?" Yoko asks. "You appeared to me as a young man a few days ago at your funeral."

"At my funeral?"

Yoko nods her head. "You died, or will die – I can't tell which anymore – at 93. You visited from the future and brought a baby with you – our great-granddaughter, Heiwa. I thought I had gone mad with grief.

"I dream about you. The images are vivid, so colorful. I smell things, and I feel what I see – like I'd really been there. John, I believe you and I may have lived several lives together."

"Maybe your dreams are glimpses of those other lives."

Yoko whispers, "I feel my spirit slipping away now. Is seeing you like this just a final wish? An illusion?"

"All of life is an illusion, my dearest Yoko. It is what we make of it, what we choose to believe. We see it all through our own eyes, and our perspective is different than that of any human being that has ever lived. There might be billions of realities."

John sits down beside Yoko and holds her hand. She leans her head on his shoulder and says, "I'm afraid, John. I don't know what to expect."

"Don't be afraid. We are not bodies with souls. We are souls with bodies for the short time we are here on earth. There is more."

"Can you stay with me for a while?" Yoko asks.

"Yes, my love. I will stay with you for the journey to the other side – for as long as it takes. John embraces Yoko, kisses her cheek, and sings, "*You're not alone, no matter where you roam, no matter what you do, the angels love you…always.*"

One by one, tiny points of light surround them, spinning faster and faster until a blur of joy lifts them away. Their life's music rises up and out through the window, mingling with the snow, drifting high into the sky past the poufy clouds, zooming by the sun deep into the inky-black vastness of space, through the majestic Milky Way, beyond infinite galaxies and on to the edge of time.

"Don't worry. Don't worry," Yoko hears John say. "I am with you. Breathe."

Sean yells into the living room, "Mom? Who are you talking to?" He returns from the kitchen carrying a tray of tea and biscuits. "Mom? Mom? Where are you?"

Afterword

But for a mere billionth of a nanosecond — too long at that — the present doesn't exist. It is a thin wisp of a line separating the past from the future. The line is fluid; behind it, everything that ever was since the beginning. In front of it, everything that can ever be — an unbounded future. But it is always elusive. Just as you reach it, it moves forward.

Reality, then, is formed only by our memories and the hope of things to come.

A Special Message from John Lennon

Time disappears in a blur. I believe that beautiful sky opened up for me when I was a child. I feel my memories; I smell them and taste them. They run amok through my dreams. There's no distinction between reality and imagination in my head. It is with my heart that I have clarity.

Perhaps I am alive today because of intervening angels and a wrinkle in time, or perhaps I am spirit. What is most important is not my form, but my message: We must love one another to thrive.

The dark side of human nature perplexes me the most. I refuse to accept such evil – in all its forms described here; a crazed fan waiting outside the Dakota on a cold winter's day to shoot me, religious intolerance, domestic violence, and terrorism.

Are we doomed to be creatures of violence and destruction? We hurt and kill one another in the name of God, to draw lines in the sand, to impose disparate personal beliefs on one another, and to own natural resources that should be shared by all citizens of the world.

We are polluting our air and water and decimating the land. Mother Earth is bountiful; if we care for her, there is enough for everyone. There is room to be free.

Every civilization, every religious entity, and leaders from almost every territory on earth have committed atrocities throughout the history of man. Why have we not learned that violence in reaction to a problem is never the answer? Never. Is our destiny to repeat the same wickedness for all eternity?

Yoko and I have dedicated our lives to the peace movement because we believe the human race can rise victorious through love.

Yes, the issues are complex and challenging; but we are blessed with astounding problem-solving abilities and ingenuity. Relationship-building and cooperation will be our salvation. Love is life itself.

Change begins with a thought; then a declaration. Words are powerful! They have mobilized grass roots initiatives, shaped the course of world history, and affected the fate of nations. Give peace a chance! Say it! Say it out loud and with conviction!

It's not necessary to time-travel to see what lies ahead if we don't decide on a better course now. Read history books. Knowledge is power. Use it to good purpose. Technology brings us unlimited information – there's no excuse for ignorance. No excuse for not doing something to help someone, anyone, in big or small ways.

It is necessary that we, guardians of the earth; we, co-creators of our life experiences; we, compassionate creatures and protectors of our children; we, makers of art, music, and literature rise to a higher level of consciousness.

You may call me a dreamer, but I know I'm not the only one! Won't you join me in building a peaceful world?

All my love

John Lennon

Join the movement!

www.SaintJohnLennon.com

ABOUT DANIEL

Daniel Hartwell is an author, concert promoter and positive living specialist. He's been the creator of niche events and large music festivals for many years. As a health and wellness coach promoting peace, love, and balance, he encourages his clients and friends to embrace life to the fullest. The inspiration for this story came to Daniel in a dream. You can find Daniel running the beach in South Florida.

Daniel@SaintJohnLennon.com

Photo by Carol Calicchio

ABOUT ROSIE

Roseanne Bottone is a writer, teacher, and environmentalist. Rosie is a former Peace Corps Volunteer and believes the means to world peace is through cooperation and communication.

Roseanne@SaintJohnLennon.com

Disclaimers:

1. The following named and unnamed characters are fictitious. No identification with an actual person (living or deceased) is intended or should be inferred:

St. Peter's Church sexton; NYPD Officer Justin Dove; FBI, CIA, NSA, Homeland Security, and World Health Organization officials; Dakota apartment guards and the Lennons' bodyguards; Majordomo Julio; Vim Vitae nurse receptionist and Dr. May Belle; Bill Maher's *Real Time* show backstage techie; Goopplezon interns Alyssa, Lexi, Gigi, and Anthony; Radio City ambassador Rockettes; John Lennon's press secretary Ioni; All reporters at Radio City press conference including BBC reporter Lorraine Mersey and internet blogger Leif Hart; Radio City security guards/screeners and man and woman would-be assassins; Wende Prison guard; Scottish Hooligan and witch burning contingent; American Airlines flight attendant Potential bed-in shooter, Omar Abadi; "Star Trek" characters; Pedestrians interviewed on the street for John Oliver's show *Last Week Tonight;* Judge Soenso and court bailiff; Overdosing drug user, Good Samaritan, EMTs at the Gramercy Theater; Jackie on Brooklyn Bridge/Dr. Jacqueline Love at Memorial Sloan-Kettering; White House Secret Service agents; Callie and Floyd Ellis and their children; Mount Sinai West Hospital nurses; Hummer driver, White Knight Three pilots, and Spaceport assistants; Reporters in New Mexico; Peace ambassadors on *Unity* flight; Baseball announcers Bob, Joel, and Jim; Baseball players Ricky Garcia, Joey Santucci, and Ben Granger; Rescuers and the captain of the *Samudra;* Jihadi John's comrades; Hostages Jack and Jenny; Hanson-IBM robot Darling; Ghosts of woman, children, and family in Syria; People on the street during the nuclear strike; John's grandson Kibo and great-granddaughter Heiwa; and Kibo's wife Kerri.

2. This is a work of FICTION. There are, however, well-documented historical facts and quotes interwoven throughout the story. Quotes are

often used out of context within the fictitious story. Please see the endnotes for citations.

3. Real living and deceased persons named in the story – including, but not limited to: musicians; television and radio personalities and guests; actors; diplomats; politicians; scientists; John Lennon's family members (Yoko, Julian, Sean, and sister Julia); the Beatles, their children and their wives; Cynthia Lennon; executives Sundair Pichai, Tim Cook, Jeff Bezos, Robert Johnson, and Sir Richard Branson; researchers; TED speakers; photographers; deceased terrorist Jihadi John and accused witch Janet Horne; journalists; managers and other associates; and Mark David Chapman – did NOT actually interact with John Lennon after his death that took place in 1980 or at any other time when John Lennon is portrayed traveling through time. Nor did they participate in or comment on any of the made-up events described within this story. Their inclusion in this story should not be construed as an endorsement.

4. The mention of real books, newspaper and magazine articles, research documents, foundations, associations and governmental and non-governmental organizations does not imply endorsement of this book by their authors, owners, publishers, founders or members.

5. The back-cover comments under "Imagine reviews like these" are fictitious. They are for entertainment purposes only and do not imply endorsement by any celebrity.

Douglas Hartwell, Jr. and Lorraine Hartwell, we thank you for your original lyrics "Always" and "I'm just a hippie" respectively.

Steven Greene, you were the coolest beta-reader ever! Your insights were invaluable. You rock!

To our many beautiful friends, your encouragement made all the difference. We felt the love.

Endnotes

PROLOGUE – ZEPHYR
[1] PAGE 2: **When I went to school… they didn't understand life.**
Commonly attributed to John Lennon but no source available.

THE EGG MAN
[2] PAGE 4: **Do it, do it, do it.** Sloane, Danielle. "Inside the Mind of John Lennon's Killer" Source: http://www.cnn.com/2015/12/08/us/mark-david-chapman-lennon-interviews/ Dec. 8, 2015 Original source cited: Recorded interview of Mark David Chapman by reporter Jim Gaines in a visiting room at Attica Correctional Facility in upstate New York, three years after Chapman killed Lennon.

[3] PAGE 5: *Who does he think he is, … heaven and the Beatles.* Jones, Jack. *Let Me Take You Down: Inside the Mind of Mark David Chapman, the Man Who Killed John Lennon:* New York City: Villard Books 1992. Print.

[4] PAGE 5: **If someone thinks that peace and love…that's a problem.** "Quote by John Lennon." *Quotery.* n.d. Thu. 27 Apr. 2017. http://www.quotery.com/quotes/if-someone-thinks-that-peace-and-love-are-just-a/

[5] PAGE 10: *Yes, I do believe in God…translations have gone wrong.* "John Lennon." BrainyQuote.com. Xplore Inc, 2017. 26 April 2017. https://www.brainyquote.com/quotes/quotes/j/johnlennon164192.html

[6] PAGE 10: **Anybody who claims to have some interest in me…they don't see anything.** "John Lennon." *Playboy* magazine interview with John Lennon and Yoko Ono: Published in January 1981 issue. "Anybody who claims to have some interest in me has absolutely misunderstood everything I ever said if they can't see why I'm with Yoko. And if they can't see that, they don't see anything."

[7] PAGE 10: **Some people are old at 18...that humans created.** "Yoko Ono." AZQuotes.com. Wind and Fly LTD, 2017. 27 April 2017. http://www.azquotes.com/quote/475269

[8] PAGE 10: **Time is too slow for those who wait…time is eternity.** "Henry Van Dyke." AZQuotes.com. Wind and Fly LTD, 2017. 27 April 2017. http://www.azquotes.com/quote/84281

NOW
[9] PAGE 18: **"The postman wanted an autograph…a piece of me."** Based on the quote "The postman wants an autograph. The cab driver wants a picture. The waitress wants a handshake. Everyone wants a piece of you." "John Lennon." AZQuotes.com. Wind and Fly LTD, 2017. 29 April 2017. http://www.azquotes.com/quote/172577

[10] PAGE 20: **"If everyone demanded peace…then there'd be peace."** "John Lennon." Brainy Quotes. May 6, 2017 http://www.brainyquote.com/quotes/quotes/j/johnlennon110003.html

[11] PAGE 21: **"Everything will be OK…it's not the end."** "John Lennon." AZQuotes.com. Wind and Fly LTD, 2017. 29 April 2017. http://www.azquotes.com/quote/492671

[12] PAGE 21: **Peace is not something you wish for…something you give away.** "John Lennon." AZQuotes.com. Wind and Fly LTD, 2017. 29 April 2017. http://www.azquotes.com/quote/843232

[13] PAGE 21: **"I'm not claiming divinity…peace, love and understanding."** "John Lennon." AZQuotes.com. Wind and Fly LTD, 2017. 29 April 2017. http://www.azquotes.com/quote/172561

[14] PAGE 22: **"Evolution and all hopes for a better world…people who embrace life."** "John Lennon." AZQuotes.com. Wind and Fly LTD, 2017. 29 April 2017. http://www.azquotes.com/quote/823195

LIKE A GAZILLION SUNS
[15] PAGE 23: **"How can I go forward…which way I'm facing.** "John Lennon." AZQuotes.com. Wind and Fly LTD, 2017. 30 April 2017. http://www.azquotes.com/quote/387606

[16] PAGE 29: **"Looking back helps me know how to go forward."** Based on the quote, "Life can only be understood backwards; but it must be lived forwards." "Soren Kierkegaard." AZQuotes.com. Wind and Fly LTD, 2017. 30 April 2017. http://www.azquotes.com/quote/158106

[17] PAGE 29: **"I'm not going to change…one of those people"** "John Lennon." AZQuotes.com. Wind and Fly LTD, 2017. 30 April 2017. http://www.azquotes.com/quote/172539

A FUNDAMENTAL PROBLEM
[18] PAGE 34: **"He's like a brother,…anything for me."** "He's like a brother, I love him. Families – we certainly our ups and downs and our quarrels. But at

the end of the day, when it's all said and done, I'd do anything for him. And I think he'd do anything for me." John Lennon speaking to RKO Radio quote Dave Sholan. Retrieved 30 April 2017 from Mirror.CO.UK http://www.mirror.co.uk/news/uk-news/john-lennons-last-day-as-told-265461

[19] PAGE 35: **"We're trying to sell peace…if you believe in it."** John Lennon on-air interview. *The David Frost Show*, June 14, 1969 Retrieved April 30, 2017 from http://urthepob.byethost24.com/pob/pob18.html?i=1

[20] PAGE 36: **"A dream you dream…together is reality."** "Yoko Ono." AZQuotes.com. Wind and Fly LTD, 2017. 30 April 2017. http://www.azquotes.com/quote/523953

[21] PAGE 43: **"Be ashamed to die…victory for humanity."** Mann, Horace. Address at Antioch College 1859 Retrieved April 30, 2017 http://www.quotationspage.com/quote/2046.html

[22] PAGE 48: **"When you're drowning,…you just scream.** "John Lennon." AZQuotes.com. Wind and Fly LTD, 2017. 30 April 2017. http://www.azquotes.com/quote/172556

THE SALVATION OF 81A3860
[23] PAGE 71: **I'm cynical about politics, newspapers…love, goodness, death.** "John Lennon." AZQuotes.com. Wind and Fly LTD, 2017. 06 May 2017. http://www.azquotes.com/quote/1447303

[24] PAGE 78: **I'm just a hippie…a hippie can't be bought** Hartwell, Lorraine. *Imagine sublime a world of peace and Harmony, a world of peace and a dream that is mine Harmony, I'm just a hippie….* "I'm just a hippie." Unrecorded original lyrics Lorraine Hartwell©2017 All Rights Reserved

[25] PAGE 78: **The quiet one.** The Beatles' nickname for George Harrison

THE BEST MEDICINE
[26] PAGE 83: **"In my book, the Beatles are the best thing…We grew up with you."** "Lorne Michaels." Spoken on April 24, 1976 on camera, SNL (*Saturday Night Live*)

[27] PAGE 83: **"The National Broadcasting Company has authorized me…that's $1,000 right there."** "Lorne Michaels." Spoken on April 24, 1976 on camera, SNL (*Saturday Night Live*)

THE PERSONAL AND THE POLITICAL
[29] PAGE 88: **The pope smokes dope...Yeah, yeah, yeah.** Peel, David. *The pope smokes dope. God gave him the grass. The pope smokes dope; he likes to smoke in mass. The pope smokes dope, he's a groovy head. The pope smokes dope, the pope smokes dope. Yeah, yeah, yeah.* "The Pope Smokes Dope." The Pope Smokes Dope album. Apple Records. 1972 Retrieved from:
http://www.lyricsmania.com/the_pope_smokes_dope_lyrics_david_peel.html
Permission for use granted by Jeffrey Levy; Orange Records Limited

[30] PAGE 88: **"I have to say that, from my point of view...honest with yourself."** Grice, Elizabeth. The Telegraph. April 1, 2015 (Interview originally published May 23, 1998) Retrieved from:
http://www.telegraph.co.uk/culture/4713954/Dad-was-a-hypocrite.-He-could-talk-about-peace-and-love-to-the-world-but-he-could-never-show-it-to-his-wife-and-son.html

[31] PAGE 90: **"Ye mak a better door than a windae."** Old Scottish slang for "You're blocking my view."

[32] PAGE 90: **"Keep the heid"** Old Scottish slang for "Keep your head."

[33] PAGE 91: **"It's gaein be awright...has gane awa."** Old Scottish slang for "It's going to be all right once the pain is over."

[34] PAGE 91: **"It's a lang road that's no goat a turnin.** Old Scottish slang for "Things will change. Don't be disheartened."

[35] PAGE 91: **"Whoever fights monsters...not become a monster."** "Friedrich Nietzsche." AZQuotes.com. Wind and Fly LTD, 2017. 06 May 2017. http://www.azquotes.com/quote/214472

SHAKE THE WORLD
[36] PAGE 94: **Shake the World.** "In a gentle way, you can shake the world." "Mahatma Gandhi." AZQuotes.com. Wind and Fly LTD, 2017. 06 May 2017. http://www.azquotes.com/quote/105852

[37] PAGE 96: **Sri Sri.** His website is www.artofliving.org for The Art of Living.

BED-IN
[38] PAGE 98: **"No one is born hating...they can be taught to love."** "Nelson Mandela." AZQuotes.com. Wind and Fly LTD, 2017. 06 May 2017. http://www.azquotes.com/quote/371806 Mandela, Nelson. Long Walk to Freedom. Little Brown & Co. 1994

[39] PAGE 103: **"Alkuffar min algharb yjb 'an yamut"** Arabic for "The infidels of the west must die."

[40] PAGE 103: **"Yjb 'an tadfae l bik—"** Arabic for "You must pay for your…"

[41] PAGE 104: …**marhabaan, kon'nichiwa, bonjour,…olá and hallå.** The Voyager spacecraft carries greetings from Earth-people in fifty-five languages: http://voyager.jpl.nasa.gov/spacecraft/goldenrec.html NASA

[42] PAGE 106: **"It's just getting out of one car and into another."** "John Lennon." AZQuotes.com. Wind and Fly LTD, 2017. 06 May 2017. http://www.azquotes.com/quote/374488

I AM I
[43] PAGE 114: **"No one controls me…just barely possible."** "John Lennon." AZQuotes.com. Wind and Fly LTD, 2017. 06 May 2017. http://www.azquotes.com/quote/710636

LOVE AND THE ODDS OF YOU
[44] PAGE 124: **"The basic thing nobody asks is…ourselves against it."** "John Lennon." AZQuotes.com. Wind and Fly LTD, 2017. 07 May 2017. http://www.azquotes.com/quote/172581

[45] PAGE 124: **"Part of me suspects that I'm a loser,…God almighty."** "John Lennon." AZQuotes.com. Wind and Fly LTD, 2017. 07 May 2017. http://www.azquotes.com/quote/172562
https://www.brainyquote.com/quotes/authors/j/john_lennon_2.html

[46] PAGE 126: ***What are the chances…*** Spector, Dina. The Odds Of You Being Alive Are Incredibly Small. June 11, 2012. Business Insider. http://www.businessinsider.com/infographic-the-odds-of-being-alive-2012-6. Statistic Source: http://blogs.law.harvard.edu/abinazir/2011/06/15/what-are-chances-you-would-be-born/

TABULA RASA
[47] PAGE 127: **Imagination is more important…giving birth to evolution.** "Albert Einstein." Einstein on Cosmic Religion and Other Opinions and Aphorisms. Albert Einstein. Page 97. Dover Publication. Mineola, New York. 2009. (This Dover edition is an unabridged republication of "Cosmic Religion and Other Opinions and Aphorisms," originally published by Covici-Friede, Inc., New York in 1931)

REASON FOR LIVING
[48] PAGE 129: **Hey there, it's time for bed…On yet another dream.** Hartwell, Douglas. *Hey there, it's time for bed…On yet another dream.* "Always" Unpublished. All rights reserved.

[49] PAGE 132: **Some dreams are built to last...they're dear to me.** Hartwell, Douglas. "Always" "*Some dreams are built to last...they're dear to me.*" Unpublished. All rights reserved.

BIGLY INVITATION

[51] PAGE 149: **"Our society is run by insane people...That's what's insane about it."** "John Lennon." AZQuotes.com. Wind and Fly LTD, 2017. 07 May 2017. http://www.azquotes.com/quote/172542

[52] PAGE 150: **"If she gets to pick her judges...I don't know."** Corasaniti, Nick and Haberman, Maggie. Donald Trump Suggests 'Second Amendment People' Could Act Against Hillary Clinton. *The New York Times.* August 9, 2016. New York City, N.Y. https://www.nytimes.com/2016/08/10/us/politics/donald-trump-hillary-clinton.html?_r=0

[53] PAGE 150: **But Trump publicly asked Russia to hack her emails.** Parker, Ashley and Sanger, David E. "Donald Trump calls on Russia to find Hillary Clinton's missing emails." *New York Times.* July 26, 2016. Donald Trump said, "Russia, if you're listening, I hope you're able to find the 30,000 emails that are missing. I think you will probably be rewarded mightily by our press." Article includes access to video of press conference https://www.nytimes.com/2016/07/28/us/politics/donald-trump-russia-clinton-emails.html

LOVE TRUMPS HATE

[54] PAGE 153: **"But my husband is real...He supports everybody."** "Melania Trump." "But my husband is real. He's raw. He tells it like it is. He's kind. He's a gentleman. He supports everybody. He supports women. He encourages them to go to the highest level, to achieve their dreams. He employs many, many women." Bradner, Eric CNN Oct 18, 2016 referencing an interview with Melania Trump by Anderson Cooper. Retrieved from CNN.com

[55] PAGE 155: **"I say, not in a braggadocious way...all around the world."** Spoken by Donald Trump at the CNN Republican debate, September 16, 2015 "I say, not in a braggadocious way, I've made billions and billions of dollars dealing with people all around the world." YouTube Video: https://www.youtube.com/watch?v=G20tjQGJ9go

[56] PAGE 155: **"Living your words, walking...talking your walk."** Trump, Donald and Kiyosaki, Robert. Midas Touch: Why Some Entrepreneurs Get Rich and Why Most Don't. Plata Publishing, LLC. Scottsdale, AZ. First edition 2011

[57] PAGE 155: **"I think if this country gets any kinder...cease to exist."**
Holodny, Elena. Trump's 1990 Playboy interview perfectly lays out his view of
the world. February 11, 2017. Business Insider.
http://www.businessinsider.com/donald-trump-playboy-interview-trade-
foreign-policy-japan-2017-2 Quoted Donald Trump in Playboy Magazine
interview, March 1990

[58] PAGE 155: **"When will our country stop wasting...focus on lower
taxes."** Tweet by Donald Trump 6:01 AM - 5 Feb 2014. Twitter.
https://twitter.com/realdonaldtrump/status/431019797040869376

[59] PAGE 156: **"The concept of global warming...manufacturing non-
competitive."** Tweet by Donald Trump 11:15 AM – 6 Nov 2012. Twitter.
https://twitter.com/realdonaldtrump/status/265895292191248385?lang=en

[60] PAGE 163: **Unpresidented.** President Trump misspelled "unprecedented"
in a 2017 tweet that he later deleted and corrected at 8:57 AM – 17 Dec 2016.
See Fox News Article: Trump trolled for misspelling 'unprecedented' in tweet.
December 17, 2016. http://www.foxnews.com/politics/2016/12/17/trump-
trolled-for-misspelling-unprecedented-in-tweet.html

THE DIVERGENT PATH
[61] PAGE 164: **"the more I see, the less I know for sure."** "John Lennon."
AZQuotes.com. Wind and Fly LTD, 2017. 08 May 2017.
http://www.azquotes.com/quote/172559

[62] PAGE 165: **"You don't need anyone to tell you...You are what you
are."** "John Lennon." AZQuotes.com. Wind and Fly LTD, 2017. 08 May 2017.
http://www.azquotes.com/quote/172546

[63] PAGE 168: **"I'm intelligent. Some people...very, very intelligent."**
Useem, Jerry. "What Does Donald Trump Really Want?" *Fortune* magazine
April 3, 2000 http://fortune.com/2000/04/03/what-does-donald-trump-
really-want/

[64] PAGE 169: **"When it gets down to having to use violence...non-
violence and humor."** "John Lennon." AZQuotes.com. Wind and Fly LTD,
2017. 08 May 2017. http://www.azquotes.com/quote/796902

THE GARDENER
[65] PAGE 170: **"Time you enjoy wasting, is not wasted."** Altered quote by
John Lennon, "Time you enjoy wasting, was not wasted." "John Lennon."
AZQuotes.com. Wind and Fly LTD, 2017. 08 May 2017.
http://www.azquotes.com/quote/172541

---

[66] PAGE 170: **Love, love, love...Love is all you need.** Lennon, John and McCartney, Paul. *Love, love, love, love, love, love, love, love, love. All you need is love, all you need is love, All you need is love, love. Love is all you need.* "All you need is love." Single. Parlophone, Capitol. 1967

[67] PAGE 170: **There's nothing you can do...It's easy.** Lennon, John and McCartney. *There's nothing you can do that can't be done. Nothing you can sing that can't be sung. Nothing you can say, but you can learn How to play the game It's easy.* "All you need is love." Single. Parlophone, Capitol. 1967

[68] PAGE 173: **"I'm not really a career person. I'm a gardener basically."** "John Lennon." AZQuotes.com. Wind and Fly LTD, 2017. 08 May 2017. http://www.azquotes.com/quote/442071

FACES
[69] PAGE 190: ***Looking at these stars suddenly dwarfed...into the unknown future.*** Wells, H.G. and Sasaki, Chris. The Time Machine. Dover Publication 1995 (Chapter 7, Paragraph 12, First edition by William Heinemann, London 1895) Retrieved from: http://www.shmoop.com/time-machine-hg-wells/time-quotes-2.html

SUNDAY, AUGUST 15TH
[70] PAGE 205: **"I have sticker books on baseball...I have baseball cards."** Source: http://www.beatlelinks.net/forums/archive/index.php/t-9665.html. Quotes from interview by Singleton, Don, December 6, 1982 edition of the *New York Daily News.*

[71] PAGE 206: **"You would think someone...the Yankees, lost, 1 to 14."** Source: http://www.beatlelinks.net/forums/archive/index.php/t-9665.html. Quotes from interview by Singleton, Don, December 6, 1982 edition of the *New York Daily News.*

HEY JULES
[72] PAGE 212: **The earth has guilt...beneath the dark blue waves.** Hawthorne, Nathaniel, "The Ocean" Retrieved from: The Poetry Foundation https://www.poetryfoundation.org/poems-and-poets/poems/detail/57286 Original Source: *The Mariner's Library or Voyager's Companion* (1833)

THE SUN RISES
[73] PAGE 224: **the dissolution of terrorist groups...** Rand Corporation. "How Terrorist Groups End; Lessons for Countering al Qa'ida." 2008 Retrieved from: http://www.rand.org/content/dam/rand/pubs/monographs/2008/RAND_MG741-1.pdf

[74] PAGE 224: **In an article published in...recorded human history.**
Hedges, Chris. "What every person should know about wars." *The New York Times.* July 6, 2003

THE IMPULSE TO SCRATCH
[75] PAGE 236: **"we live in a world where we have to hide...broad daylight"**
"John Lennon." AZQuotes.com. Wind and Fly LTD, 2017. 12 May 2017.
http://www.azquotes.com/quote/440426

[76] PAGE 242: *You say you want a revolution...it's gonna be alright.*
Lennon, John and McCartney, Paul. *You say you want a revolution, well you know, We all want to change the world, You tell me it's evolution, well you know, We all want to change the world. But when you talk about destruction, Don't you know that you can count me out? Don't you know it's gonna be, alright...* "Revolution." Single (B-side of "Hey Jude"). Apple. 1968 Retrieved from:
http://www.azlyrics.com/lyrics/johnlennon/revolution.html

[77] PAGE 242: **"You're all geniuses, and you're all beautiful...as soon as you like."** Partial quote. "John Lennon." AZQuotes.com. Wind and Fly LTD, 2017. 13 May 2017. http://www.azquotes.com/quote/687492

[78] PAGE 242: **"Declare it. Just the same way we declare war...need to declare it."** "John Lennon." AZQuotes.com. Wind and Fly LTD, 2017. 13 May 2017. http://www.azquotes.com/quote/474621

LADY GAGA IS BUSY RIGHT NOW
[79] PAGE 244: **"Produce your own dream...You have to do it yourself."**
Modified from original quote by John Lennon: "Produce your own dream. If you want to save Peru, go save Peru. It's quite possible to do anything, but not if you put it on the leaders and the parking meters. Don't expect Carter or Reagan or John Lennon or Yoko Ono or Bob Dylan or Jesus Christ to come and do it for you. You have to do it yourself." "John Lennon." AZQuotes.com. Wind and Fly LTD, 2017. 13 May 2017.
http://www.azquotes.com/quote/468368

[80] PAGE 245: **"Never doubt that a small group of thoughtful, committed citizens...the only thing that ever has."** "Margaret Mead." AZQuotes.com. Wind and Fly LTD, 2017. 13 May 2017.
http://www.azquotes.com/quote/196005

[81] PAGE 245: **Deffo.** London slang: definitely

[82] PAGE 245: *flat roofin.'* London slang: to be overworked and stressed.

KISMET

[83] PAGE 246: **"I'm ready to start all over again…Who knows what's going to happen next?"** John said this to Dave Sholin, a reporter for RK radio, who interviewed Lennon on the day he died. Heller, Billy and Kane, Michael. "We were there on the awful night John Lennon was shot." *New York Post. December 4, 2005.*

WE BELIEVE IN MAGIC

[84] PAGE 250: **"Do not pray for easy lives…you shall be the miracle"** "Brooks, Phillips." https://www.goodreads.com/author/quotes/232518.Phillips_Brooks. American Episcopal clergyman, author, and lyricist of the Christmas hymn, "O Little Town of Bethlehem"

BREATHE

[85] PAGE 262: **You're not alone…always.** Hartwell, Douglas. *You're not alone, no matter where you roam, no matter what you do, the angels love you…always.* "Always" Unpublished. All rights reserved.

Made in the USA
Columbia, SC
23 February 2019